The Woman in the Wires

By Susan F Banks

LEGAL

Books by Susan F Banks

Red Souls of the Underworld

Red Souls

Wall of Unknowing

Wheel of Augustus

THE LISTENER SERIES

The Woman in the Wires

The Circle of Augustus

Willet Du Place – the Listener and Guardian of the Gate in Los Angeles

Audrey Du Place – the Ring Thrower

Dean Simmons – the Golden-Hearted Warrior

Thomas (TJ) Barlow – the Silver Warrior

Gem – the Guardian of California

"Why do you sing HU?" she asked the Guardian. "What does it do for you?"

Gem smiled. "HU is the Sound of all Sounds, the ancient name of the Spirit of All. It brings me to a place without shadows, where joy and love are all there is." She closed her eyes, remembering it. "There I find peace."

"Yes," Willet said. "I want that too."

Chapter 1

The Circle of Augustus destroyed the Dragon Head Building in downtown Los Angeles, but its members were scattered. The Ring Thrower is trapped in the Lightning Worlds. The Golden-Hearted Warrior is reliving a treacherous past life in ancient Rome. The Silver Warrior is spending his time in the Hollywood Hills, dealing with a jealous woman who won't leave him alone. And the Listener has been promoted to Guardian of the Gate in L.A. The situation has given Willet a terrible headache. A tornado howls in her head, driving her through the halls of Pine Siskin House like a wraith, unable to settle down anywhere. Memories too raw and losses to awful made her heart pound and her body tremble. *The Circle is broken. The Ring Thrower is gone, my sister. Audrey.*

The truth hit like an ice pick to her brain, so sharp, it hurt to turn her head. Her eyes wouldn't focus, and her scalp burned. She tried to move, but her temples throbbed so much that she felt she would pass out. This house, the one Audrey had found for them, had seemed like a haven of peace in a world filled with clamor and noise. Now it felt empty, alien. She was alone.

Blood pounded in her head like a sledgehammer, but her migraine meds were in the kitchen. Could she get there without falling? She wasn't sure. She stumbled through the halls, touching the walls until she found her way back to her bedroom and climbed in bed, pulled the covers over herself and shuddered. Maybe this was where she would stay for the rest of her life.

She moved her hand across the mattress and touched a warm hand. Yes. Thomas was there. She wasn't completely alone. The soft flutter of his breath whistled in his nose, a reassuring sound. His arms around her could drive away the remnants of any nightmare, but she didn't want to wake him. Thomas needed rest. Yesterday, the Circle of Augustus – herself, Thomas, Audrey and Dean - fought a bruising battle against Jat the Deceiver in downtown Los Angeles. They stopped the tornado from spinning inside the ninety-story Dragon Head Building before it sucked the city into the dark of the Underworld. The victory had taken every ounce of energy they had. Two members of the Circle hadn't returned from the fight. It made her want to pull the covers over her head and cry.

The need for migraine relief could not be ignored. Breathing slowly to control her queasy stomach, she swung her legs off the bed, found her feet, and wobbled in place, trying to get her balance. Her head rolled heavily on her shoulders. She groped for her robe at the foot of the bed and slipped it on, wrapping it tight around her waist, put her hands out and found the dresser near the bed.

The round gold-framed mirror above the dresser faced her from the wall. She caught a glimpse of herself. Shadows around her eyes gave her a haggard, depressed look. Her skin was pale, and her long blonde hair was stringy.

Ugh. How long have I looked like this? Pull it together, Will.

The migraine could not be ignored. She backed away from the mirror, trying to keep her balance. Holding on to the dresser, she felt for the wall, followed it out the doorway and staggered along the hallway until she found the kitchen. When she reached the cupboard, she pulled out the plastic bottle and managed to drop two white pills into her palm without spilling them on the floor, then groped for the sink and filled a glass with water. Two pills were twice the recommended dosage. The last time she took that much, she had to go to the emergency room to get her stomach pumped. *Audrey would be mad if she knew.* That thought stabbed her heart. Audrey won't be here. The pain of loneliness gripped her. No medicine could cure it.

Willet couldn't imagine her world without her sister. Audrey took care of her through their childhood when their mother couldn't cope with Willet's supersensitive hearing and all the side effects it produced. Nausea, migraines, bad dreams and phantom voices – it was Audrey who sat by her bedside, brought cold packs for her neck, and held her hand when Willet had night terrors. Audrey brought lessons home from school so Willet could keep up with her studies. They studied computer science together. Audrey brought the world into Willet's darkened bedroom, giving up dating and parties and the social activities of a teenager to keep her sister company. Willet was just beginning to understand what a sacrifice she had made.

After the battle in the tornado, members of the Circle made choices. Willet returned to her physical life to be the new Guardian of Los Angeles. Thomas followed her. Dean chose to remain in his Light body and visit a past life in ancient Rome. Audrey chose to stay with Dean, rather than return to physical life. Willet couldn't blame her for wanting more for herself, but it was a shock. Audrey didn't choose her.

She stood at the kitchen sink and hung her head, not sure what to do next. Anguish drained her. Her piteous dependency on Audrey was embarrassing. *You're a Guardian now. Act like it.* She *was* the Guardian, but she felt like a zombie. She could barely walk through her own house. The walls and ceiling flowed in waves as if the house was under water. Even the furniture rippled. Her mind raced. *What has happened to my vision? How am I supposed to guard L.A.?* She concentrated on her breath, slowing it down from its frantic pace until it found a manageable rhythm. A plan of action formed. *I'll go to the bedroom and fix my hair.* That was simple enough. She stumbled out of the kitchen, back to the bedroom, and picked the comb up from the dresser. She tried to drag it through her hair, but the comb caught on a thick matt, right at the scalp line behind her neck. *OW. That won't work.* She tried to brush the matt out, but it was a dense tangle. She found manicure scissors in the top drawer and cut out the matt, then found another matt and cut that out too.

At this rate, I'll be bald.

Absorbed in the problem, it took her a moment to notice the second pair of eyes in the mirror. Eyes that weren't hers. Dark brown eyes floated over her right shoulder and stared at her. The scissors slipped out of her fingers and hit the floor. She turned her head to look behind her. No one was there. She turned back to the mirror, peered into it, and squinted. Now there were two pairs of eyes floating inside the frame, a pair over each shoulder. She blinked rapidly and stared. The eyes still floated in the mirror.

Is this double vision? A brain tumor?

The eyes in the mirror split again. Four pairs of eyes stared at her. She leaned closer, turning her head left, right, up and down, looking for a trick of the light that might cause the apparition. Sometimes migraines caused flashes of light in her eyes. Could that be it? A migraine had never caused anything like this.

The most disturbing thing – there was fear in those eyes.

What are they afraid of? Is it me?

Mesmerized, she swayed on her feet and stepped backwards. The eyes grew larger and came toward her as if they would burst out of the frame. She took another step back and shut her own eyes. When she opened them again, the eyes in the mirror were bloodshot and bleeding from the corners. She clapped her hands over her mouth to stifle a scream and closed her eyes again. When she peeked at the mirror again, the bloody eyes were gone. All she saw were her own bleary, blinking eyes and haggard face.

She had to get away from the mirror before her knees buckled. She stumbled out of the room, made her way back to the kitchen and grabbed for the kitchen table, pulled out a chair and dropped into it. A sliver of morning sun streamed through the window over the sink. Dawn. The kitchen shimmered and reflected thin early light. The nickel-toned appliances undulated in silvery streaks. Black and yellow tiles on the floor hopped up and down like squares of a jigsaw puzzle. Everything she looked at seemed to be moving, and the migraine was taking its sweet time going away. Her stomach lurched.

She looked around the kitchen, and her eyes watered. This was Audrey's kitchen, her pride and joy. Her sister loved to cook in it. Willet pictured her moving from stove to refrigerator to sink, chopping vegetables and stirring pots, all with her usual graceful efficiency, turning out delicious food for whomever sat at her table. Now the kitchen was just another room, empty and devoid of energy.

The void left space for memories she didn't want to relive. Every sight and sound of the Circle's last battle against Jat was still a visceral sensation inside her. The deafening roar of tornado winds, the downward pull of the tornado's vortex. Jat's leering dragon face and fire-red eyes were burned into her retinas. She felt the heat of his fire breath on her skin. Now that she was Guardian, Willet needed the Circle's unified power behind her. She couldn't defend the city against the forces of the Underworld with two members missing. Overwhelmed by despair, she dropped her forehead to the kitchen table and wrapped her arms around her head, sobbing, until the sleeves of her robe were soaked. She would fail as a Guardian.

Not much certainty beyond that, apart from a few important details. The towering mountain of black sand left behind by the collapse of the Dragon Head Building still remained in downtown L.A., a threat to everyone who came near it. There was an open Gate inside the sand that served as a portal between the physical world and the Underworld. Her responsibility as a Guardian was to close the Gate before demon Souls from the Underworld came through it. *Are they already here?* Her own lack of offensive skills was embarrassing. She was just the Circle's Listener, after all. What could she do against demons? Willet looked up from the kitchen table. The room wavered and blurred in shades of black, yellow, and white. She was on the verge of another blubbering breakdown, but then she remembered. There were guests in the house. She couldn't let them see her like this.

Bart Johnson slept in the guest room last night. He helped the Circle bring down the Dragon Head Building. After the building was reduced to a pile of sand, he drove Willet and TJ home to the desert. And Jonah was here, a young boy who got separated from his mother during the melee. They couldn't leave the boy alone in the city, so he came home with them too and slept on the couch in the living room.

Everyone in the house was a survivor of the battle against Jat. She needed to be strong for them. She pressed her palms against her temples and closed her eyes. The last vestiges of the migraine lingered, unwilling to release her.

Someone spoke her name. Startled, she looked up. A woman sat in the chair across the kitchen table. Everything about her glowed. Her brown skin was lustrous. Her blonde-tipped brown curls reflected light. Her brown eyes were diamond bright. She wore a gold silk dress embroidered with green vines and red and pink flowers that made her look like a Queen of the Tropics. The light of dawn seemed to emanate directly from her, and the scent of cinnamon and clove filled the room. It was Gem, formerly the Guardian of Los Angeles and now the newly appointed Guardian of California. Dora, the big black Labrador and Gem's devoted companion, was at her side as always.

"Gem!" Willet brushed tears off her face with the backs of her hands, and the hint of a smile bloomed on her lips. "You're here!"

Gem studied her. "Why do you cry?"

"Audrey's gone." Willet hung her head. "I'm a mess."

"Do not fear," Gem said gently. "Soul never dies. The Ring Thrower is on her own path."

"I'm useless by myself."

"I would never abandon you," Gem said. "You are still my Listener. Certainly not useless. You are a Guardian now, baby girl. You must behave like it."

Gem had called her 'baby girl' since they first met. Willet objected at first, until she began to understand why Gem would think of her in that way. Gem was over 170 years old. All the people in her original life had passed away long ago, and the life of a Guardian could be a solitary one. Gem treated Willet with the same gentle love of a mother to a child. Willet came to cherish that affectionate term, but to hear herself referred to as Guardian by her teacher and guide was hard to accept.

"I can't call myself a Guardian. I can barely walk around without bumping into things. I saw phantom eyes in the mirror. How can I be a Guardian if I can't see straight?"

"The mantle of Guardian comes with enhanced senses. You will see more, hear more, and sense more than ever before. It will take time to adjust, but new strengths come with it."

"How long, exactly? How long did it take you?"

Gem's loving smile made her glow even brighter. "The sensations you find troublesome now will become the tools you will use in the future to fulfill your mission as Guardian. Early in my life, I did not understand the pieces of ice forming in my mouth. I tried to swallow them and nearly choked. One day, a man threatened me with a club, prepared to strike me for helping people escape from a slave owner. Ice formed in my mouth so fast that I couldn't swallow. I blew them out and hit him in the face. He went limp and fell to the ground. I learned that my cold breath could freeze violent or extreme emotions in human beings. When I accepted the feeling of ice on my tongue, I began to create many forms of cold out of my breath. Not only ice, but sleet, hail, fog, and cold rain. It is my unique ability as Guardian. The Freezing Breath helped me seal the Gate when it was breached, as you have observed. You too will find your way."

"But I'm not like you! I have no special way to stop an attack by a demon. Do I use my fists? Throw furniture?" Frustration brought new tears. She tried to rub them away, but they kept coming.

Gem leaned over to stroke Dora's smooth black head, and the big dog snuffled. "The way will become clear, but you cannot wait for clarity. You must go forth and be the Guardian you are meant to be. The dangers increase by the moment."

"I guess I can use my winning smile," Willet said miserably. "You have imagination, strength of character, and a clear purpose. The Silver Warrior is with you. Use these benefits to your advantage."

Willet thought of Thomas, sleeping in her bed. A knot of tension in her chest eased.

"The Gate to the Underworld has been breached," Gem said. "You know where that breach is. Your city is in danger, and its people will need protection. Sing HU as I have taught you and prepare for a new challenge. But never fear. You have the support of the Guardian Enclave, and mine most of all. Never fear..." Gem's voice and form faded as the Guardian of California and her hound disappeared from the kitchen, leaving an empty chair.

Willet stared at the chair and felt a chill across her skin. She didn't know what the Guardian Enclave was, but Gem's message was clear – there could be no delay. She had to return to downtown L.A. and face the mountain of black sand, by herself if necessary.

Chapter 2

She crept back to the bedroom and climbed into the warm cocoon of her bed, wiggled close to TJ's chest and inhaled the scent of him. His was the fresh scent of the ocean clinging to his skin. The essence of their love was like spice in the sheets. She never wanted to leave this fragrant space or think about how things had changed in their lives. After what seemed like months of traipsing through the streets of Los Angeles, chasing specters and fighting demons in an interminable, impossible war they didn't fully understand, they were back home, safe in each other's arms.

"Thomas," she whispered. "Are you awake? I've got things to tell you."

"Nooo," he groaned "Problems can wait. We've been away so long. I need you." He reached for her, nuzzled her neck, let his hands slide down her body to her backside and pulled her close while he bit at her ear and kissed her lips hungrily. "Mmmm, you smell good. I love you," he said in a whisper.

His warm breath on her neck was so agonizingly beautiful that she couldn't hold back the moan that escaped her. He was all around her and inside her, overcoming any hesitation. She gave in to his heat. For the moment, the difficult things faded, the uncertainty and loss, the dread of a future without her sister. They rocked together in a rhythm all their own until ecstasy poured through them. It was warm and sweet and complete, her heart open to him so wide that it hurt. Her doubts eased. Life would move ahead like a wave, carrying them forward into the unknown. They would be together. They would find the answers.

In a few minutes, he fell asleep again, if she could judge from the long rise and fall of his breath and the soft whistle through his nose.

She slipped out from between the sheets as quietly as she could, slipped into her robe, and felt her way carefully back to the kitchen. She fumbled in the refrigerator for the pitcher of cold lemon water that was always there and carried it back to the kitchen table. She poured herself a glass, stared down at the glistening surface of the water, and took a long swig. It was quiet in the house, but not for a Listener. Sound waves bombarded her ears. They weren't loud, so she allowed them to vibrate her tympanic membranes at full strength. The familiar sounds of desert life outside were soothing. As the sun rose, buzzing bugs and chirping birds were starting their day. All happy sounds, but some sounds were missing. Audrey's sounds.

Willet felt that deep ache in her chest again. In the warmth of TJ's arms, it eased, but now it gripped her in a stranglehold. A taste of bitter ash burned the back of her throat. The emptiness was too much to bear. Tears ran down her cheeks again. She couldn't stop them.

Stirrings of activity in the living room reminded her - *Oh, our guests.* Bart Johnson walked into the kitchen wearing the same rumpled t-shirt and jeans he arrived in the day before and gave her a cautious look. "Am I up too early? I can go back in the bedroom for a while if you need alone time." He scratched at his brown hair, uncertain, and noticed her tears. "Sorry, didn't mean to interrupt. Are you okay?"

Willet sniffled and pulled it together. "Thinking about Audrey," she said. "I'm ok." The quiver in her voice said otherwise.

Bart sat down at the table. "Yeah. I miss her too. She cooked me dinner here. It was our first date. And our last. We didn't have a chance to really get to know each other. I can't believe she's gone. It really hurts."

She dropped her head in her hands and started crying again, her shoulders shaking.

Bart was mortified that he made her cry. He got up and went to her, put his arm around her shoulders. "I'm sorry, Willet. You must miss her terribly." Then he put both arms around her and hugged her gently. The tears stopped.

"I'm a mess," she said. "A total mess. You shouldn't have to see me like this."

"I could grab us both a cup of coffee at the minimart…"

She sniffled and wiped her cheeks. "Don't be silly, Bart. Please. I'll make coffee. Making coffee is still within my capabilities. I think."

Bart was an ally in the Circle's fight against Jat. They owed him a lot. He cultivated a powerful crystal on his farm and brought bags of it to the Dragon Head Building, then spread pieces all around the base. The crystal weakened the foundation of the building. When the Circle reversed the spin of Jat's tornado inside it, the building dropped, leaving a mountain of black sand in its place. The crystal pieces that surrounded it absorbed so much of the sand's negative energy that they grew to boulder size. It was the only thing keeping the sand under control.

Willet stumbled around the kitchen, trying to see through all the blurriness, groping in drawers and cupboards for the makings of a pot of coffee. She could feel Bart's eyes on her. "Maybe you should sit down, Will," he said. "You seem a little unsteady. I could make the coffee…"

"Just a pulled a muscle in my leg. No worries."

She tried to sound cheerful as she opened a bag of coffee. The grounds looked like they were rolling in the bag, but she managed to scoop a cup into a filter. She shuffled to the sink and filled a carafe with filtered water and then poured it into the coffee maker. The perking machine soon sent the aroma of brewing coffee through the kitchen. Thin morning sunlight got brighter and warmer. She turned to Bart but stopped short of speaking. A light reddish-purple color glowed around him, like a watercolor wash. She blinked her eyes several times to make sure she was really seeing what she thought she saw. The color remained.

Before she could comment, TJ shambled into the kitchen in t-shirt and pajama bottoms, drawn by the smell of the brew. "How did you know I needed coffee?" he mumbled and pulled a mug out of the cupboard. A sheen of silver with a green tinge at the edges glowed around him. She blinked again to test her eyes. Yep, the colors were really there on him too.

Seconds later, Jonah appeared in the doorway. He was almost thirteen, skinny, with brown curly hair and serious hazel eyes. He wore one of TJ's voluminous white tee-shirts that covered him to below his knees and made him look like a ghost. A nimbus of pink color surrounded the boy. They would have to figure how to reunite him with his mother, if they could find her. Jonah thought TJ walked on water and wanted to be at his side constantly. Now he looked at him expectantly. "Good morning, Mr. Tom, Ms. Willet. Mr. Bart. What are we doing today?"

"Good morning, boy," TJ said. "Are you hungry?"

"Um, yeah, I guess so." Jonah's eyes shone.

"I can whip us all up some eggs. Do we have eggs, Will?"

Willet shook her head. "No one's been home in over a month. I wouldn't trust anything in that refrigerator."

TJ opened the fridge and bent down to sniff. "There is a questionable odor, but I see bread. We could make toast, and here's peanut butter and some jams. They don't go bad, right?"

"The bread is questionable. There's another loaf in the freezer. Use that."

"PB&J," Bart said. "The breakfast of champions."

TJ pulled a carton of eggs and two cartons of milk out of the refrigerator. He poured the milk out in the sink and ran hot water after it, and then carried the eggs and containers to the outside trash. Willet toasted four slices of whole wheat bread and put them on plates. When everyone sat down at the table, they spread their toast with peanut butter and strawberry jam and were soon munching open-faced PBJ and drinking mugs of coffee. Willet prepared another round of toast when they were done. She tried not to stare at the colorful glow around each person sitting there but stole glances to see if the colors would change or fade. They did not.

"So, what's the plan?" Bart asked. "Is there a plan? Pretty soon, I need to go see what's going on at my business. The crystal fields have probably spread across state lines by now."

"Willet and I have no working wheels," TJ said, "so we'll have to buy some kind of vehicle. You've been totally awesome to us, Bart. Of course, you have to get back to your life. Can you take us to a car dealer before you leave town?"

"Sure, man, is there a dealer around here?"

TJ looked at her. "Is there a dealer in Hemmings, Will?"

"No clue," she said. "Maybe Riverside."

"That's too far. We'll find out where the closest one is. Bart has already given us so much of his time. Thanks a lot, dude."

"What am I gonna do, Mr. Tom?" Jonah asked.

"You can stay here and watch TV," TJ said, "if it's alright with Willet."

"But I wanna go with you," Jonah said in the whiney tone of a preteen.

"You need to stay and keep an eye on things while we find a car. We'll come back and get you when we have wheels." The job sounded important enough that it satisfied Jonah. He settled back to his PBJ without further protest.

Willet looked at the three men sitting around her table and felt the heaviness in her heart ease. Their presence in her home made her happy. Never before in her isolated life were there friends other than her sister, and of course the Circle, but she didn't know what to think about the colors swirling around each of them. It was disconcerting. She tried opening her eyes wider. The colors got even brighter. "I'm seeing colors around each of you," she announced. "It's like someone painted halos around you. Maybe it's a trick of the sun. Do you see any color around me?"

They all shook their heads. Jonah licked crumbs and jelly off his lips. "What colors?"

"Bart glows light magenta. TJ is silver with a hint of green. You're pink, Jonah. Maybe I'm developing cataracts. Do my eyes look cloudy to you, Thomas?"

TJ leaned in and studied her blue eyes, then gave her a quick kiss on the lips. "Not at all."

Jonah stuck out his chin. "I don't want to be pink. That's a girlie color."

"What do you think it is, Will?" TJ asked.

"Gem said my senses might change, and they definitely have. Migraines can mess with my vision, but I took meds earlier, and things still look screwy. I've heard some people see auras."

TJ squinted at her. "When did you talk to Gem?"

"What's an aura?" Jonah asked.

Willet preferred to avoid TJ's question for the moment and answer Jonah's. "An aura is said to be the color of a person's energy that glows around them. Someone with a special type of sight can see it. The color is supposed to indicate a person's state of consciousness."

"What does a magenta aura mean?" Bart asked. "If colors mean different things..."

"Yeah, what does pink mean?" Jonah piped in. "Can I change it?"

"Magenta is a combination of red and blue. Bart is balanced between physical and emotional energies. Gem always called TJ the Silver Warrior, so his silver-green color makes sense. Pink is innocence, I think. I'm no expert."

"I'm not innocent," the boy protested with his mouth half-full of PBJ. "I'm a warrior. I fought monsters, like the spider and the lizard. They were really scary. I didn't even cry."

"You're a warrior in training," TJ patted him on the shoulder. "I'll give you that.

"If I can detect auras on other people besides you three, then I can call it a new Guardian sense. Knowing when to avoid someone could be a useful defensive skill, I guess. Right now, I've got nothing else except early sonic warnings."

"You don't have 'nothing', sweetheart." TJ reached out and took her hand in his. "You've got me."

"I'm going to need you, because we have to face that big problem waiting for us in L.A." The guys looked at her expectantly. "Don't tell me you've forgotten the huge pile of black sand we left downtown. If we don't get rid of it, Jat might use it to create another monster building. Or something worse."

After the Dragon Head Building shook itself apart, the Circle and friends left downtown in a hurry. Now that Willet was officially L.A.'s Guardian of the Gate, it was up to her to go back with a solution. She hoped somebody at the table had a good suggestion, because she didn't.

TJ cleared his throat. "The sand. Yes. That *is* a problem."

"Why is it black?" Jonah asked. "Sand isn't supposed to be black. I never seen it like that."

Bart was a professional geologist, so he had relevant information. "Lava out of a volcano can disintegrate into black sand. Like on some beaches in Hawaii." He was the one who discovered the crystal's ability to digest pollutants, both physical and psychic, and turn them into electricity. A crystal like that had never been seen on earth before. Jat grew it underground as a passageway out of the Underworld for Red Souls. That's where the first pieces came from.

"But there's no volcano," Jonah protested. "So why is it black?"

Silence around the table. "Good question," Bart answered. "I'll take samples of the sand and find out what it is. Augite and Biotite are black minerals. Semi-precious stones like tourmaline, onyx and obsidian are black. Understanding the mineral content could help us get rid of it. No guarantees, though. The stuff is completely unusual."

Willet waited for more commentary on the subject. None was forthcoming.

"I suggest we deal with the immediate problem first," TJ said after a minute. "Willet and I both need wheels." That was a problem they could actually solve.

Chapter 3

It wasn't true that TJ and Willet had no wheels at all. Gem's broken-down Jeep was parked on the circular driveway in front of Pine Siskin House. Its roof had caved in, bumpers sagged, and side mirrors dangled. Jat hurled boulders at the Jeep when the Circle made a frenzied escape out of the San Gabriel mountains north of L.A. The Jeep was too useful to just sit idle. They needed to tow it into Hemmings and get it repaired. It would be Willet's ride when it was road worthy. But was it even possible to repair it? The extent of the body damage was considerable. Any internal damage was unknown.

TJ went out to inspect the Jeep, remove valuables, and prepare the vehicle for towing. When he returned to the house, he had an odd story to report. "There's a cat in the Jeep. How long has it been in there? I wonder."

"The Jeep's been locked for two months," Willet said. "How could a cat survive in there?

"When I opened the door, it jumped out and ran away into the brush. I don't see any openings underneath the chassis for it to crawl through. The doors were locked. It's too weird."

Another 'too weird' thing was something they didn't need. After breakfast, Bart hitched the Jeep to the back of his truck. Willet and TJ climbed in the truck and they towed it into Hemmings where a General Motors dealership was located. At the car lot, there wasn't a single car. They drove through the empty lot and looked in the big windows of the dealership to see if it was open. A young man wearing a gray suit and orange tie came out to greet them. Bart rolled down his window.

"Morning," the man said. His nametag said, 'Nicolas'.

"Are you open?" Bart asked.

"We are, but we're out of stock, as you can see. We're hoping for a delivery this week, and we already have a long waiting list. You might try Walt's Auto Repair. People sometimes leave cars behind when they can't pay their repair bills. It's just down the road." Nicolas pointed.

"Thanks, we'll give it a try." Bart turned back onto the road in that direction.

"That guy had color around him. I would call it puce," Willet said.

Walt's repair shop was two blocks away. Bart parked, and everyone got out. A gray-haired man in a cap and overalls covered in grease walked out of one of the repair bays. He held a wrench and puffed on a cigar.

TJ called to him. "Are you Walt?"

"I am. What can I do ya for?" A gray cloud swirled around Walt. Willet wasn't sure if it was an aura or just cigar smoke.

"Do you have any cars for sale?"

"I do not, sorry."

"How about rentals?"

"Nope, none of those either."

TJ looked around the lot. "What about that one?" he said, pointing at a white car parked to the side of the shop. It had two black racing stripes down the hood.

"That's my car," Walt said. "Not for sale."

"What would you take for it? If it were for sale…"

"That there's a vintage machine. Dodge Charger R/T Hemi Coupe, 1969 model year. Rear wheel drive, V-8 engine, 16 valve, manual 4 speed, 425 horsepower at 5000 rpm, 490 foot-pounds of torque at 4000 rpm. It can tow a thousand pounds. Great traction. It's a beast." Walt nodded proudly at his ride.

"How much?"

Walt scratched at his scrubby gray beard with grimy fingers. "This is a vintage automobile. It ain't cheap.""

"$3000."

Walt guffawed and looked at the ground, shaking his head, before he glanced up at TJ. "For the Zinger? You're kiddin' me."

"The body weighs a ton, and it eats gas. How long do you think you can keep it running?"

"I'm a master mechanic, son. I can keep it runnin' forever. It does eat gas, but it snarls like a tiger and does 130 mph without breakin' a sweat."

"Can I take a closer look? Under the hood?"

"Knock yourself out, but it's still not for sale."

TJ walked over and strolled around the car, checking the body. He crouched down and looked underneath it, opened the driver side door, and stuck his head inside, then popped the hood and examined the engine. After his perusal, he came back to Walt.

"I'll give you $6000."

"It's worth at least $25,000. We're talkin' muscle car here."

"The body is banged up. It needs paint, and the upholstery looks chewed on. It smells horrible in there. How about $8000?"

"Can't do it."

"Walt, that car's a load. Wouldn't you like to drive something lighter, easier to maneuver and brake? Automatic transmission and brakes. Not to mention, better gas mileage."

A pensive look washed over Walt's eyes. "My sciatica does act up when I drive too long. Burns like hell."

"$9000. Can't do more…"

Walt scratched at his beard. "Too low. And it would have to be cash."

"We don't walk around with that much cash. We have a credit card."

Walt studied TJ a moment. "$10000 and you got a deal."

"Done." They shook on it, and TJ waved Willet over. "We bought a car," he said, pointing to the Hemi. "Can you give the man your card?"

Willet took in the big metal beast. "Oh. Racing stripes, huh? That's fun…" The stripes wavered in her vision. They seemed to jump up and down on the hood.

"I'd prefer cash," Walt reiterated.

"The card will clear," TJ said with a side glance at Willet. "We won't take the keys 'til it does. We'll leave this Jeep here with you for repairs. And collateral."

Willet withdrew the card from her wallet, looked at it uncertainly, and handed it to Walt. After all was said and done, the pink slip was signed over, keys changed hands, and Willet became the proud owner of a gas-guzzling hunk of metal named 'the Zinger'. Bart unhitched the Jeep and left it in Walt's capable hands. It was time to say their goodbyes.

"Bart, I don't think L.A. would have survived without your help," Willet said and hugged him TJ clapped him on the shoulder. "You helped us bring down the Dragon Head. We can't thank you enough."

Bart heaved a heavy sigh. "I just wish…Audrey and Dean. I feel like I failed them. Wish it could have ended differently."

"Don't worry, Bart," Willet said, putting on a brave face. "They had reasons for what they did. Good reasons."

"I wish I had your faith, Will," he said, shaking his head. "It just feels like a tremendous loss."

"If you saw what we've seen, then you'd know. Soul never dies. It just changes state."

TJ shook his hand. Willet hugged him again. Bart got into his truck with a wave and headed off to his crystal fields. They watched him until he disappeared down the street.

"OK, girl," TJ said. "Are you ready to take the Zinger for a ride?"

They climbed into their new wheels and adjusted the black leather bucket seats. TJ fired up the engine. He put it in gear and eased out onto the road, then stepped on it. The Zinger did indeed snarl like a tiger. It was a smooth ride. On the way back to Pine Siskin House, the subject of finances had to be addressed. "Will, I'm sorry for putting this on you. Jonah gave my wallet away to some guy when I was unconscious. I'll have to get new credit cards and new driver's license. I swear I'll pay you back for this. Can you cover the charge short-term?"

"Honestly, I don't know. Audrey handled all the money. I'll have to come up to speed pretty quick before I miss a major payment on something. Nobody's working the business right now, so I don't know if cash is coming in."

"I feel like such a eunuch. I should be taking care of these things for us."

Willet held her nose and opened her window. "We need air fresheners. It smells like sweat and dog in here. And a lot of tobacco."

"Yeah, it's a little funky. We'll get rid of the smell."

"I'm glad you found a car you liked, but why this car?" Willet said. "It's kind of old and so - aggressive. We could have looked around more."

"Walt kept this machine in top shape. No leaking or burning oil. The engine hums, the hoses are brand new, and the tires are good. The brakes feel solid too. It'll give us at least a couple of years of good service if we stay on top of it." TJ slid his arm around Willet's shoulders and pulled her closer. "This is a car that will protect us, Will. It's built like a tank and flies like a cannonball. If something gets in our way, we'll run it over. We don't know what's going on in L.A, but we do know we'll have to go there soon, so you can do the Guardian job. At some point we may have to flee for our lives. I want to be sure we can do it."

The Zinger flew through Hemmings and on to the outskirts of town. TJ didn't push it to 130 mph, but the car accelerated to 95 on the open road as if it had a mind of its own. They turned up Pine Siskin Road and came to a squealing stop on the circular drive at the house. Jonah was already opening the front door. He ran outside and beheld the Zinger with wide eyes and a big smile.

"Wow, this is so cool! I heard you comin' a mile away. I wanna ride in it"

Willet regarded the Zinger with new appreciation. She hugged TJ around the waist. "See? You do take care of me. I didn't know you knew so much about cars."

"I was a car geek as a kid. Got it from my dad." TJ kissed her. She kissed him. It turned into a long, passionate melting of lips.

"Ewww, You guys…" Jonah retreated into the house.

Chapter 4

Willet had gained some ability to move out of her physical body into a Light body, but only when other members of the Circle needed her help. She had to develop more control over her movements. Each night, she practiced conscious out-of-body movement, sitting in the bedroom chair and doing the contemplation exercise Gem had taught her. She closed her eyes and focused on the space between her eyebrows, projecting her consciousness through that space to a point outside her physical body. Sometimes she was behind her body, sometimes above it, sometimes in another room. Sounds and sights had the clarity of physically being there. When she felt established in a place, she tried to look around and move in her environment. At first that would push her right back into her physical body, but with several nights of practice, she began to walk through her house in her Light body as if it were natural. On the seventh night, she stepped out of her body, and Gem's Light body was standing in the bedroom with her, wearing the gold dress embroidered with green vines and colorful flowers she wore the last time Willet saw her. An aura of pale gold light surrounded her. As always, Dora stood attentively at her side.

"Are you ready to meet your fellow Guardians?" Gem asked with a smile.

Willet was nervous. "What do I do?"

"Move your Light body to the desert outside your house. You know how it looks. Picture it in detail. Project yourself into that place. Be there."

Willet closed her eyes and pictured the broad expanses of desert around the house, the saguaro cactus and dry brush, and the dark rolling hills in the distance. Soft calls of night creatures echoed in the quiet. Those sensations grew stronger. She felt a subtle movement, and then she was standing in front of her house in her Light body. The crescent moon illuminated the night sky and cast shadows over the undulating contours of the hills, highlighting them in silhouette. The quiet of the desert was deep. It vibrated inside her. Everything seemed even more real and immediate than when she was out there physically. She turned 360 degrees as Gem had instructed her to do to become fully present in the desert.

Gem stood near her, looking up at the moon. "You have made good progress," she said. "Now we must reach the mountains. Take a leap and follow me."

Before Willet could ask what 'take a leap' meant, Gem and Dora jumped into the air and flew off. Willet jumped without thinking and was soon flying over the desert in Gem's wake. The desert floor streamed past far below her. The feeling of flight exhilarated her. The dark and empty desert gave way to a large city lit up like an amusement park. They veered north and east, and the city faded from view. Campfires dotted the dark lands. They soon entered a region of massive, craggy mountains white-tipped in snow. Willet felt a touch on her shoulders. Gem motioned to her and headed downward. They picked up speed into the descent. Willet wondered if they would hit the ground head-first. She couldn't look. The sound of the wind whooshed in her ears. Coming to a sudden stop and landing gracefully on her feet on something solid, she opened her eyes.

They stood on a broad, flat ledge of rock leading into a large cave cut deep into the side of the mountain. The rock was black with specks of white and gray. Heavy, indestructible granite. Inside the space, lights twinkled and glowed, and violins softly played. It was a different world. She suspected that if she stepped into that space, it would change her in ways she couldn't anticipate.

Gem and Dora stood beside her on the ledge. "Welcome to Blanca Peak," Gem said. "a gathering place for the Guardian Enclave of North America. The granite of this peak is almost two billion years old. It repels intrusive energies. Only a pure heart in a Light body may enter here and must be invited. Please come in."

Willet took the step over the threshold. The atoms of her Light body hummed, as if they were singing for joy. Her whole being vibrated. The Light bodies of the Guardians in the room glowed in shades of gold, white, pink, and blue. Men and women gathered in small groups. Soft murmurs of their conversations drifted. Crystal globes of light floated high in the dome of the cave, and plumeria scented the air. The Guardians wore all manner of garb, from t-shirts, dresses and business suits to saris, Indian and African tribal dress, and sarapes. It seemed odd to Willet that Light bodies wore clothes. Why would they need to? She asked Gem about it.

"At this level of vibration, our Light bodies reflect our physical appearance. Our clothing identifies us and our origin. In higher worlds, we are simply Light."

A Japanese man with short, straight black hair wearing a navy-blue kimono approached them with a warm smile. "Dearest Gem, is this the new Guardian we have heard so much about? A gifted Listener, instrumental in saving her city from three devastating attacks by the Deceiver. We are so glad she is finally among us."

"Willet, this is Hideo Takama, Guardian of San Francisco," Gem said with a gesture. "Hideo, this is Willet Du Place, a Listener like no other and of course, the new Guardian of Los Angeles." Willet felt her Light Body glow warmer at this introduction.

Hideo gave her a deep bow, and Willet bowed in return. She was flustered to be introduced with such fanfare by Gem. "Pleased to meet you, Hideo. I have much to learn."

"Hideo has been Guardian of San Francisco for two hundred years. He helped his people survive the perils of earthquakes, fires, floods, and attacks by denizens of the Underworld. As you know, Jat can target earthquake fault lines when he wants to cause fear and panic. Not only does Hideo drive Jat back into his Underworld domain and seal breaches in San Francisco's Gate, but he also inspires people to draw on their highest inspirations when such challenges arise, so they don't lose heart."

Hideo bowed to this assessment by Gem and walked with them into the midst of the other Guardians. All conversation stopped, and every head turned in their direction.

"Guardians, this is Willet Du Place, Guardian of Los Angeles," Gem said. "Willet, these are your fellow Guardians."

"We welcome you!" they said in one ringing voice.

Willet was on the verge of crying. "Thank you all. I'm honored to be here with you."

Gem introduced her to a tall black man with a short black beard named Sebastian Ibbis, Guardian of Atlanta. He was at least six foot five and wore loose drawstring pants with sandals and a jacket woven in magenta, orange, and gold silk. "It is a pleasure to meet you, Willet," he said in a rich, melodious voice. The spark of humor in his eyes made her smile.

"Now, let me introduce you to our leader." Gem gestured toward a tall woman standing nearby. "This is Gaia Philendra, Guardian of North America and leader of the North American Enclave."

A tall, willowy woman, brown-eyed and slender, approached them. She looked like a Grecian goddess come to life in a pale green gossamer gown. A gold lariat encircled her waist, and another wove through her long brown hair. The aura of light around her was white gold. "You may call upon me at any time," Philendra said in a soft vice. "If you have questions." Willet looked into that Guardian's eyes and felt as if she were falling into deep space. There was something so remote and unfathomable about Philendra that Willet felt herself floundering. Her mouth struggled to form words. She hoped some of the words that came out would be 'thank you', but she wasn't sure. Finally, with better control of her tongue, she said, "What kind of questions?"

Philendra stepped closer and bent toward her. The large room seemed to shrink to a small space containing just the two of them. Sounds around them were silenced, as if they were in a sound-proof booth. "Someone in your city may ask you, 'Why am I alive?' What will you tell them?"

Willet stared at her and felt a chill run up the back of her neck. "What *should* I say?"

Brown eyes pierced her with a look that was urgent and without compromise. "Think about why *you* are alive, young Guardian," Philendra said. Her voice chimed. "It is a good place to start."

Suspended in that moment, Willet felt an eternity passed, locked in Philendra's eyes. She couldn't even take a breath until the room expanded again, and the murmur of conversations resumed. A man in a gray suit touched Philendra's elbow and guided her away to another group seeking her company. Willet watched her go with jaw hanging.

"The Guardian of North America has been on this earth since the earliest days of humankind," Gem murmured. "She escaped the continent of Atlantis before it was devoured by the sea. When European settlers first came to the New World, she offered her services to Augustus. A clash of cultures with the Native Indians and between European nations could cause enough emotional upheaval to breach the Gate to the Underworld. A steadying hand was needed before that occurred. She has served here as Guardian of this Continent ever since."

"I didn't know what to say to her," Willet said. "She's kind of scary."

Gem nodded. "Philendra does have that effect on people."

"Has anybody ever asked you 'Why am I alive'? While you were Guardians, that is." She looked at Gem and Hideo, hoping the question didn't seem too odd.

"Ah," said Hideo. "People say that kind of thing when they stand on the Golden Gate Bridge and think about jumping off. It requires a delicate response."

Gem studied her. "Why do you ask, Listener?"

"Philendra told me to think about it."

"She has her reasons, I am sure," Gem said. "It is wise to heed her."

A hush fell over the room like a soft blanket. The Guardians began to chant 'HU' in voices low and deep. The song swelled through the room in a wave that rushed up against the rock walls. Willet listened with her whole attention and felt the wave flow through her. She sang HU softly at first. The sound strummed the core of her like a harp. She sang louder until she vibrated with it. The light in the cave turned from gold to white, then to a hue so pure it was beyond color. The Guardians floated with their heads thrown back in ecstasy. She floated too. Love overwhelmed her heart and healed all that was broken inside her. The intensity was almost too much to bear, but she never wanted it to end. Light and Sound was all there was, divine and perfect.

How much time passed, she didn't know and didn't care. The sound of the chant finally faded away. She became centered in herself again and turned to Gem, but Gem wasn't there. Neither was Hideo nor any of the other Guardians. The granite cave had disappeared. She suddenly dropped into her physical body in bed, opened her eyes, and sat up.

TJ was sitting in a chair by the bed, watching her. "Welcome back," he said with a curious smile. "I'll tell you where I went if you tell me where you went." He had learned the importance of focus in the work of the Circle, and he saw what it had done for Willet. He practiced his HU chant when she practiced hers.

It took a few moments to gather body, mind, and emotions into a cohesive whole. It would take a while longer to realize all the changes in herself, but two things were clear. She had a lot to measure up to as a Guardian, and she had to embrace that role without fear. When she finally felt like herself, she wasn't ready to talk about the experience. She managed to say, "You went someplace? Where?"

TJ chuckled. "To my parent's place in Santa Cruz. They were sitting in the living room watching TV. Dad was asleep in his chair. Mom had Bruno, our pug, in her lap. They seemed fine. I was glad to see that. I've been worried about them since the Walls closed in on L.A."

"Did they know you were there?"

"No, though Bruno did look up in my direction. He sensed me. Where were you?"

Putting the experience into words would be difficult. She wanted to share it with him but wasn't sure she could do it justice. "I went to the Guardian Enclave in the Rocky Mountains. Guardians from all over the continent were there. It was amazing, Thomas, like another dimension. I met the Guardians of San Francisco and Atlanta, and the lead Guardian, an awesome woman who lived on Atlantis! Then we did a HU chant. The light got so bright, and the sound was so intense, it was overwhelming. I can't describe how beautiful and wonderful it was, but I 'became' the light and sound. That sounds strange, I know, but it doesn't even do it justice."

He studied her face. "You seem different. Kind of lit up."

"I'll never forget it." The effort to talk suddenly drained her. "I'm really tired." She lay down on her side and gathered the pillow under her head. TJ covered her with a blanket and crawled in beside her with his arms wrapped around her. She sighed in contentment before dropping into a deep sleep.

Chapter 5

After the visit to the Enclave, Willet felt an even greater sense of urgency to go out and face Los Angeles as its new Guardian. The massive pile of black sand was a disaster waiting to happen. She couldn't believe Jat would leave it behind without a destructive purpose. What effect was the sand having on people? How could they get rid of it? And most important, was the crystal they laid around the bottom of the pile still eating it? The sand could qualify as a pollutant. The crystal ate pollutants. She hoped it would devour the whole pile.

TJ insisted on going into L.A. with her this time, but they also had an opinionated preteen to deal with. Jonah refused to be separated from TJ. After some contentious discussion, they negotiated an agreement whereby they would take him to his old apartment to see if his mother, Evelyn, was there. If she was, TJ and Willet would hand Jonah over to her custody. They would ask her permission for Jonah to work with them as an apprentice. If she agreed, then he could come along with them until school started. It seemed like the responsible thing to do, although Jonah was looking less and less like a child and more like a teenager every day. He was taller and more muscled than when TJ first met him. His voice was dropping, and stubby whiskers had sprouted on his chin. If Evelyn wasn't at home, then they gained the responsibility of a growing teen, at least for the moment.

They set out in 'the Zinger' early in the morning. Jonah was ecstatic to be with them in the new car. Whenever TJ accelerated, the car growled and Jonah woop'ed with appreciation. Yes, the car was crazy fast. They blew by traffic like it was standing still.

"You remember where your apartment is, right Jonah?" Willet asked.

"I guess," the boy said, sounding unenthusiastic.

"I first met you and your mother east of Riverside," TJ said.

"What town did you live in?"

"Umm..." Jonah stared into the air.

"What school did you go to?"

"Magnolia Elementary."

"OK," TJ nodded. "I'll head to Magnolia. Hopefully you'll recognize where you are when we get there."

They found the elementary school in the town of Magnolia and stopped the car. TJ and Willet both turned to Jonah in the back seat. "Look familiar? Which way to your place? If you don't tell us, we'll take you to the police station as a runaway."

Jonah got wide-eyed and pointed reluctantly. They followed his directions until they came to an apartment building. "I live here," he admitted. "Number 34."

They walked up a metal stairway to the second floor and knocked on the door. No answer. "Evelyn? Are you in there?" TJ called out. Still no answer. It looked dark inside.

Jonah had a big smile on his face when they returned to the car. "Where we goin'?" he said. "I wanna fight bad guys."

As they drove through the town of Magnolia, Willet realized her senses were changing by the minute. The barrage of sound hit her hypersensitive ears louder than usual, but she also saw things she'd never seen before. What normally looked like empty air was actually full of flashing particles. The blurriness resolved into fast-moving waves of energy, cutting and crossing each other in crazy patterns. Color swirled around every person she saw. Some in soft pastels, some in bold primary colors, and others in colors that looked disturbed - bilious greens, angry reds, and unsettled grays. There was so much visual activity, it was difficult to focus on any one thing. Information overload. It made her head spin.

"Magnolia doesn't look like a hotbed of psychic activity," TJ said. "Seems pretty tame."

"You'd be surprised," Willet said, squinting at the streets. "A Guardian needs to notice small signs before they become bigger problems. That's something Gem told me. I'm realizing the truth of it now."

A woman walked down the sidewalk at a rapid pace, surrounded by an orange-pink glow. A man standing by his car at the gas station emanated a muddy brown aura. What did it all mean? "She looks happy, and he's in a bad mood," Willet murmured. "Or maybe she's excited and he's sick. I'm spying on people. Do I have a right to know when someone is sick?"

"It's good for you to see people's true colors, isn't it?" TJ said. "Small signs lead to big signs. The price of gas might send the guy over the edge."

"It isn't funny, Thomas."

"Just trying to help." He patted her knee.

"There's so much sensory information coming at me, I don't know what's important. Gem could see breaches in the Gate in the sky. She knew where to go. I have no clue. All I see is a jumble of stuff in the air."

A moment later, she felt pressure shift in her head and heard a soft pop, followed by the loud ringing of a gong. She found herself standing outside the car in her Light body. The onslaught of sound and light became even greater than before. She tried to dodge the waves of energy, but they passed right through her. Colors around people were more vivid. They churned and pulsed and spiked out in long projections poking at the air like the legs of an octopus. The aura of the woman striding down the street turned bright orange-gold. Streamers of color writhed around her head. She looked like Medusa with her snakes on fire. Ribbons of dull red like old blood unfurled from the man pumping gas and waved in the air. A battered blue Chevy pulled into the gas station parking lot just then, and four teenagers spilled out the doors, bubbling with shrieks of laughter, surrounded by a carnival of colors. A thin girl with brown curls wearing cut-off short-shorts and a white tee shirt walked to the back of the car, opened the trunk and leaned in. The man at the pump turned his eyes on her. Long red wires shot out of his forehead and aimed straight at the girl. One wrapped around her waist and slid between her legs. Another went up her shirt. The girl pulled a bag out of the trunk and handed it to one of her friends with a laugh, totally unaware of the visual assault.

The audacity of his stealth intrusion made Willet gasp. "Stop that, you pervert." Her voice echoed, and she was about to cross the street and interrupt the man's mental groping. Before she could take a step, she realized she was not alone. Gem was standing beside her, bathed in her soft gold light. The Guardian of California gave Willet a stern shake of the head. "The mission of a Guardian is to maintain the Gate and protect the living from Underworld attackers. It is not her mission to police the thoughts of individuals. I hope this is clear, dear one. To intrude on the consciousness of others is a violation of their spiritual space."

"I can't let the guy think that way about a young girl, can I?" Willet said, looking to Gem for confirmation. "He could turn dangerous. And where is the Gate anyway? I don't know where to look."

"The Gate is everywhere. You will see the breaches in time. If an individual is directly in harm's way, the Guardian may intervene. Then and only then."

"But what if that man acts out later?" Willet said. "Isn't it better to stop him now while he's thinking about it?"

"People think about all manner of things. Future actions cannot be anticipated from current thoughts. We all have free will to act or not act on them. The girl was unaffected by the man's thoughts, and so, a Guardian must remain neutral in that situation. Seeing manifestations of people's thoughts and emotions is a rare and difficult gift. Be careful how you use it. Focus on your mission and remain alert to Underworld entities that threaten your city. Stop them and send them back, then close the breach from which they entered. You remember how we dealt with the Red Souls, I trust."

How could Willet forget the Red Souls? The chaos they caused in L.A. and the problems they caused for the Circle set the stage for their first confrontation with Jat. Red Souls trapped her in an underground mine. They screamed in her ears and tried to drive her insane. It almost worked. Gem blew the them back to the Underworld using the freezing gale of her breath.

The man at the gas station finally took his lascivious gaze off the teenager, and the long red wires of lust snapped back into his forehead. He finished pumping his gas, got into his car and drove away. Willet turned to Gem, but Gem was gone. She found herself back in the passenger seat of the Zinger with a pounding headache. "Can we go home now, please?" she said. "I don't feel good."

"What just happened?" TJ said. "You seemed sort of gone for a minute there."

"I just got a lesson in Guardianship from Gem. Hard to explain…"

TJ drove them back to Pine Siskin House, parked, and looked to the back seat. Jonah was zonked, eyes closed and snoring. "Let's take the kid in and then we can talk about what happened."

Willet looked back at Jonah too. "What are we going to do, Thomas?" she murmured. "Are we adopting him?"

"The last person we know who saw his mother was Arhat. Any way you can ask him where Evelyn went? Maybe he took her somewhere."

Arhat was 'The Arahata' or Teacher. He was centuries old in the service of the Circle of Augustus. He protected her when she was blinded by the Needle Men and drove her through Los Angeles to find TJ and Gem. "I wonder how I can get in touch with him…" She pictured the dark-haired man and remembered his gracious care of her. In the next moment, he was walking up the driveway toward the car. *He knew I needed him.* "Arhat! You're here!" She scrambled out of the Zinger and ran to greet him. They embraced like old friends.

"Yes, Guardian," he said with a short bow. "How can I be of service?"

She felt odd being referred to as 'Guardian' by Arhat. That was always Gem's title. "It's so good to see you. Come inside so we can talk."

TJ roused Jonah from his slumber and ushered him into the house to the guest bedroom. Arhat followed Willet into the living room. They sat down on the couch in front of the fireplace. "Arhat, that boy, you know him, right?" she said, referring to Jonah.

"Yes indeed, young Jonah. He ran away from us."

"Do you know where his mother, Evelyn, is?"

"The Traveler and I brought her to the Hollywood Hills. She said she was supposed to meet Mr. Barlow there."

TJ returned to the living room and sat down with them. "Evelyn said she was meeting *me*? Where did you drop her off exactly?"

"To a home perched on a cliff in view of the ocean," Arhat nodded solemnly.

"She went to my house!" TJ exclaimed. "What did she do when she got there?"

"Ms Evelyn had keys to the house. She unlocked the front door and went inside. That is where we left her."

"Damn! She has my keys!" TJ looked sheepishly at Arhat, who showed no reaction. "She must have taken them out of my pocket when she kidnapped me. I thought I dropped them somewhere."

"She might be there now," Willet said. "Thank you, Arhat. This will help."

"Of course, Guardian. Is there any other service I can offer?"

"Not at this time. Thank you again."

Arhat got up and walked out the front door, closing it quietly behind him. Willet had seen Gem leave the house this way a few times. Guardians and other high beings came and went through the ethers effortlessly, but they made it look as natural as possible. Willet knew if she opened the front door, Arhat would be nowhere in sight.

TJ immediately pulled out his phone. "I'll call the house to see if she's there." He dialed and waited, then got the answering machine. "Evelyn, are you there? Pick up, please."

After a moment, Evelyn answered, and TJ put his phone on speaker. "Tom," Evelyn said, "when are you coming home? I'll make dinner."

"How did you get my keys?"

"They fell out of your pocket when you were sleeping in back of the van. I didn't want you to lose them."

"We need to take you and Jonah home to your apartment."

"Jonah's with you? Oh, that's nice. He adores you. We make such a good family."

TJ was visibly grinding his teeth. "We're not a family, Evelyn. Stop thinking like that. I'm taking you and Jonah back to Magnolia. I'll be there as soon as I can." He hung up and looked at Willet. "She's in denial. I hope she doesn't make a scene."

"Oh, she'll make a scene." Willet scoffed. "She locked me in a bathroom, kidnapped you and almost got you killed. Does any of that ring a bell? If she offers you something to drink, don't take it. I wouldn't put it past her to drug you and have her way with you. Please be careful."

When the Wall of Unknowing spread across L.A., TJ found Evelyn and Jonah wandering near Riverside. The static of the Wall had surrounded them with shadows and addled their brains so much that they forgot their own names. They were unsure of where they were or how to get home, TJ led them out of the mass of static, but not before he fell victim to the Needle Men in those shadows. They were demons with needles for fingers. They stabbed their needles into every muscle of his body until he lay in the street in excruciating pain, unable to walk on his own. It was Evelyn and Jonah who shouldered his weight and helped him stumble out beyond the border of the Wall. He would have perished without their help.

"I feel conflicted where Evelyn is concerned, you know that, Will. After the way she helped me, I owe her all the help I can give."

"I understand that, Thomas, but she's not rational where you're concerned. She won't give up until she creates the happy little family she imagines. I should go with you."

"I can handle Evelyn. You've got other responsibilities, don't you? I'll be back in no time. Is your phone working?"

"Yes, but…"

"Then we'll be in touch. I promise."

Chapter 6

TJ got a text from Walt that repairs on the Jeep were finished. Incredible turn-around time. The guy really was a master mechanic, and his timing was perfect. With the Jeep available for Willet, it was possible for TJ to take the Zinger and go pick up Evelyn. He told Jonah to get ready to go back home. The boy dragged his feet, visibly. "I don't wanna go back to the apartment. Why can't I stay here with you guys?"

"Your mother will need you with her. Maybe we can work something out for the summer months before school. You're a minor. You can't just leave home without her permission."

TJ, Willet, and Jonah drove into Hemmings in the Zinger to meet Walt. Willet paid the bill and took possession of the Jeep. She climbed in and adjusted the seat, mirrors, and seat belt. Was she actually going forth to do Guardian work in Gem's Jeep? It seemed surreal.

TJ stood beside the Jeep, watching her through the open window. "I'd prefer it if you just drive home and stay there until I get back. You don't need to go out alone on any crusades. Not yet."

"I do know how to drive, pretty much, but I'm not experienced," Willet said. "Audrey did all the driving. I had to wear headphones because of the traffic noise. If I can get this Jeep back to Pine Siskin House, I'll consider it a successful test drive, but I will stay put after that. Please call me after you get to your house. I want to know Evelyn doesn't have you tied up in the garage."

"I'll be fine," he said. "It's you I'm worried about. If any problem at all comes up, call." He turned the Zinger around and roared out of Walt's parking lot with Jonah riding shotgun.

Willet started the Jeep. At the sound of the engine roaring to life, her body shook. She took a deep breath and clamped her fingers around the steering wheel, eased off the brake, then gave it some gas. The Jeep rolled slowly forward into the street. *OMG. I'm really driving. Haven't done this since high school.* Her hazy memory of the streets in Hemmings kicked in. Pine Siskin House was twelve miles away. She headed in the direction she remembered, keeping to the surface streets and avoiding the freeway. The crazy visual distortions flashing at her eyes might make her drive off the road if she wasn't alert. *Keep breathing. Just keep breathing.* By the time she pulled up at home, she was dripping sweat, but she felt pretty good about herself. "See? Like riding a bike," she said out loud as she parked, opened her door, and stepped out.

A fluffy gray and white cat walked out of the garden, all feline grace on its dainty paws. Probably a full-grown cat, but small. The tips of its ears were tufted with white and black fur. It meowed at her.

"So, you're the cat," she said. "What are you doing out here? You appear and disappear like smoke. Are you hungry?" The cat meowed again. It followed Willet to the front door. When the door opened, the cat trotted inside like it owned the place. She went to the kitchen, filled a dish with milk, and put it on the floor. The cat lapped at it sedately.

"You don't seem to be starving. Someone's been feeding you, I guess. You shouldn't roam around out there. There are coyotes and hawks in the desert. They'd have you for lunch." The cat looked up at her with serious blue-gray eyes and studied her face in a way that was disconcertingly aware. Willet took a peek underneath and saw he was a male. "You can stay here if you like. I always wanted a cuddly friend. Audrey had allergies, so I never could." She reached a tentative hand down toward the furry head. The cat allowed himself to be stroked and responded with a steady purr. "I'll call you Smoke if you don't mind. If the name doesn't suit you, let me know. We can change it." Smoke walked out of the kitchen into the living room. Willet watched from the kitchen doorway as the cat jumped onto one of the couches, turned in a circle and plopped down. His head tucked into his tummy, and his body relaxed. With a big sigh, he fell asleep.

"I guess it's official. We have a cat."

Chapter 7

The Zinger flew down the freeways and crossed L.A. from desert to coast in record time. TJ pulled into the driveway of his house in the Hollywood Hills and steeled himself for a confrontation. "Stay here," he said to Jonah. "I'll bring your mother out, and we'll take you guys home." If Evelyn was going to throw a fit, he didn't want her son to witness it. He got out of the car and slammed the door shut to let Evelyn know he was there. He walked up to the front door and knocked. He didn't have keys, but the door was unlocked. Inside, Evelyn was standing in the kitchen.

"Evelyn. Good," he said. "Ready to go?"

Evelyn looked thin and pale in a blue house dress that hung on her gaunt frame. Her hair was a messy tangle of red curls. She always seemed rather lost since the first day TJ met her in the Wall. Now her eyes were wild, and she looked unhinged. Her red rimmed eyelids suggested she'd been crying. She gave him a sad, beseeching look. "Why are you doing this, Tom? You know we belong together. For Jonah's sake. I could take care of you if you'd let me. We could love each other."

"This was never about you and me. I care a lot about Jonah. I care about you too, but it doesn't make us a family. It's not good for you to be in my house, I'm sorry. If you go back to your apartment, you can live your own life again. And please hand over my keys."

"It's that woman, isn't it?" Evelyn's wan face twisted into an ugly sneer. "She only thinks about herself. She'll never love you the way I do." She pulled the keys out of the pocket of her house dress and put them on the counter.

"Leave Willet out of it. This isn't about her. Besides, she and I were together before I met you. I love her. You have to accept that."

Her bottom lip quivered as tears welled in her eyes. TJ would have to lie to himself to say he wasn't affected by it. Maybe he should just let her stay in the house. "Can we go now? Please, Evelyn," he said gently. "If your old apartment doesn't work, we'll find another place for you."

Evelyn's shoulders wilted, and a dejected sigh escaped her lips. "I'll get my coat. It's in the bedroom." She headed to the master bedroom. Five minutes later, she hadn't returned to the kitchen. He went into the bedroom to see what was taking so long. Evelyn was standing beside the bed holding a small black revolver, the one he kept in the bedside table. She stared at it.

"You don't want to do this," he said in as calm a voice as he could manage. "It will hurt Jonah. He'll never get over it." She looked up at him and pressed the barrel of the gun to her temple with a shaking hand. "I can't live without you, Tom. I won't. Now you'll see how much I love you."

She pulled the trigger. The windows rattled, and the explosion echoed through the house. Evelyn fell to the floor, bleeding from the head. He ran to her and dropped beside her with his heart pounding in his ears. "Evelyn, can you hear me?" He leaned in close, not sure he would hear her speak.

Her eyes fluttered open for a second. "I'd die for you." Her eyelids drooped and closed.

He ripped a pillowcase off a pillow and pressed it to the side of her head to stop the bleeding. His hands shook. He couldn't hear her breathing, and her pulse barely registered under his finger. "God, Evelyn." He started giving her CPR. until he felt her chest rise and fall.

The front door slammed open against the wall in the hallway, and Jonah ran through the kitchen into the bedroom. "I heard a loud noise, like a gun." He saw his mother on the floor and the blood streaming from her wound. He swayed on his feet, going into shock. "Mom."

"Jonah!" TJ barked at him. "Call 911. Now." He continued breathing into Evelyn's mouth until her chest rose and fell on its own, and then he threw a blanket over her to keep her warm.

Jonah found the phone in the kitchen and called 911. TJ shouted out the address. Despite paralyzing panic, the boy managed to convey the facts of the situation and where they were. An ambulance arrived at the house seven minutes later. Paramedics charged in through the front door carrying a stretcher and an oxygen tank. Within minutes, Evelyn was on the stretcher with a mask over her mouth, headed out the door. Jonah jogged along at his mother's side. "Mom! Mom! Don't die. Please don't die."

"Stay back, kid," said the paramedic. "We'll take good care of her, don't worry."

TJ watched them load the stretcher carefully into the ambulance as Jonah stood by, white-faced. The ambulance roared away moments later, lights flashing and siren blaring. TJ went to the boy and hugged him. "Your mom had an accident. She needs to go to the hospital."

Jonah pulled away and looked up at TJ, searching his eyes for answers. "She had blood on her head. It was a gun, right? How did she have a gun?"

It was pointless to withhold the truth. Jonah had already seen too much, and he was too old to accept fabrications. "Your mom made a mistake. She found a gun in my room and fired it. The bullet hit her head. That's where the blood came from. She's breathing, so that's good. The ambulance got here fast. That's good too."

Jonah looked shaky and uncertain like he just woke up from a deep sleep. "I want to go there, where she went…"

TJ considered taking Jonah back to Pine Siskin House instead of letting him see Evelyn in her current state but thought better of it. Evelyn might not make it. Jonah deserved to have any time left with his mother. "We'll follow the ambulance," he said. "Let's go."

Chapter 8

The office at Pine Siskin House was another one of Audrey's domains. Willet seldom went in there, but she had to go in today to figure out what bills to pay, investments to manage, accounts to pay and receivables from their computer engineering business. She sat at the desk in Audrey's chair, swiveled on it, and surveyed the raft of papers on the desk. Rifling through the drawers, she found labeled folders full of papers. She would have to go through them carefully, but she turned on the computer instead. Her head started to swim. *Where would an obsessive-compulsive woman like my sister hide financial records?* She took a deep breath and started searching through folders for files with names that suggested money. Invoices and yearly statements popped up. *OK, we're getting somewhere.*

She was digging into the details of a spreadsheet when she heard a voice muttering, low and disgruntled. Willet was well-accustomed to hearing voices that others could not, but this one was right there in the office. She tuned in. The voice was female, familiar, and complaining about a cat. And allergies. Odd things for a ghost to worry about if that's what it was.

The cat in question entered the room and sat next to the desk. "Smoke, I hear someone talking about you," Willet said to him. "Do you hear that?" Smoke meowed his noncommittal response and yawned.

The disgruntled voice seemed to be talking to herself. "Where is he? He said he'd be here. Is he ghosting me?" Willet closed her eyes and listened closely. The grumpy ghost grumbled about a variety of subjects Willet didn't understand. The voice got louder. "Dean, I'm waiting. Where are you?"

No way. It was Audrey. Willet jumped up from her chair and searched the empty air. "Auddie, is that you?"

The voice stopped grumbling. "Why is there a cat in the house, Will? You know cats make me sneeze." Definitely Audrey.

"Smoke lives here now." Willet's voice shook. She couldn't believe she was actually talking to her sister. "Where are you? Why can't I see you?"

"Pretty sure I'm in the Lightning world. Remember where Gem took us when we first met her? It's dark, and lightning shoots right past me. I can't rise above it, and I can't get back to where you are. I'd really like to get out of here."

"What can I do to help? To bring you back? I miss you so much!"

"Miss you too, sweetie. Dean said he'd meet me at our house, but he's a no-show again. You're the Listener. Can you hear Dean anywhere close by?"

Willet listened. "Sorry, no. Should I be worried about him too?"

"He went to visit one of his past lives in Rome, circa 180 AD. He said he'd meet me here after that. I haven't seen or heard from him since."

"I thought the visit to Rome was a dangerous idea from the beginning. Besides, we're two members short of a full Circle. How am I supposed to do the Guardian work? I have no backup, except for Thomas, of course, and Gem, but she has all of California to deal with."

"Now you have *me* worried."

Willet's voice rose an octave. "I need the Ring Thrower!" The phone rang at that moment, and she clicked on. "Thomas! You'll never guess who I'm talking to!"

TJ's voice cut in. "We have a situation, Will, just as you predicted. Evelyn shot herself in the head, and with my gun no less, the one in my bedroom. The ambulance took her to the hospital. She may not make it."

"Oh no… That's horrible… Poor Jonah. Where are you?"

"Jonah and I are at the hospital. The doctors rushed her into surgery. Jonah won't leave, and I can't leave him. Not sure when I'll be back to you."

"OK, don't worry about me." Willet tried to be reassuring, but her heart sank. She had counted on him being with her.

"What's going on there?" he said.

"Well, remember the cat you found in the Jeep? We've adopted him. Also, Audrey is here, sort of. We're talking. She's waiting for Dean."

There was silence on the other end.

"Thomas. Are you there?"

"If it was anyone but you, I'd say you'd been doing drugs. What does Audrey say?"

"She wants to get out of where she is, but she's stuck."

"Where is she?"

"Lightning World. Apparently, Dean's gone AWOL on the time track. She's mad at him, and worried about him too."

"Stop talking about me like I'm not here," the grumpy voice said. "I can hear you."

TJ cut in again. "Sweetheart, I have a big favor to ask. I can't come to pick you up right now. Do you think you could get to my house? It would really help me to take care of Jonah. He's pretty shook, and I don't think Evelyn is getting out of the hospital any time soon. If we lose her, it will be very difficult for him. A gentle female presence could help with that."

The thought of driving across L.A. by herself made Willet gulp. "Drive in L.A. traffic? I've never done that." TJ lived in the Hollywood Hills near the coast of the Pacific Ocean, as far from the desert as he could be and still live in Los Angeles. Her skin was already crawling. "I guess I have to drive on my own sometime if I'm going to do my Guardian thing." She gathered her courage and resolve. "I'll be there. Somehow."

"Thanks, Babe. Take your phone. Call me if *anything* goes wrong. I'll get help if you need it."

Willet hung up. The thought of the long drive across L.A. terrified her. She put the chilling thought aside for the moment and focused on what was in front of her. Was her sister still around? "Auddie, can you tell me about the finances, bills I need to pay or deposits I need to make?"

That got an impatient huff from the grumpy ghost. "You can figure out the money. I'm a disembodied Soul floating in the stratosphere. Can we get back to me now?"

"I don't know what to do about you. Helping Souls move between planes is not in my job description. Okay, maybe that does sound like my job description, but I don't how to do it." Audrey huffed again. "You have a direct line to Augustus now, don't you? Ask him these questions, about Dean's whereabouts and me getting stuck in limbo."

"I'll try. What about the Traveler? Did you ask her for help?"

"I've tried. Sonrisa isn't answering."

An idea dawned on Willet. "Maybe there is someone who might know about Dean. Gaia Philendra. She's the Guardian of North America and was alive back in ancient times. She told me to seek her out if I have questions."

"See, I knew you could help. How's the Guardian thing going?"

"I haven't even begun to guard. I need to do what Gem did, go out into L.A., look for breaches in the Gate, but I have no idea where to find them or what I would do if I did. Wish you were here, Auddie. I need you more than ever."

"Not sure how this in-between state works. I keep feeling like I'm on the brink of moving out of it, but I can't quite make the move. Don't know where I'll end up." Audrey's voice faded to an echo and then ceased.

"Audrey?" No answer from the grumpy ghost. Willet felt the emptiness of her sister's absence all over again. "Well, Smoke," she said, reaching for the cat's gray and white head and giving it a gentle stroke. "I'll have to face Los Angeles traffic by myself.. Wish me luck."

Chapter 9

***** Dean ****

Rome. 180 AD. The height of the Roman Empire. Dean could hardly believe he was there, seeing and hearing it. He floated in his Light body down a narrow street of hard-packed mud, pockmarked with holes and lined with furrows. Squat, reddish mudbrick buildings rose on each side. The street was filled with people on foot and ox-drawn carts rumbling and creaking on wooden wheels. People weren't aware of him in their midst, watching them. They talked among themselves or walked silently, with purpose, to other destinations. It was as real and immediate as a lucid dream. The Traveler, Sonrisa Degas, was at his side, a tall and imposing woman in red robes. She had brought him here to view his past life. Augustus said he might learn something important from the experience.

Sister Maria Sonrisa Degas de Megaro had mastered out-of-body travel as a nun in fifteenth century Spain. The King of Spain did not like her talking about her visions and experiences on inner planes. He thought she was possessed by the devil. To prevent said devil from getting loose and roaming through his country, he condemned Sister Maria Sonrisa to be locked in a coffin, permanently. There she lay in a death-like repose as her physical health faded until she was visited by the Guardian of Spain, who taught her how to rise from her physical shell in full consciousness and travel at will through all the worlds beyond her coffin. She became especially familiar with the World of Cause where the records of past lives are kept for all Souls. She accepted the mission to escort Souls along the Time Track to view their past lives. Sonrisa Degas has served the Guardian Enclave as a Traveler for centuries.

Dean's journey on the Time Track began with snapshots of his many past lives rolling past his view like a fast newsreel. When the Track came to a stop at the time of his long-ago life in first century AD Rome, he stepped off into his old stomping grounds and felt an eerie familiarity about the place he couldn't put into words. From the viewpoint of his Light body, he took it all in and tried to absorb every detail, so he could remember the experience later. He sensed the Traveler at his flank, a Light body like himself and a powerful presence. He was very glad she had his back.

People walking down the street seemed not so different from those in modern time. Most but not all were men, short by modern standards, no one over five foot seven. They were dressed in tunics, most overlaid with togas in neutral shades. The cloaks were pinned to their shoulders by metal broaches or wrapped around the body and thrown over an arm. Leather sandals on dusty feet. Hair oiled and curled. Women pulled their cloaks up to cover their hair. Dean looked at people's faces and into their eyes, trying to fathom their thoughts and emotions. The language they spoke was Latin. *Doesn't sound like it does in church.* Young, old, fat, thin, rich, and poor. Some people stood against the walls of the buildings lining the street. Many were bent over, leaning on walking sticks or completely crippled and unable to stand, their bodies clothed in rags. Some had milk-white blind eyes, or an eye-socket sewn shut with a long scar. Others sat on the ground and held their palms out. Coins dropped into those palms with a clink.

"Do not let what you see mislead you," Sonrisa whispered in his ear. "Everyone in Rome at this time receives support from someone higher in society. It is expected that people of means contribute to the living of those less fortunate who come as supplicants, in coin, in food, or by some other means. It begins with the emperor. He has a wide circle under his patronage. His largess filters down to the lowest levels of society."

Dean and Sonrisa followed the crowd into a wide courtyard with a large red terracotta brick building at one end. A shaded portico surrounded the building supported by fluted stone columns with Corinthian capitals. Elegant statues of human figures stood between the pillars. Dean followed the flow of people to a wide-open doorway in front of the building and looked inside. It was a bath house. Multi-colored mosaics covered the floor around a large pool beyond the doorway. Panels of red marble on the walls alternated with paintings of people and scenes of nature. Men sat in the heated pool, chatting amiably or soaking with eyes closed and heads tilted back against the side of the pool. On the right through a wide doorway, clouds of steam billowed. Hotter pools beyond, or saunas. Wood fires in tunnels underneath the floor heated the water in the pools. Dean wasn't sure how he knew that, but he did. He floated in to take a closer look.

To the left, in another room, men dipped gingerly into cold pools. One pool was empty. Workers wiped it out with rags. *What disinfectant are they using to kill bacteria? Boiling hot water kills most bugs ... OK, I'm getting too analytical. Where are the women?*

Sonrisa's voice answered his unspoken question. "Women have separate bathing houses. The Emperor of Rome builds the baths as gifts for his people. Communal bathing is an important activity in the Romans' social life. They go to the bath houses every day."

It was all coming back to him, his memories of life in Rome. Dean turned back to the doorway and left the bath house, drifting into another flow of foot traffic moving down the street. The street opened up into a market full of color and noise. Before he could move into it, he heard Sonrisa whisper again. "Wait," she said. "There is danger here for you."

"What kind of danger? No one can see me. Can they?"

"You may meet yourself here. If you and that incarnation of yourself see each other, you could be drawn into that body and become locked into this time of history. You will not return to your life in the modern world until this life ends."

If he didn't get a good look at himself, he'd never know what he needed to learn, and the chances of actually running into himself among all these shoppers seemed pretty slim. Dean forged ahead into the crowd. He would try to avoid eye contact with anyone that might be him.

Chapter 10

Driving the east-west L.A. freeways was a whole different ballgame from driving the few miles of surface streets between Hemmings and home. Willet had bad memories of the last time she was on the freeway and Arhat drove her through the Wall of Unknowing. Big battle-armed trucks, called 'Chuckers', chased them and tried to smash them to smithereens. If it wasn't for Arhat's nimble driving, they would have been crushed. Now she contemplated getting in the Jeep and driving across L.A. alone. If there was something in the Guardian manual about dealing with L.A. traffic, no one told her. *A Guardian can't hide in the house. I have to get out there.* She dressed in her Circle work clothes – gray hoodie over a green tee shirt, faded jeans and gray Skechers. She filled a bag with energy bars and water and stuffed it in a backpack along with a pair of noise-cancelling headphones just in case she needed them. She went to the kitchen and scooped a couple of tablespoons of canned tuna onto a plate for Smoke. "Be good, Smoke," she said and headed out the front door.

The Jeep stood ready in the driveway. The day was sunny, and the sky was pure blue as usual for July in Southern California. The optimism of the weather didn't match her mood. She sang HU under her breath to settle her nerves, climbed in, and buckled the seat belt. Her hands were already trembling. A thought occurred to her. *I could ask Arhat to drive me around like he did before. That would be safer, wouldn't it?* She felt elated at the idea for a moment, then embarrassed. It was the coward's way out. Gem never had a chauffeur. She drove herself and Dora around L.A. all hours of the day and night searching for Underworld demons that had broken through the Gate. That was what the Guardian did. That was what Willet had to do.

Steeling her nerves, she steered the Jeep carefully around the circular drive and headed toward the main road to the freeway. The entrance north to Riverside was not far away. She followed the signs for Freeway 10 West. Her heart tap-danced in her chest and sweat broke out on her forehead as she merged into the flow of traffic in the slow lane. Cars whizzed by so fast she couldn't believe they could stay on the road. Her knuckles squeezed the steering wheel tight enough to snap it, and a flush of pinpricks ran over her skin. Yeah, she was in the thick of it now. Her crazy senses weren't helping. Steams of light and choppy wave forms poured through the windshield, right into her eyes. It was very confusing, and sunglasses didn't help. On top of the visual barrage, traffic noise roared. Her eardrums could barely keep up with the vibrations. Putting on her noise-cancelling headphones would have helped, but she couldn't do that while driving. Even she knew it was dangerous.

She squinted straight ahead at the car in front of her, praying she could avoid a rear-end collision. Then she heard a 'meow' from the back seat. Her heart jumped, and she almost lost control of the wheel. At the next exit, she pulled off into a gas station, parked the Jeep, and spun around to the back seat. There was Smoke. The tip of his gray tail flicked. He gave her a calm stare, as if to say, 'what's the problem?' She had a tough time not screaming at him. "What are you doing here, cat? I just left you in the house!" She hoped the frantic tone of her voice conveyed her displeasure, but he seemed unperturbed. She was too far down the road to turn around and take him home, so he was along for the ride. "Don't distract me, Smoke. I'm nervous enough as it is." She inhaled a few deep breaths, took the wheel again in her shaking hands, and maneuvered the Jeep back onto the freeway, hugging the slow lane with grim focus.

Cars weaved in and out of lanes, trying to make time through the traffic. 'Lane commandos', Audrey used to call them. Drivers were willing to risk everyone's lives to get somewhere five minutes sooner. She never truly appreciated the challenges Audrey faced when driving through L.A., and she did it almost every day. Her heart started to ache all over again for the loss of her sister. *Pull yourself together! You're driving. Concentrate.* She passed the cities of Colton and Bloomington. Traffic around her picked up speed. *How far am I from the Hollywood Hills?* She didn't want to think about the many miles she still had to go.

A sports car veered suddenly into her lane right in front of her and caused her to swerve and hit the brake. She was perilously close to a panic attack. *I have to calm down before I crash.* She took the next exit and headed north into Fontana, a small city in the foothills of the Jurupa Mountains. Mt. Jurupa rose ahead of her. A dusting of snow covered its rolling shoulders. She passed strip malls and small businesses on long streets dotted with palm trees. Red-roofed stucco dwellings clustered in housing developments landscaped with sturdy gray-green foliage. And traffic. Lots of traffic. Like many California towns, the setting was beautiful, but Fontana was a zoo on a sunny Saturday afternoon. Ahead of her, the flow of traffic turned right into a commercial mall. She followed it and ended up in front of a large Indoor Swap Meet. She managed to park the Jeep across the street near the mall. Her body shook. She took several deep breaths to settle her jangled nerves, relieved she had been able to come to a safe stop.

"I need to walk around, Smokey," she murmured. "Get control of myself. Wait for me." Smoke jumped into the front seat and sat beside her. "Meow," he said, licked his front paw and stroked it against his ear.

The air pressure shifted in her ears as she stepped out of the Jeep, and the now-familiar sound of a gong rang twice to announce a lucid dream state. Her Guardian senses were wide awake to all the different energies flowing around her. She crossed the street to the sidewalk and entered the Swap Meet parking lot. It almost felt like slow motion. People strolled among canopied stalls offering colorful crafts and novelties. Ethnic foods of various types roasted on grills. A Mariachi band in black and silver costume stood on the edge of the lot, strumming their big-bodied guitars and singing with gusto. Girls in long red, green, and yellow skirts and headdresses twirled in an open space near the musicians. Friendly greetings rang out. "Hi Nicky, Hi Tomas, Hi Jin, how ya doin'?" People knew each other. They smiled and hugged. Ribbons festooned the area in a riotous display of pink, yellow, and orange.

She floated through the kaleidoscope of color, sound, and movement, and began to realize that the ribbons she saw weren't actually ribbons but connections between people, forehead to forehead and heart to heart. Little lights traveled along the ribbons, carrying something between them that was beyond words. Feelings, intentions, thoughts not easily expressed but understood. An air of general goodwill prevailed. It calmed her. *This is nice. Glad I stopped.*

It was nice until it wasn't. At the corner of the lot, a pinwheel of black color caught her eye. It entered the lot from the side street, spiking black ribbons, and seemed so out of place in the happy crowd. A hollow feeling in her chest started to grow. This was going to be a problem.

Willet focused on the dark swirl and edged through the throng of shoppers to follow it, uncertain of what she would do when she caught up. In the center of the swirl was a man who entered the Swap Meet building through the front doors. She trailed him at a safe distance. He melted into the jumble of noise and activity inside, and she lost track of him momentarily. The sensory overload was enough to agitate a normal person. Brightly lit displays lined the walls offering athletic shoes, handbags, and jewelry. Long tables laden with homemade soaps and body lotions ran through the center space. Aromatherapy products and incense scented the air. Vendors hawked their wares while people slow-walked the aisles, checking out every product. Rock music played over speakers. For someone with Guardian senses, it was overwhelming.

She located the black pinwheel again. The man was deep into the throng of shoppers. His head swung left and right, scanning the room, and the black ribbons waving out from his forehead had pointed arrow tips. They projected into the crowd. She saw them pierce the foreheads of other people. Gem told her not to interfere in the free will of others, no matter what their colors revealed, but this felt like an attack. She had to stop it. The man wore a gray puffer coat over jeans. *A bit warm for a puffer coat, isn't it?* She tiptoed up behind him. Sharp black wires sprung at her from the back of his head, hitting her forehead and chest. She yanked them away. He turned and looked at her. His cold dark eyes glittered with malice. In that crowded space, there would be no margin for error if he acted on bad intentions.

"What's your problem?" she murmured when their eyes met. Not the most diplomatic words. They triggered a reaction in him. His lips spread into a rigid perversion of a smile, and a swirl of black emotion spun out of him. Wires wrapped around her throat and squeezed tight enough to strangle her. She choked, unable to speak or breathe, and swayed on her feet. The man opened his coat. In one fluid movement, he pulled a large gun from under his shoulder and aimed it in her direction. She took one look, dropped to the floor, and rolled between two tables.

Mass shootings were dismal fodder for the evening news. She could become another statistic right there. She grappled with the wires around her neck and tried to get a full breath. New wires sprung from him and wrapped around her body. She was pinned to the floor and skewered through the chest. His violent emotions bombarded her heart as she glimpsed his thoughts in her mind's eye. She had to do something, but she was incapacitated. Her mind raced. *How can I get the gun? If I slow him down, it might buy time before he targets other people in the store*

As she lay on the floor, she wondered why he hadn't shot her already. She peeked out from between the tables and saw a large gray animal jumping into the air. The man froze at the sight, and the barrel of his gun tilted lower in his hands. The animal leaped at him, hitting him in the chest with all four paws. The man staggered backwards, and the gun dropped to the floor, fired off a shot with a deafening bang, and spun in a lazy circle on the ground. The man grappled with the animal. While his attention was off her, his wires loosened. She was able to rip them from her arms and neck, and roll to her hands and knees, crawling toward the gun. The man pushed the animal away and made his own move toward the gun. He would get to it first, but before he could pick it up, she barreled-rolled hard into his lower legs and knocked him off balance. The animal, it looked like a cougar, jumped at him, and took him down to the floor with the full weight of its body, then lay on top of him and snarled in his face, showing a mouth full of long sharp teeth. The man stopped moving. Willet pushed the gun out of reach.

A cascade of screams had flooded the room after the gunshot. Shoppers ran for the exit in a thunderous herd. If anyone noticed the large feline in their midst, they were too busy escaping to react. Just as well. There was another problem. Everyone's chaotic emotions streamed through the store and hit Willet from every direction, trapping her in a color-coded barrage of their worst fears. There were so many, it turned into a massive tangle. The more she tried to rip the wires away, the more they tightened around her. Panic, anger, confusion, all the raging reactions to a crisis hooked into her consciousness. Mental images raced through her mind like an out-of-control news reel. What do people think about when they fear for their lives? Children, family, pets, friends, visions of home. Their yearnings rushed into her head and heart. The web of their emotional wires brought her to the floor and bound her tight. It was exhausting. She could barely raise her head.

The cougar rose from the man's prone body, stalked over to her, and started ripping away the emotional bindings with its claws until the web of wires thinned. She was able to shake off the last of them and got to her feet. They had to get out before she was caught in another web, or the man went for his gun again. "My hero," she said to the big cat. "Let's get out of here before someone questions us."

Police and paramedics arrived. Uniformed men and women ran in with their SWAT gear and surrounded the man who had the gun in his hands. He collapsed when they tased him. They relieved him of the gun and dragged him to the exit in handcuffs. Willet and the cougar followed the police at a discrete distance and slipped out the front door behind them, then stepped to the side to let the rest of the crowd run past. It felt good just to be out of the building.

Just beyond the doorway, a girl sat in a wheelchair. A small banner mounted on a stick was attached to the back of her chair. 'Creations by Carla' it announced. She had a green scarf around her brown hair and wore a long, dark green skirt down to her sandaled feet. Balls of gold yarn sat in her lap. She was knitting, seeming unfazed by all the shouting and people stampeding out of the building. Her needles clicked so rapidly they were a blur. A long swath of knitted gold yarn trailed out of the needles and draped to the ground.

It was a precarious spot to sit and knit. Willet felt the need to speak to her. "A gun went off inside, and people are running away. You might get trampled sitting there."

The girl looked up with a calm expression. "I'm fine. Are you fine?"

"Did you see what happened?"

"I heard," the girl nodded "You're the woman in the wires. People were scared, but you took care of them. You and your cat."

It was a surprisingly accurate report. Willet guessed that Carla was no ordinary knitter. "You could say it that way," Willet said. "This cat appeared out of nowhere. He's not mine."

Carla gave her a quizzical smile. "Are you sure?"

Willet looked down at the cougar. Its ears flicked. The big cat studied her with intense blue-gray eyes that projected wild energy. Those eyes had a familiar look to them.

"No one really owns that kind of cat," the girl said. "He's not of this world, but he's yours, nevertheless."

"He saved my life. I guess that makes us friends. I'm Willet, by the way."

"Carla," she said, pointing to the little sign above her head with a giggle. "Great to meet you. It's an honor."

Willet wasn't sure what that meant. "Why would it be an honor? I'm not special."

"You take care of the city. You see and hear what others don't. It's your job, isn't it?"

Willet wasn't sure what to say. "I'm a Guardian," she admitted. "You know about Guardians?"

"Yes. Some others do too. The Ice Breather protected us from dark things that come through the cracks. Now it's you, it seems."

It surprised Willet to hear the truth stated this way. She would have liked to know more about Carla, but fatigue was getting the best of her, and she had to get to TJ's house. She stammered some last words, said goodbye, and headed toward the street. The big cat walking beside her suddenly bolted ahead of her and disappeared into the crowd.

Chapter 11

Willet hauled herself into the Jeep with a weary huff. Her head hurt, and her heart pounded so hard it felt like it would crack her ribs. Smoke was sitting on the front seat, staring at her with his usual pensive innocence. Tufted ears, blue-gray eyes. There was something in his eyes that said "Yeah, it was me. You're welcome."

"'Fess up now, cat. What kind of animal are you, really?" Smoke hunkered down and became absorbed in cleaning his paws. She called TJ. "Thomas, you'll never believe what just happened. I can't even describe it."

Muffled voices spoke urgently in the background. TJ sounded agitated. "Sorry, Will. The situation got more serious here. Evelyn's in a coma. The doctors had to put her on life support. Jonah's distraught, and I'm being called upon to make decisions on her behalf that I'm not really qualified to make. She doesn't seem to have any relatives. I'll need to bring Jonah home at some point, and your presence there could help calm him. Hope you're on your way."

"Of course, I'll be there, but you need to know Smoke is with me. OK for him to visit your place? Hope there's no cat allergies."

She heard TJ exhale a long breath. It whistled through his teeth. "Why is the cat with you? Never mind, just bring it. Explanations later." He hung up.

She slumped lower in the seat and closed her eyes. Too tired to drive. Too tired to think. Smoke stepped into her lap on delicate paws and plopped down. She pulled his warm body to her chest and hugged him, laid her cheek on his head, and rubbed his soft ears. His presence was comforting. "That was a close call, Smokey. No matter what kind of cat you are, I'm glad you're here. It's lonely being a Guardian. I never realized that so much as now. Gem told me she appreciated my company. She might have been lonely too." Smoke's purr vibrated against her chest, and her breath slowed to its rhythm. They breathed together in steady inhales and quiet exhales. The tension in her muscles melted.

She became aware of a buzzing sound. The buzz kept getting louder until it was right in front of her face. She opened her eyes. An oversized wasp hovered in front of her, flapping its transparent amber wings. Red bristles covered its legs and a stinger an inch long jutted out of its backside. Its bug eyes bulged and stared at her. The eyes were blue. *Can wasps have blue eyes?* Smoke hissed at the wasp, and the wasp buzzed back in a sound she could understand as words. "Stay away from Tom and me." The tone was downright nasty.

No way. She knew that voice. "Evelyn? I thought you were in a coma..."

"That's none of your damn business. Tom is here with me where he belongs, and my son is with us. If you try to interfere with our family, I'll sting you. It'll hurt a lot. I promise."

I'm more tired than I thought. After what happened in the Swap Meet, this confrontation was the last straw. It made her mad. She snarled at this insect manifestation. "You're delusional, Evelyn. Thomas and I are together, and we'll be together in the future. So, get well soon, and then go home where you belong. Besides, things have changed. I'm the Guardian of the Gate in L.A. now. I will shove your venomous bug-body into the Underworld and shut the door until you either wake up or die. Sorry to be blunt, but those are your options. Now buzz off."

The wasp's buzz rose to a high rate of vibration. "You bitch!" It dive-bombed Willet and turned its stinger toward her right eye. Smoke raised his right paw with claws spread and batted the wasp away in one smooth swipe. The wasp somersaulted backwards against the windshield and righted itself, wings flapping furiously. "I'll sting that cat until it convulses!"

The wasp took a dive at Smoke. Willet curled over him and wrapped her arms around him. She felt the wasp's stinger jab into her scalp and forehead. It might be psychic pain, but it sure did hurt. A lot. She gritted her teeth, wondering how long the wasp could keep stinging her. Didn't they lose their stingers after a while, or was that just the bees? Hovering protectively over Smoke, she waved her arms and slapped her hands at the wasp, trying to smash it against the windshield. She got several stabs in her hands for her trouble. Tears of pain came to her eyes. *Can the stings make my hands swell?* A sharp knocking sound interrupted her thoughts, and the blue-eyed wasp disappeared. A policeman was tapping his knuckle against the driver side window. She rolled the window down and tried for a bright smile while she steadied her panicked breathing. *So not ready to answer questions.* "Hello, Officer. What's up?"

The policeman bent down to peer at her through the open window. "Are you alright, miss? We just had an incident inside the store. You looked like you might be in some, uh, distress."

It was embarrassing. "I'm fine. Really. There was a bug flying around in here. I was trying to swat it." *I probably look deranged. Can he arrest me for that?*

He squinted at her, scanned the inside of the Jeep, and then noticed Smoke in her lap. "It's not safe carrying an animal loose in the car. It might interfere with your driving. Do you have a carrier for it?"

"I don't, but you're absolutely right, Sir. I'm going right home. I'll bring a carrier with me next time."

The policeman gave her a dubious stare, but nodded and moved on, leaving Willet to collect her wits. She took a closer look at Smoke. "What's the deal, little one? Do you have extraordinary senses? You saw the wasp just like I did."

Smoke responded with his usual yawn, showing all his sharp little white teeth and long pink tongue. He curled up on her lap with a deep sigh and went into a snooze. *Cats are Souls. They could have supernatural senses just like humans, couldn't they?* She faced the steering wheel and thought about getting back on the freeway. After facing an armed gunman, the thought of L.A. traffic didn't seem quite so ominous, but pinpricks of fear still ran up her arms. She needed to get to the Hollywood Hills before TJ brought Jonah home. She started the Jeep with some trepidation. If Evelyn went on some kind of rampage, who knew what her wasp might try to do. She pulled carefully away from the curb with a gulp of courage and headed toward the freeway.

Chapter 12

**** Dean ****

The sound of drums, hand bells, and finger cymbals drew
Dean into the market square. The spritely music was hypnotic
in a way that made him want to dance through the
marketplace. Vendors lined the square behind wooden tables,
hawking pots of oils, live birds, and grains heaped in tightly
woven baskets. Casks of wine. Stacks of gourds. The air
glistened with flies hovering over dried fish, cheese, and some
kind of baked buns. Wares he couldn't identify looked like
tools made of wood and rope. A man led a gray donkey
through the crowd carrying two straw baskets suspended
across its back. The man bought fruits, vegetables, dried fish,
and olive oil and stuffed them into the baskets. The beast
swatted flies away with its skinny tail.

Dean watched coins of real silver, gold, and copper pass between the hands of shoppers and vendors. He stopped short at one table that displayed pomegranates cut open in halves. The woman behind the table had long straight black hair. Her eyes were dark brown and lined with black kohl. She wore a loose brown tunic with a leather pouch slung across her chest. She made an ululating sound in her throat, wagging her tongue and beckoning to customers to check out the fruit on her table. There was something about her. She didn't look like the other Romans. She had full lips and high cheek bones, and her skin was golden. A foreigner, then, maybe Egyptian. Rome was the crossroads of the known world at this time. People from countries around the Mediterranean, northern Africa and into Asia brought their wares to trade. The pomegranate seeds looked red and juicy. He would have purchased fruit from her if he could, but he had no coins and no hands with which to offer them. He studied her face and came to a surprising conclusion. He knew this woman, though he couldn't quite put his finger on what it was about her that was so familiar. A whisper in his ear warned him, "Do not stare too long, Warrior. You should not get drawn into life here."

Dean averted his eyes and didn't argue. *Could I have been a woman in this life? Never considered that.* He kept walking down the row of wobbly tables. A short man in drab peasant garb with a frayed rope around his waist stood behind a table that held an array of small drums for sale made of brown hide stretched across round wooden frames. Colorful bird feathers hung from each frame. The man held a drum in his left hand and used the palm of his right hand, the back of his hand and his fingers to tap and thump the drum. He popped it off his knee, keeping up a sprightly, clipped tempo and danced a jig with a smile on his face that showed a couple of missing teeth. Dean was curious how he made so many different sounds on such a rudimentary drum, so he moved closer to the table. As a drummer himself, Dean would have loved to pick up a drum and try it out.

A man in a white cloak wrapped over a light brown tunic walked up to the table and spoke to the drummer. The man had shoulder-length dark brown hair liberally spangled with silver and carried a wooden walking staff. The two men seemed to know each other. Dean moved closer to hear what they would say. The older man suddenly turned his head and looked straight at Dean. His silver-frosted brown mustache framed smiling lips, but it was the piercing blue eyes that startled Dean. Unmistakably Augustus. Could *he* see Dean floating there in a Light body? Dean held his breath, waiting for Augustus to say something, but Augustus turned back to the drum vendor and resumed their conversation. Another thought occurred to Dean – *maybe I was the drum vendor. Augustus said we knew each other. Don't look in his eyes. Don't look in his eyes.*

Dean quickly looked away. A rustle in the crowd caught his attention. The crowd parted in front of him, and two men walked through their midst dressed in the uniforms of Roman centurions. They wore leather breastplates and leather-paneled skirts over red tunics, and the laces of their leather sandals wrapped up their ankles. Daggers hung on their belts, a short one on the right and a longer one on the left. One soldier held a staff of twisted wood in his right hand. He was older than the other soldier and seemed to be of superior rank. The soldiers stood out beyond just their uniforms. They were taller and more muscled than any of the shoppers. The soldiers came to stand in front of the drum vendor's table. The younger soldier picked up a drum and began to pound on it clumsily. The soldier with the staff laughed. The first one said something to the vendor and held up the drum. A negotiation in price began, but there seemed to be a language barrier. The vendor held up four fingers of his right hand. The soldier held up two fingers and wiggled them. The vendor clasped his hands against his chest in a beseeching gesture and raised three fingers. The soldier banged his hand on the table and raised two fingers again. His voice rose to a shout. Silence fell around them as other shoppers turned to look. The soldier with the staff laid a hand on the younger man's shoulder and said something in a low voice. The young soldier shrugged the hand away and leaned across the table. He grabbed the vendor by the front of the tunic, shaking him. A murmur went up in the crowd. *Uh oh.* The older soldier raised his staff and pounded it on the ground. The young bartering soldier threw the drum on the table and turned around with a glare at his superior officer. Words were exchanged. Dean got the gist of the conversation but wished he understood it all.

The older soldier turned suddenly and looked at Dean. Their eyes met, and Dean felt a sudden pressure in his heart, as if a hand had grabbed it. Time stood still, and all sound stopped. He was pulled forward toward the soldier's brawny body. It absorbed him like an ink blotter. In the next moment, he was looking out at the world through the eyes of the soldier.

He settled into the solid physical reality of the soldier and realized *I am now this body.* He became aware of what was on the body and within it. The strong, fit physique bristled with energy. His broad chest flexed under his leather chest plate. The daggers on his belt lay heavy against his thighs. The heat of the hard-packed earth radiated over his sandals and up his legs. The skin on his muscled arms felt dry, baked brown by long exposure to the sun. Barely healed wounds in his left leg and the right side over his ribs ached. A partially digested meal sitting in his stomach made his abdomen feel tight, and his bearded face itched. He lifted a finger to scratch the chin under his beard. His thick wrist, perhaps accustomed to swinging that long sword, felt heavier than his own wrist ever felt.

The conscious being of the ancient soldier was inside the body with him. Although they were two incarnations of Dean himself, they were two different beings with their own thoughts and feelings. Was the soldier aware of him? Could they communicate with each other? He wanted to understand his previous life, but he never expected to be trapped in it. Sonrisa had warned him about this. He should have left the market when he saw Augustus.

Dean hadn't experienced Rome fully with all physical senses until that moment. Now it was overwhelming. Dust flew into his eyes. The warm, stultifying air made his body drip sweat under his armor, and smells assaulted his nose. Roasting meats, sweat and piss mixed with patchouli and the taint of sewage. This ancient world was raw, visceral, and unrefined. He had an urge to throw up violently. The body heat of all the shoppers pressed against his skin, and amazingly, he now understood what everyone was saying. In Latin. The body swayed on its feet. He tried to recover some sense of his identity. *I'm Dean Simmons. I live in Manhattan Beach. Dean. Remember Dean.* Another voice echoed. *I am Lucius Avitus of the Roman Guard, son of Crassus. My people come from Tarentum.* Lucius Avitus, the soldier, was struggling to hang on to his own identity. 'Dean' and 'Lucius' fought to control their shared body and guide its movements.

Sonrisa's voice whispered in their left ear. "Warrior, what have you done?"

"I'm trapped," Dean whispered. "How do I get out of here?"

"Who is that?" Lucius shook his head, trying to clear his ears. He heard the voices, but didn't understand them, and he was distracted by a situation going on in front of him in which he was personally involved. The younger soldier – Dean knew him now as 'Silas' – was yelling at the drum vendor again, threatening to overturn his table if the vendor didn't sell a drum for one denarius. Silas was a trainee. Lucius was the commanding officer. It was up to him to bring order. He spoke to the vendor, who held out a drum to Silas with a trembling hand. Silas took the drum, slammed one denarius on the table and walked off. Lucius fished under his leather skirt for a pouch, pulled out two denarii and plunked them on the table. He strode off through the crowd after Silas. As his superior, he had to stop the hothead before he caused more trouble.

Dean had no control of their movements. He directed thoughts to the Traveler, hoping she could hear him. *Sonrisa! I'm seen enough. Get me out of here.* He was desperate to get free of the soldier's body.

Lucius was aware of Dean's thoughts. He blinked his eyes, listened, then looked around, wondering if someone nearby was speaking to him. *Too much wine last night?* He trudged on through the market, taking Dean along for the ride.

Chapter 13

TJ's house in the Hollywood Hills seemed like a million miles from Fontana. Willet's stomach did flipflops just thinking about the distance, and her crazy senses didn't let up. Waves of energy streamed around her, through her and through the car. Pinpoints of light flashed at the corners of her eyes. She could hardly see the road. How was she supposed to drive this way? Gem said the new sensory manifestations would become her Guardian tools. It couldn't happen soon enough. She gathered her wits and resolve, clamped the steering wheel in a death grip, and tried not to think too hard about what she was doing. Smoke stepped into her lap for a snuggle. "Smoke, I need to concentrate right now." He jumped into the back seat like the excellent kitty he was. Cruising down the long street through Fontana, she began to breathe calmly.

The GPS was set for TJ's address. She could just relax, follow directions, and the Jeep would take her there. No problem. After fifteen minutes, it became clear that the Jeep had another destination in mind. They were heading toward downtown L.A. as surely as if a magnetic tractor beam was pulling them. She tried to tap the brake and turn the wheel, but the Jeep would not alter its course. She shouldn't be surprised. It was Gem's Jeep after all. Willet had a suspicion of where they were going, and she didn't want to go there, certainly not alone. The mountain of sand in the middle of downtown L.A. called to her with the heavy drumbeat of its black heart pounding in her ears.

But I'm not ready.

Exit signs for 'Downtown Los Angeles' came up on the right side of the freeway. Sure enough, the Jeep slowed down by itself and took that exit, despite GPS instructions to the contrary. It drove her down 5th Avenue. She caught sight of the massive mountain of black sand looming above the tops of other buildings. Her heart beat double time. She put a foot to the brake, not wanting to get any closer, but the Jeep wouldn't stop until they reached Hope Street. Then it slowed and allowed her to park. The sand mountain was straight ahead.

"Smoke, can you stay here? Please?" Smoke opened one sleepy eye and meowed, then went back to sleep. She got out of the Jeep, and walked into Hope Place, a shady little courtyard tucked into the middle of the busy downtown. A 3-foot statue of a naked woman made of bronze stood on a round granite pedestal in the middle of a circular pond. Water bubbled in the pond. A plaque on the pedestal said the statue was called *Source Figure*. The sculptor was Robert Graham. The water of life supposedly poured through the woman's fingers into the pond. It was an uplifting image, in contrast to the threatening black sand towering above it.

The courtyard was not as she had last seen it. Crystal boulders surrounding the sand were now ten feet high by ten feet wide. They had grown from small pieces of crystal scattered there by Bart Johnson. One boulder right in front of the mountain was bigger than the rest. It had to be fifteen feet high by fifteen feet wide. All the boulders had grown in size by eating into the sand and digesting its negative energy. They had consumed a lot, but the pile still rose to the sky, and the heartbeat coming from the sand pounded louder than the last time she heard it. She pressed her fists to her ears. Fear fluttered in her chest.

Wire fencing had been raised around the sand pile with red *Warning* signs on it. Some kind of construction work was in progress. Men in hardhats and reflective vests were shoveling sand into separate piles. A giant backhoe with a bucket attached to a long mechanical arm reached in from the street and scooped up the piles and dropped them into a dump truck parked nearby. This was bad on so many levels. Everyone was oblivious to the danger the sand posed, and it should absolutely not be removed from the courtyard. It would be dangerous wherever it ended up. *Where are they taking the sand?*

Willet searched the area for someone who looked like a site foreman. She spotted a tall man in jeans and a blue plaid flannel shirt holding a clipboard. From under his white hard hat, a long blond ponytail trailed down his back. She hurried over and stood right in front of him, making herself impossible to ignore. He was tall and muscular. She barely stood higher than his elbow, bent as he scribbled on the clipboard.

She cleared her throat. "Excuse me, sir, are you the foreman? I need to talk to the person in charge here."

The man looked down at her. "This is my dig. I'm Lars Lake. What can I do for you, miss?" The label on his shirt said, 'Lake Construction'.

"How much sand have you taken from this site?"

He gave her a puzzled look and pointed at the dump truck.

"This is the third load today."

"What are you doing with it?"

"The sand is going to a paving project in Bel Air. We're mixing it into cement before we pour. Why do you ask?"

She decided to plunge right in. "You can't use this sand. It will hurt people."

The man stared at her. "What do you mean? What's wrong with it?"

"It's contaminated." That was as good an explanation as any.

"Yes, contaminated. It needs to stay isolated until it can be disposed of."

"How do we *dispose of* this much sand? If we were inclined to do so, that is?"

"Bury it. Dissolve it with acid. Send it into space. I'm not sure, but we have to figure out something. Do you remember the big building that used to stand in this spot? We don't want another one of those."

"You mean the Dragon Head Building?"

The Wall of Unknowing spread static over L.A., courtesy of Jat the Deceiver, and caused a sort of amnesia in everyone in the city. The US Bank Tower that stood on this spot for decades was suddenly replaced by the Dragon Head Building without anyone realizing the change. Lars was giving her a strange look. She had to be careful, or she'd sound like a lunatic.

"Yes, the Dragon Head. Do you know *how* it turned into this pile of sand?"

His blue eyes glazed over. "I think I was out of town at the time." Another convenient alteration of memory. Jat covered his tracks well.

No point debating it. "The sand was contaminated. By radiation. People can't be near it."

"How do you know that?"

She searched for words and decided that continuing the lie was her best option. "I'm with the EPA. We've already tested this site. Radiation is off the charts. Dangerous for you to be near it."

The man studied her face and then snapped back to business. "I'll have a test engineer recheck the radiation levels. Thanks for the tip." He resumed writing on the clipboard.

She had hoped for a better response. "Mr. Lake. Lars. You don't understand the seriousness of the situation here. This sand is dangerous."

Lars sighed and gave her a bemused look. "Sweetheart, I have customers who want the sand mixed into concrete for construction at their properties. The mixture of black sand and quartz is part of the design. It's become very popular. We signed off on it, so I have contracts to fulfill. You understand."

They were getting nowhere, and what's more, Lars was awfully good looking. Lots of muscle evident under the flannel shirt, white teeth in a tanned face, strong jaw, and blue eyes that twinkled with intelligent good humor. It was distracting. Willet didn't notice other guys since she and TJ got together, but it was hard not to notice Mr. Lake. A shiver ran over her when he smiled. *Get ahold of yourself, Will. You're here on Guardian business.* "Could you delay the projects? Until we have more information. If it is radioactive, you wouldn't want to spread the sand around, would you?"

"No, of course not, but contracts have deadlines. Delays cost money. I have to have a good reason to delay a project. I'll have the sand tested like I said, but I can't promise much beyond that."

"What about the crystal boulders? You're not touching those, are you?"

"The city conveyed the boulders to me as part of this job. I have bids for two of them. A designer in town who makes custom art pieces wants one. And a businessman wants another. We'll close the deals by the end of the week. They'll net enough income to finance my company for the next two years."

Even worse news. Removing the boulders was a disaster. The crystal was the only thing keeping the sand in check. "The boulders should not be removed under any circumstances," she said, trying to keep the emotion out of her voice. "They er, keep the contamination of the sand in check!"

The smile on his face turned perplexed. "You realize that makes no sense, right? I can't turn down the amount of money I've been offered for the boulders. That would be even crazier than what you just said."

Willet was at a loss for more convincing arguments. "OK, but can we talk more when you have time? About the sand and the boulders. I need you to understand what I'm trying to tell you. My name is Willet, by the way."

"Willet." He smiled that smile again, a genuine smile tinged with sly humor. "We could have lunch. Then we can talk, if that's what you want," he said with a wink.

A sneaky reddish wire of emotion sprung from his chest, then quickly retracted. She didn't feel any jeopardy. She was just wary. This was unfamiliar territory, and she wasn't sure how to act. Her experience with men prior to TJ was zero. Despite the distracting blue of his eyes, she couldn't lose sight of the need to stall the project. "Sure. Lunch sounds good." They nodded at each other. She watched him walk away, not sure she liked what just happened. Lunch with a man she just met – *does he think it's a date? How will I explain this to Thomas?*

All of a sudden, a red-hot poker of pain hit her in the back. Heat ran down her spine and radiated through her nerves all the way to her fingers and toes. She spun around and faced the sand mountain. The mountain sat silent, but very much aware of her. "I know it's you," she accused it. "Whatever you are." Beams of red light shot out and strobed around her like search lights, then hit her in the abdomen. The sudden pain drove her to her knees, and the burn of it spread through her body. The heartbeat from inside the mountain boomed like a bass guitar. Black ichor oozed out of the sand, dripping down the sides of the mountain. The black liquid twisted, turned, and morphed into shapes both humanoid and inhuman before melting back into the sand.

She looked around. *Does anyone else notice what's going on here?*

The construction crew working on the sand pile seemed unaware of all the psychic activity happening right near them. She heard a deep voice, like tumbling boulders, speaking in a foreign tongue. It came from the mountain. She didn't understand a word, but she realized the sand was probably the location of a major breach in the Gate. Even though the Circle had destroyed the Dragon Head Building, the breach was still in there, wide open. Souls from the Underworld could walk right through it into the physical world and probably had done so already. She folded forward and groaned, curled in tight with hands over her head, trying to protect herself from the hot red lights and deafening heartbeats. When she shut her eyes, afterimages of the red lights burned on her retinas. The onslaught of energy made her head swim. Someone was calling her name, but she couldn't respond. *Sorry, too dizzy. Call back later.* The relentless bombardment of lights and sounds was a sure recipe to incapacitate the new Guardian of Los Angeles.

She heard a voice shouting at her. 'Stand up! Run, Will!' *Who was that?* She couldn't move or respond.

A hand touched her back, and then an arm dropped over her shoulders. Lars knelt beside her. "Willet? What's going on? Do you need a doctor?" Concerned pink-orange streamers swirled out him, circling around her without touching.

She peeked up at him from her huddled posture. "Red lights are coming off that sand. They're hot as lasers, and they hurt. You have to be careful." A hot beam from the sand hit Lars in the head, then two more. He didn't seem to notice. "It's hitting you too, here, here, and here." She touched a fingertip lightly to his cheek, jaw, and temple. "You have to protect yourself. If you get a headache, don't be surprised."

He drew back with a suspicious look. "I don't get headaches, but now that you mention it, the side of my head does hurt. How did you know that?"

"I have a lot of experience with headaches. And I can see what's hitting you, even if you don't." She could tell by the look in his eyes that curiosity and disbelief were battling in his brain. She was trusting him with more information about herself than she intended, but there was no other choice.

"Look, I know this sounds crazy. There's a lot you don't know about me, and it's not important, except to say that the sand is dangerous to people. It shouldn't be spread around. Your crew is getting hit by the same hot beams you and I are. They will feel the pain eventually. You need to understand what you're up against and get everyone away from here, including yourself. How soon can we get together and talk?"

Lars sat back on his haunches, studying her. "We take a break in fifteen."

"Good. Your men need distance between themselves and the sand before they're all seriously hurt. Maybe you could let them go early."

Lars rubbed the back of his neck. "You are one strange lady, ya know that?"

"Wait 'til we talk at lunch…"

Chapter 14

**** Audrey ***

Audrey felt so cut off from everyone and everywhere she wanted to be that she couldn't help feeling grumpy, and she had to dodge lightning left and right. It was getting old. She worried about Willet's safety and pictured her alone, fighting demons without the full Circle behind her. As soon as she had that image, she found herself floating over Hope Place courtyard, a place of bad memories for the Circle. Willet was walking across the courtyard, away from the black sand mountain. Red lights shot out from the sand and hit her in the back. She spun around, and the lights hit her in the chest. She sagged to the ground like a sack of rice.

Audrey was at her side immediately, shouting, "Will! Can you hear me? Get up! Run!" It was like shouting from the other side of the planet. Willet didn't respond. She tried to touch her sister's shoulder but couldn't make physical contact.

A low voice came out of the sand mountain. "This city is mine for the tasting," the voice chuckled. "I will eat its fruits and gain physical life."

Audrey couldn't tell if Willet heard the voice or not, so she answered on her behalf. "The Guardian of the Gate will stop you, and the Circle of Augustus will defeat Jat as we have done before. Whoever you are."

"The Circle is broken, Ring Thrower. Its days are past. Begone."

Willet lay in a heap on the ground. Audrey tried shouting at her sister again. Willet was the Listener, after all. The Listener heard everything. Willet turned her head, but then, a tall blond man came to kneel beside her. He put his arm around her and raised her to a sitting position. Willet spoke to him. She was conscious, at least.

A fluffy gray cat walked into the courtyard, padded over and sniffed Willet, then sniffed the blond man. The man looked surprised at the sudden visitor. Willet reached out, stroked the cat's head, and said something in a low soothing voice. Whatever the cat was looking for, it was satisfied with the sniff. The cat walked out of the courtyard as casually as it had arrived.

Is this the new cat? He comes and goes as he pleases. I wish I could talk to Augustus about it. Audrey pictured Augustus in his light blue suit and full white beard, standing in his light-filled office in Samhasa. And then she was there in front of him. It happened as fast as a thought.

Augustus smiled at her. "So. You have found your way here at last. Welcome back, Ring Thrower. What took so long?"

"You - you- can... see me?" She was so happy to be seen.

"Of course, my dear. Please, sit down, and tell me how you are." He gestured toward a white settee in the middle of the room. She took a seat. A plush blue chair appeared in front of her. Augustus sat there. His countenance beamed.

The love in his eyes encouraged words to pour from her. "I've been stuck in an in-between place for so long it drove me crazy, but then I was in that horrible courtyard, watching Willet get hit by red lights from the sand. I'm so afraid for her. She's in trouble, and she didn't hear me when I spoke to her. How is that possible? She's the Listener! What do I do now? And how did I get here anyway?"

Augustus nodded as she got everything off her chest. Then he reassured her. "The Listener has her senses. She heard you but could not respond. As for your recent movements, Soul follows the focus of its attention. You will move to the person or place you envision. You may return here anytime by putting your attention on me."

Audrey took a deep breath and looked around the office. "It's that easy? Just think of you and I'm here?"

"Yes. Now, what troubles you most?"

"Dean and I were supposed to meet up. I don't know where he is, and I worry about him too. I would really like to get my physical body back like TJ did. Instead, I just float around like an untethered balloon. I should be doing something useful, right? But I don't know what. Or how."

"What would you like to do?"

"I'd like to be back in the Circle. My sister needs help. The black sand is hurting her, and she seems to have no defense against it."

Augustus studied her and stroked his white mustache. "A reunited Circle would benefit all concerned. You wish to be a Ring Thrower again? Or something else?"

"I didn't know there was a choice."

"There is always a choice, if we are willing to pay the price for it." His gaze was unwavering.

"What's the price for being Ring Thrower again?"

"You must forgive yourself, Audrey. Guilt darkens your light. It will hold you back from the greater things of which you are capable. You will not be able to manifest a new physical body until you are able to let that guilt go."

She wanted to argue, but it was pointless. There *were* things she felt guilty about. She wasn't able to save Nick Hardman before he had a heart attack while he was caught in the Spider's web inside the Dragon Head Building. His death devastated his best friend, James Jain, who still suffered from the loss. And then there was Matt Gregg. He was TJ's friend before he fell for Jat's promises of power and turned into a demented lizard-man. She actually cut Matt's head off with her energy ring before he could kill her and Dean. It seemed like self-defense in the heat of the fight, but she felt miserable afterwards. They were all casualties of Jat's vicious deceptions. Delusions of power, pride, guilt, despair. Jat knew every person's weakness and played them to perfection.

"I don't know what to do about Nick or Matt. Their lives ended. What can I do to help James Jain? Nick's death has brought his life to a standstill."

Augustus nodded. "He is in despair. Show him a path forward. That is the mission of the Circle after all."

"I thought our job was to drive Jat out of Los Angeles and slam the Gate shut behind him."

"It is, of course, but what good does it do to drive out the Deceiver if people cannot recover from his attacks?"

A valid point. How to help James Jain recover, that was the question. "So, what would help? What do I do?" It seemed like she asked that question over and over lately.

"Demonstrate to the man that Soul never dies and let him know he can find his purpose if he seeks it."

She pictured Jain, his close-cropped black hair and strong shoulders and the stubborn set of his jaw, secure in his own street smarts. She hoped she could be persuasive enough. There wasn't much time. Augustus and the office around her were already fading from her view.

Chapter 15

Willet wanted the reassurance of TJ's voice before she had lunch with Lars, but her call went to voicemail for the umpteenth time. She didn't know what to say anyway, so she hung up. Regretting that, she called again and left a terse message. "I'm downtown. You know where. The sand is acting up. I need to talk to you." She realized she didn't ask about Evelyn, but at the moment, Evelyn was not high on her priority list.

The thought of lunch with Lars made her nervous. Fifteen minutes went by fast. She met him at the construction site, and they walked to a nearby coffee bar. Inside, there were two stools next to a window. They ordered avocado and tuna sandwiches and coffees and sat down to wait. Lars leaned forward on his muscled forearms and smiled at her. Their knees touched, and the table suddenly felt way too small. Yellow streams waved around his head that looked like they might be curiosity, along with some fuchsia romantic fantasies. One purple plume lightly touched her cheek. She brushed it away as discretely as she could.

"I don't usually let anyone hijack me when I'm working," he said, "but I made an exception for you. Can we go out sometime?"

Uh oh. This was already getting tricky. "That's flattering, Lars, really, but I'm' here to talk about the sand. It's important for you to hear what I have to say, so no one gets hurt."

The smile faded from his face. He sat back and eyed her. "Well?"

She plunged right in. "I've got two questions. First, have you ever looked at a map of the Hope Place courtyard from two years ago? What building was there? Second, what color was the Dragon Head Building before it fell?"

He looked puzzled. "That's three questions. I haven't looked at a city map from two years ago."

"Can you think back and tell me what building was there two years ago?"

Lars stared into space. "The Dragon Head Building has been there forever, as long as I've lived in L.A."

"OK, question two: what color was the Dragon Head Building?"

"The color of the buildings in that area is Light Oyster Gray like a lot of other downtown buildings. Why?"

"It leads me to another question, and you're a good person to ask since you're in construction. What would cause a ninety-story building made of Light Oyster Gray stone turn into a pile of black sand?"

A vertical crease folded between his eyes. It got deeper the longer he thought about the question. "Oil sand? Maybe tar?" He fell silent again. "Is this some kind of trick question?" he said after a minute. His stare turned into a glare.

"It's not a trick. I would like you to think about how oil or tar would get in the debris from a fallen building. An underground leak? The La Brea Tar Pits? Does something like that sound plausible?"

"I have no idea," he said with a grunt and an irritated shrug of the shoulders. Sandwiches and coffees were delivered to the table. He took a sip of coffee and bit into his sandwich.

"One more question, and I'll stop. Where do you think the crystal boulders came from? Is there any record of someone installing them around the sand?"

His hands and feet twitched, and his annoyance grew visibly. "I don't know. They were there when I started the project. They belonged to the city. Now they belong to me. What do you want me to say?"

"I'd like you to think about the questions, that's all. Take your time. When you're ready to consider the possibility that something might be off about the sand, we should talk further. In the meantime, please don't use it for any new building projects. Please."

Lars put down his sandwich. "That's a lot to ask. I don't make scheduling decisions on a whim. There are other people involved. How would I justify it? I can't just take your claims on faith."

"Like you said, you'll have the sand tested for contamination. That's not unusual, is it?"

His eyes grew icy. "Don't tell me how to run my business, *Willet*. I don't like being manipulated, even by someone as hot as you."

"I apologize if I made you feel that way. My intention is to alert you to a serious danger and hope you make the right decisions." She fumbled in her pack for paper and a pen and jotted down her phone number. "Here's my cell. If something unusual comes up regarding the sand, anything at all, you can call me immediately. Any hour."

He took the paper and then into her eyes. "Ordinarily, I'd consider this a good sign. Now I'm not sure what it is."

"Well, I want to keep in touch. Is that good? I hope it is."

Lars wrapped up his food and drink. "I guess so. Not sure where this conversation is going, but I've got to get back to work. Have a nice day." He stood up and walked out of the café, leaving a chilly breeze in his wake.

Willet watched him go and sipped her coffee. She didn't achieve all her objectives with him, but at least he had her number. When things started to hit the fan, he'd know how to reach her.

Chapter 16

**** Dean***

Two voices in one head is the essence of schizophrenia. The inner voices of Dean and Lucius battled for supremacy. Their thought streams collided, and there was a third voice, that of the Traveler. "Warrior," she whispered. "Listen. Focus. Remember who you are. Remember where you came from." Dean struggled to do as the Traveler instructed. Lucius was beginning to wonder if he was going crazy.

Dean remembered his life in the future, but the world he was in now was all too real. The sights and sounds of ancient Rome exploded in his face, overwhelming his senses. He became interested in what was around him and wanted to walk this way and that, checking out what he saw. Lucius had different plans and pulled him in other directions.

It was Lucius who controlled their physical movements. He walked down the aisle of tables and stalls in the market, back to the dark-haired woman selling pomegranates, and stood in front of her table, staring at her. She was beautiful. Not Egyptian, Dean now realized, but Sicilian, with Egyptian ancestors. "Amisi," Lucius said. "Your fruits look inviting as always." From the double entendre, Dean surmised that Lucius and Amisi knew each other well. Images flickered through Lucius' mind's eye, of Amisi naked in bed, her arms and legs wrapped around Lucius. Another girl with long black hair and the same golden skin was climbing into bed with them. Lucius was a busy man.

Amisi's dark eyes met his. "You flatter me, Lucius. You devil." A blush came to her cheeks under the golden tone of her skin, and she gave a coy shrug of the shoulders. Her long black eye lashes fluttered over her eyes. "Banafrit asks for you. She misses you."

"Tell your sister I will see her anon." Lucius picked up a cut wedge of pomegranate and pressed it against his lips. He stared at Amisi and sucked the sweet, juicy seeds into his mouth, scraping the rind with his teeth. Amisi gave him a knowing smile. Images flashed again of the dark-haired girl with pert breasts smiling at him, kissing his chest. The lovely Banafrit. Blood flushed under Lucius' skin, and Dean felt the heat of it. *OK, too much information.*

Another image floated through their shared mind, of a woman with honey blonde hair and direct blue eyes smiling at them. Audrey. The image was gone after a few moments. Dean savored the memory of Audrey. Lucius wondered who she was.

A hand touched their left arm. A tall woman stood beside them and spoke. "Warriors. Walk with me." She wore a white toga with an embroidered blue band around the neck, and her long brown hair hung loose on her shoulders. The expression on her face was stern.

Lucius stared at her, wondering who she was and what she wanted.

The Traveler read his thoughts. "I am Sonrisa Degas. We will be acquainted. Come with me now."

The intrusion irritated Amisi. "Who is this woman, Lucius? Tell her to leave us."

Dean and Lucius struggled over what to do next. Dean demanded their body follow her. Lucius resisted, but then curiosity got the better of him. "We will be together, Ami," Lucius said to Amisi. "Do not fear."

The tall woman walked off into the crowd. Dean and Lucius watched her white toga proceed down the aisle of the market like a flag. Lucius followed her until suddenly the crush of shoppers disappeared and the mouth of a large tunnel opened before him. The tall woman walked inside the tunnel and turned back to beckon them with her hand.

Lucius entered the tunnel slowly, one foot in front of the other. "What is this manifestation? What do you want of me?"

The Traveler fixed serious eyes on him. "I will show you what will become your memories."

Wind rushed through the tunnel. Images swirled on the walls, of people and places, some familiar to Lucius, others familiar to Dean. An image of the blonde-haired woman appeared again. Dean longed to hear her voice.

Lucius felt the longing too but didn't know why. "These memories are not mine. Why do I see them?"

"Because you will inhabit another body, another life, one day," she said calmly. "Dean, speak to me. You live in California in the 21st century. Do you remember this?"

"Yes."

"Focus on the images of that life. Find a touchpoint, someone, or something that can pull you from the body that holds you. If you linger any longer, you will be trapped in a life you have already lived. You will not be free until the death of this body."

Dean understood the words, but Lucius didn't. Frustration and confusion short-circuited their decision-making. They couldn't move forward and couldn't go back. The one image that held their attention was the blonde-haired woman, her blue eyes looking at them, so direct and confident. A proper Roman woman wouldn't look at a man in such a bold way. Lucius felt Dean's longing and wondered how he knew the woman. He reached his arms out, trying to touch her, but the image faded, replaced by the laughing eyes of Amisi. A different kind of longing grew in Lucius, raw and hot. He wanted to run back to her where things made sense. Dean resisted. Lucius prevailed. "This is the life I know," the soldier said. "I must return to it." He turned his back on the tall woman and ran in the opposite direction, out of the tunnel into the dusty market, carrying both of them.

Dean glanced back to the Traveler, but she and the tunnel were gone. "I'm Dean Simmons," he repeated to himself over and over. "This isn't my life. I don't belong here, stuck in the first century in another lifetime." The closeness of the crowd felt suffocating and smelled foul. He was caged and desperate. His breath rose and fell rapidly in his chest. His feet were planted on solid ground, and his muscles felt heavy and warm. *This is my body too.* He wrenched control of the body from Lucius and started elbowing his way through the shoppers, not sure of a destination and not caring if Lucius objected. He had to get out of that crowd, or he'd go crazy. Shouts rose nearby and people pushed toward the voices. Dean tried to run away, but Lucius took back control of the body. If the young Silas was in the thick of another bad situation, it was his responsibility to get him out of it. He muscled his way to the edge of a crowd encircling two men who confronted each other with bare fists raised. Silas bled from the nose. The other man bled from a nasty cut on his forehead. Blood dripped into his right eye. It would be an insult to Silas' manhood for Lucius to intervene now. He had to let the fight come to its conclusion, so he stood firm and watched. Dean had no choice but to do the same.

Silas was trained by the Roman Guard. His fighting skills would be superior. The other man looked brawny enough, but his fighting style was clumsy. He was probably a farmer or tradesman, wearing dirty brown pantaloons and a loose shirt. His black hair and bushy eyebrows framed brown eyes. He threw round house punches without precision. If he landed one, it would hurt, but the punches that hit were few. Silas jabbed, feinted, and jabbed again, moving in closer and closer. The other man backed up against the wall of the crowd. They pushed him forward. Silas closed in fast and delivered a blow to the man's nose that probably broke it and rattled his brain. The man threw a wide punch, missing its mark, then swayed and fell to his knees. Silas moved in to deliver a death blow. It was time for Lucius to step in. "The fight is over," he said. "You've won." He took the young soldier by the arm and led him out of the circle. When they were out of ear shot, he hissed into Silas' ear. "You have injured a citizen in the marketplace. Ignoramus! This is not how a soldier of Rome conducts himself among citizens. There will be consequences."

What consequences? Dean wanted to find out.

Chapter 17

TJ still wasn't answering his phone. Coma or no coma, his continued involvement with Evelyn was aggravating. It wasn't safe to be around that nasty wasp of a woman. Willet had to get to his house to warn him or Evelyn might hurt him out of spite. How could she defend him? Feeling vulnerable and useless as a Guardian, she thought of Gem and yearned for the days when Gem was by her side, reading situations and making the right decisions for the Circle. They didn't realize how lucky they were to have her. Gem was a true Guardian, experienced and powerful, with a mastery of breath she couldn't imagine.

Smoke had been in the Jeep a long time. His blue eyes had a look of urgency. She let him out to relieve himself, then he jumped back in the front seat. She pulled out of downtown and headed north toward the Hollywood Hills. When she reached Santa Monica Boulevard, she remembered that the road led to Santa Monica Beach. She wasn't sure how far that was, but she turned west, stopping to buy a can of cat food at a minimart. When they got to the beach, she parked the Jeep, opened the can, and put it down on the front floorboard. Smoke devoured the chicken treat with relish. She gathered him up against her chest and sat, watching the waves. Smoke dozed in her arms and began to snore. Guardian and cat breathed together, quietly in sync. It was the first calm moment she had in this frantic day. The gentle roll of the waves soothed her throbbing head. Her eardrums relaxed. She closed her eyes, but some thoughts would not stop. The black sand – what to do about the black sand? There was something inside it trying to break out. She was sure of it. Another round of havoc would be unleashed on L.A. Did she make any progress convincing Lars he was in danger? Who knew. And TJ seemed to be more concerned about Evelyn than he was about her. Anger and hurt clashed in her heart. She sang HU in her head to ease the feeling of desperation, but her mind wouldn't stop. *Maybe a walk would help, before I jump out of my skin.*

She laid Smoke's slumbering body on the passenger seat and got out of the Jeep. Walking across the sand seemed surreal, like she was on another planet. This was the first time she had come to the Pacific Ocean by herself. Last time she was on the beach, TJ was with her, holding her hand. She had worn her headphones then because the waves sounded like thunder against her ears. So much had changed in the way she managed her ear drums and their response to sounds. Here she was, standing at the edge of the crashing waves, managing to enjoy it. Blue-green water shattered and spread veils of white foam on the sand in a soft shush. All that water, wild and glorious, heaved with energy. She inhaled the mist and drew strength from its awesome presence, but the day was fading into dusk. She had to reach TJ's house before dark.

Her ears popped just then, and a gong rang once, twice, three times. *Something's gonna happen.* The wind picked up, and darkening clouds swirled over the horizon. A shape floated across the water, coming closer, growing larger. It was an enormous silver-white bird flapping wide long-feathered wings, approaching at great speed. The closer it got, the clearer her view of its huge feet with claws extended. *Is it going to snatch me off the ground?* It looked big enough to carry her off. She wasn't sure if she should run or get out of the way and let the bird land.

The bird reached the edge of the shore, stopped, and hovered in the air with the full length of its wings extended. It had to be eight feet in height with a ten-foot wingspan. Gold and white feathers on its breast looked like a sun rising against the darker sky. The sunburst of feathers swelled, and a figure emerged from the bird's chest, floating forward in a halo of bright light. Gaia Philendra, the Guardian of North America, stepped out of the halo and touched her slender feet onto the sand. Her long black hair and saffron robes swirled in the ocean breeze. The bird rose into the sky beating its massive wings. It backed up, flew away toward the horizon and disappeared.

Philendra's dark eyes focused an eagle sharp gaze on Willet. Her imposing height and stern countenance were as intimidating as the first time they met. The power of her persona was even more frightening. Willet found it difficult to breathe. Her voice shook. "Guardian, are you part bird?"

The Guardian's robes settled around her. "That was Olanthe. She is a gift of Spirit. When I must move far and quickly in the physical world, she carries me."

"How did you know I was here?"

"I am aware of all Guardians on this continent," she said with a hint of a smile." I felt your anguish in the depths of my being. Your tears ring like bells in the heavens. I am here to assist you."

The offer of help was so unexpected that words spilled out of Willet's mouth in a rush. "I'm lost. I don't know what I'm doing, and I have no skills to be a Guardian. Not like Gem. How can I be a Guardian if I can't defend myself or anyone else?" She knew that she was raving and didn't want to lose her cool completely in front of Philendra, but she couldn't help it.

Philendra's expression was unreadable. "Do not compare yourself to any other Guardian. Each of us builds upon our own strengths, and you possess many. Your physical and superphysical senses are exceptional. You read emotional energy in all its shades. And you have found *your* spirit animal already." She pointed at the sand beside Willet's feet. "He is devoted and strong. You can depend on him."

Willet looked down. A bobcat stood there beside her. His tufted ears flicked, and his blue eyes stared up at her with rapt attention. Another one of Smoke's guises "He saved me from being shot. I'm just not confident I can protect myself."

Philendra's eyes looked deep into her. Those eyes missed nothing. "Your heart is warm, and you have strength of purpose. These characteristics become power in a Guardian. Heat and gravity are yours to command. The Spirit of Life supports you in this."

Willet couldn't imagine how those words applied to her. "I don't feel any of that."

"Think about all that you perceive."

She thought about it. "I hear a lot, sure, and now I see stuff flying through the air that I never saw before, lights and waves, little flashes. I get so dizzy, I have to close my eyes, even when I'm driving. Is that supposed to be helpful?"

"Think of yourself as a planet exerting the pull of gravity. Elements of creation - carbon, hydrogen, dust, water, metals – come to you through the air. From those building blocks, you can create whatever you need to protect yourself and others."

Willet's mind was spinning. "I don't get it. Sorry."

"Let us try an exercise. Imagine a barrier blocking the sounds of the waves from reaching your ears. What kind of barrier would do that?"

As preposterous as that sounded, Willet couldn't ignore the direction from Philendra, so she pictured a stone wall in front of her. Nothing happened. The waves sounded as loud as ever. She pictured a steel wall. Same result. Trying to stop the sound of the ocean seemed as futile as trying to stop ocean water itself. "The waves never stop. I don't see what I can do to stop them."

"Focus on the barrier you want, not the waves."

She pictured the stone wall again, but the ocean waves continued to crash and pound as loud as before.

"I don't understand what I'm supposed to do."

"You visualize the barrier, but you do nothing to create it. What materials do you have to work with? What energies?"

Willet looked around the beach. "There's lots of sand, and an ocean of water. Is that what you mean?"

"Yes, there is sand and water. Do you wish to build a sandcastle?" Ha. The Guardian of North America has a sense of humor.

"I need more defense than a sandcastle."

"Well then, what can you make with sand and water that will protect you?"

"Uh… Glass is made out of sand and water. I'm pretty sure." Philendra gave her a patient nod. "Sand and water are in the air. Draw them to yourself. The heat of your being will melt the sand and water together. Glass will form according to your vision and command. That is a power few can claim."

"I'd have to get really hot to melt sand, like, 3200 degrees Fahrenheit if I remember my chemistry correctly. There's no way."

"You are like a small sun. Hot enough to transform matter." Willet did see grains of sand and drops of water flying through the air. She imagined them coming to her. Just that quickly, a dense, sandy cloud formed in front of her. *What am I supposed to do with this?* Her concentration broke, and the cloud dissipated into nothing. "I wasn't sure what to do next."

"You drew sand and water to yourself. A worthy start. Take control of the elements and exert your heat on them until they melt and reform them into the substance you want to create."

"You're kind of scaring me here," Willet said sheepishly.

Philendra continued on as if she hadn't heard. "A visualization will guide your manifestation. The vision must be clear. A command word can focus the process. Otherwise, what you create may not be what you expect."

Willet didn't know what to expect. She felt foolish but tried again. She saw the sand and water in the air and imagined it forming a cloud, close enough to touch. A vibrating sensation coursed through her, flowing into her arms, and out her fingers. She extended her arms. The cloud formed and rushed into her outstretched hands. She squeezed it between her hands until the heat became intense. She didn't know how long she could actually hold on, but she compressed the cloud until it liquified. She pictured clear glass and said, "Quiet". The liquid burst out of her hands in a clear spray. It cascaded down in front of her and hardened as it cooled. She touched the hard surface that had formed with a fingertip to test its solidity. It felt smooth and warm. She tapped it with a knuckle. Already hard. And she could see through it. Yep, it was glass. She saw long, slow sound waves from the ocean hit the other side of the glass and bounce off. The sound was effectively blocked, but waves of light passed right through. She could hardly believe it worked. It was amazing, but her hands were scalded. "Yow," she muttered, blowing on her enflamed palms. "*That* was painful."

"No need to hold on to your creation too long. Let it go as quickly as possible."

"Is this permanent? What if I want the thing I create to go away?"

"The barrier is subject to your visualization," Philendra said. "See what you want to see."

Willet imagined the wall disappearing. It dissolved into empty air. With the glass gone, ocean breezes rushed over her, and the sound of ocean waves rolled in loud as ever.

Philendra nodded. "I have not witnessed this command of the elements in centuries. It is wondrous to see."

"I want to try it again." Willet went through the same steps and used 'cover' as her command. The cloud formed between her hands, burning hot. She squeezed it and tossed it up fast. A fountain of liquid glass spread over her and turned into a solid dome that covered her on all sides. Ocean sounds were effectively silenced, but the heat of the sun started cooking her like a bug under a magnifying lens. She imagined empty space around her and let go of the dome before she burst into flame. The dome disappeared.

The Guardian was brilliant. Powerful, compassionate, wise beyond time, she seemed to understand physics. "I wish Dean was here. He loves to discuss the fundamental forces of physics. I bet he'd have some clever suggestions for all this, but we've lost him. I wish we could bring him back to the Circle."

"Your warrior is lost?" Philendra's dark eyes narrowed. "When did this occur?"

"We haven't heard from him since he went to visit his past life in ancient Rome. The Traveler took him. Gem said you're familiar with those times. Can you find him and bring him back?"

"The Traveler is responsible for his location in space-time. She is his only link with the present. If he becomes lost in his old life, even she will not be able to bring him back."

"How would that happen?"

"If he meets his former self, he may reunite with the body holding that old consciousness. He will not be able return until…"

"Until when?"

"Until the death of the body that holds him."

That sounded bad. "So, there's nothing we can do for him from here?"

"It is in his hands, and in the Traveler's."

"Then I have another problem. Audrey is floating around in a place between the physical world and the worlds beyond and can't get out."

The laser stare of the Guardian of North America became sharp enough to drill a hole through Willet's forehead. "The Ring Thrower is not in physical form either?"

"She and Dean had to give up their bodies to defeat Jat's tornado. Now she's trapped in the Lightning World."

"Nonsense. She can travel wherever she wishes. It is the nature of Soul."

It sounded like good news for Audrey. "Could my sister find Dean in the past?"

"Not alone. She would have to be escorted. Only the Traveler can venture that far into the past without losing her way. It is not an easy journey." Philendra gathered her robes around her. It seemed like she was getting ready to depart.

Willet had so many more questions. "What do I do now? About the black sand?"

"Use what you know and the abilities you have demonstrated. Do not be afraid. The Guardians of the Enclave will support you. Simply ask."

The silver bird, Olanthe, dropped out of the clouds and swooped down to a halt behind Gaia Philendra. The Guardian stepped back into the mass of gold and white feathers on its chest and melted into it. The bird lifted off the beach, soaring high into the sky. It was soon out of sight.

Willet looked down for the bobcat, but he had disappeared too. She wasn't sure which problem to attack first. Getting to TJ's house as fast as possible seemed to be the immediate priority. She ran back to the Jeep and climbed in. Smoke sat up alertly on the passenger seat and looked at her. "Don't look so innocent, Smoke. I know you're the bobcat. You can be more than one type of cat. I get that now. It's a handy trick. Right now, we've got to move fast." She backed out of the parking lot and took off, found Santa Monica Boulevard, and headed up to the Hills as fast as traffic would allow. "I'm a speed demon. If Auddie could see me now, she wouldn't believe it."

Chapter 18

Deepening darkness did nothing to ease her anxiety on the drive to the Hollywood Hills. The sun had set, but to her eyes, the air was lit with showers of glowing particles falling through the sky like burning embers. Glowing waves of energy crisscrossed in front of the windshield. By some miraculous luck and a cooperative GPS, she found her way to TJ's house. The house was dark. TJ and Jonah were probably at the hospital with Evelyn. She grabbed Smoke and got out of the Jeep, walked to the front door, and tried the doorknob. Locked, as it should be. She had her own key. Inside, it was quiet except for the refrigerator running in the kitchen. She flicked on lights and put Smoke down on the floor. "Don't scratch the furniture, please. You don't want to start off on Thomas' bad side."

She walked through the kitchen to the master bedroom and switched on the recessed ceiling lights. The palette of green and white colors TJ chose to decorate his room was a pleasant memory of their time together there. TJ said the colors reminded him of the ocean. She began to relax, but the large angry blood stain on the pale celadon rug next to the bed drew her eyes and made her gasp. It had to be Evelyn's blood. The intrusion made Willet mad. Wasn't this day difficult enough? She had been shot at, driven to her knees by Jat's burning lights, almost killed on L.A. freeways, and challenged by Gaia Philendra to do impossible things, all in less than twelve hours. Now she had to deal with this?

She went to the kitchen, found rags under the sink and vinegar in the cupboard, and returned to the bedroom armed with those and a bucket of water. She wet the rags and doused them with vinegar. Down on her knees, she rubbed the stain with rags in both hands, desperate to erase the brazen red of the blood that reminded her too much of Evelyn's hair. Rubbing and rinsing over and over, she made progress. She poured out the bloody water and rinsed the rags in the master bathtub. With a fresh bucket of water, she returned to the rug to rub some more, hoping she didn't bleach out all its color. By midnight, her elbows and back ached, and the blood stain was reduced to a shadow. A professional rug cleaner could remove the rest, but some things could not be removed by vinegar and water. The sight of the stain. The smell of it. The reason it was there.

Sound prints hung in the air, remnants of voices that had spoken in this room not so long ago. She could hear Evelyn's voice threatening and crying. TJ trying to calm her down. The crack of gun fire and Jonah's anguished cry. Willet heard it all as if it was happening in the present at that moment. She wasn't sure she'd be able to sleep in the room, but she was determined not to let Evelyn's antics keep her from TJ's bed. After a hot shower and a change of clothes, she lay down on the bed, too exhausted to do more. Smoke jumped up and curled against her. She fell into an uneasy sleep.

She stood outside the Hope Place courtyard. Black birds flew around her, screeching. Lights glinted in their dark eyes, and their black beaks snapped. Feathered wings brushed against her skin. She waved her arms to repel them. They flew off, but she floated into the air and followed them, unable to stop herself. They drew her to the black sand mountain. A man stood there in front of the sand – Lars Lake. The birds attacked him and drove him to the ground. He shouted in terror, and then in pain. She tried to draw energy into her hands and create a barrier to protect him, but nothing happened. She fought her way through the dense black flock and dropped to her knees beside him. He lay curled on his side, silent and still. She turned his head toward her, and a wail broke from her throat at the sight of his face. 'Oh my god, Lars! I'm so sorry!'

She fell into a long dark tunnel. Her cry echoed all the way down.

***** Audrey *****

Audrey floated out of Augustus' office into the rose garden with hope in her heart. The scent of roses uplifted her. She felt at peace, but when she pictured Willet's distraught face, she started worrying again. *If only I could speak to her.* Everything blurred, and she found herself in a rain forest, standing beside a grotto of blue-black rocks. A waterfall poured out from between the rocks into a deep blue pool. Lush ferns, flowering orchids, and green-leafed trees surrounded the pool. The sound of burbling water echoed under the tree canopy, refreshing her heart and mind. She sat on a rock beside the pool, closed her eyes, and let the sound soak in. Worries washed away. She existed in just this moment with all of creation balanced and waiting. A soft rustle interrupted her reverie. Willet was sitting near her beside the pool, watching the falling water.

"Will!" she said. "Can you hear me?"

Willet looked her way, startled. "Of course I can hear you. I'm right here."

"I was at Hope Place, shouting at you and you didn't seem to hear my voice."

"Oh. That was you? I heard a voice, but that damned sand shot me in the back with hot lights. I was incapacitated. Where are we?"

"We're in a rain forest outside Samhasa. This water carries life force. That's what Gem told me the first time she brought me here. Dean and I came after the Circle stopped the tornado. It was so wonderful..." A momentary glow of happiness was overshadowed by the thought of happiness lost. She shook it off. "What are you doing here?"

"I had an awful dream. Birds were flying at me, trying to... hurt me. A man I know... He died in the dream... I couldn't save him. Then I was here a moment later." Regret haunted Willet's eyes.. "If the dream was a premonition of what happens in real life and I can't stop it, I don't know how I'll live with it."

Her sister nodded. "We're a fine pair. We both suffer from the same affliction. Guilt. Augustus told me I had to forgive myself. You need to do that too."

"What are you guilty about? You haven't done anything wrong."

Audrey shook her head and said one word: "Nick."

"That wasn't your fault, Auddie. It took all of us to bring the spider down. You couldn't have stopped her by yourself even if you were with him."

"You didn't see Nick in that spider web. The threads were wrapped around his head, but I could see through them. His eyes and mouth were open wide, like he was screaming at the end. I can't stop seeing it."

Audrey dipped her hands into the water and ladled it to her lips. She closed her eyes, sipped it down, and sighed, then looked back at her sister. "What are you doing about the sand?"

"I don't know what to do about the sand."

"It's dangerous and evil. TJ's helping you, right?"

"TJ hasn't exactly been available lately." Willet's face couldn't hide how she felt about that.

"I'm sorry, Will. With Dean in another life and me in limbo, you're facing the sand alone.

"I feel like the sand is pulling me into a deep hole. Maybe that's its purpose. Disable the Guardian, then send every deviant from the Underworld into Los Angeles." Willet dipped her fingers in the pool and splashed cool drops over her eyes and cheeks.

Audrey trailed her fingers through the blue water and watched the ripples spread. "Drink the water, Will. It will raise your spirits. You'll feel better."

"I don't think anything will make me feel better."

"Just try it. Please." Audrey said.

Willet stared straight ahead and didn't reply.

"Will, can you hear me?" Audrey watched her sister's form fade out of the grotto. Frustration ached inside her. She wanted to do something but didn't know how or what. She dipped her hands into the blue pool and filled them again, then splashed her face with the bubbling water and spilled it into her mouth. The cool water ran off her chin and down her throat. It eased the ache, but the concerned about her sister would not go away.

Chapter 19

A wailing voice drowned out Audrey's last words. Willet recognized it as her own. She was in the dark again, desperate and afraid. The flapping wings of the birds beat on her. She knelt beside Lars and threw herself over his body to protect him. Sharp beaks stabbed at the back of her neck. Someone was shaking her shoulder. Hard.

"Wake up, Will. Wake up! Willet!"

When she opened her eyes. TJ was standing over her, trying to coax her out of sleep. He looked tired and upset, and ribbons of concern waved around his head in shades of yellow and red. Jonah stood behind him, peering at her with wide, worried eyes in a pale face surrounded by brown curls. Soft pink ribbons of emotion from the boy touched her gently. He looked confused. Had she been crying out loud? She sat up, trembling, and buried her head in her hands. "That was a horrible dream."

TJ sat beside her and put an arm around her shaking shoulders. "I'm here. Take a breath. What were you dreaming about? And who is Lars?"

She wasn't eager to discuss the details of the dream. Happily, there was something else to focus on. "Thomas, you're home, good." Then she got concerned. "Why are you home?" She looked from him to Jonah, wondering if the worst had happened.

TJ sat back and ran a hand through his sandy blond hair. His emotions turned dull green. "The docs took Evelyn off life support. She's breathing on her own now. They think she'll make it. Jonah and I came home to grab a shower and food. Hopefully some sleep, before we head back to the hospital. Jonah wants to be there when she wakes up."

"That's good news," she said and meant it. "Let me get myself together and I'll cook something for you guys." She pulled the covers back and revealed a furry gray form curled into a snug ball – Smoke in what had become his new favorite sleeping spot.

A big smile broke out across Jonah's face. "Oh! A cat! Can I pet him?"

"This is Smoke. Smokey, Jonah wants to meet you. Can he give you a rub?" Willet wasn't sure how Smoke would react, but she waved the boy over. "Rub his back, Jonah. Gently, until he gets to know you."

Jonah extended three fingers and rubbed the cat very carefully along the spine. "I love cats. Mom never let me get one." Smoke didn't seem to mind Jonah's touch. He began to purr and rolled on his back, inviting a belly rub. Jonah obliged with gentle fingers, and the cat purred even louder, a vote of approval.

"He likes you," Willet said. "Would you like to feed him?" The look on Jonah's face shouted 'yes'. "There's a can of cat food in a bag on the counter. Open it up and put some in a bowl on the floor. He'll come running."

Jonah went to the kitchen. When the lid of the can was pried open, Smoke jumped up and off the bed, heading for the smell of fish.

Alone together now, Willet could tell TJ what was really on her mind. "Why haven't you answered your phone? I left a dozen messages. You couldn't answer just one? I was shot at and almost killed. I needed to talk to you!"

TJ shrugged with a weary sigh. "I'm sorry, Will. There was a lot going on at the hospital. It was touch and go for a while. Jonah was on the verge of falling apart." Then her words registered. "You were shot at? How did that happen? Is that why you were crying in your sleep?"

"No, it was an attempted mass shooting at a swap meet. Long story, no one got killed, but I wish I could say the shooting episode was the worst thing that happened to me today. At least it would be over and done. The mountain of black sand is the problem. It's loaded with evil, destructive energy. Red lights blasted out of it and hit me. It really hurt. Black stuff is oozing out in shapes that look like they're not of this world. It's a total freak show, Thomas. Other people are getting hit by the lights and they aren't aware of it."

"Will, I told you not to confront the sand without me being there. What were you thinking?"

"I had to go. I'm the Guardian now, and besides, the Jeep wouldn't let me go anywhere else. I'm glad I went, because if the sand wasn't scary enough, a construction company is taking that sand by the truckloads to building projects in other parts of the city. They're putting it into other structures! It'll be a disaster if we don't do something."

She got out of bed and started pacing around the room, trying to organize her thoughts. "Gem's Jeep headed downtown like a homing pigeon, straight to the sand. I couldn't steer it. When I got there and saw what the construction crew was doing, I tried to talk the site manager out of moving the sand. Lars is kind of arrogant. He thought I was nuts."

TJ gave her narrowed eyes. "You're on a first-name basis with him? Let me guess – Lake Construction? I know Lars Lake. His company was involved in one of my real estate projects. Tall, muscle-bound, thinks he's God's gift."

She couldn't argue with the description. "Lars didn't accept what I was saying, but at least I convinced him to have the sand tested for radiation before he spreads any more around. It buys some time, though not much. We have to stop him! Do you know Lars well enough to talk to him?"

"I know him purely in a business context. If your angel face couldn't convince him, I'm not sure what I could say. He's into the ladies."

"Thanks, but that doesn't help. I need suggestions I can use."

"I'll give him a call if you think it might help."

"Yes. Please do that."

They peeked into the kitchen to check on Jonah. He sat cross-legged on the floor with Smoke lying in his lap. Jonah stroked the cat's back with a smile. Smoke's eyes were closed, enjoying the rub. They could hear him purr. Willet and TJ backed up into the bedroom and quietly closed the door.

"The cat is good for Jonah," TJ said. "Like a therapy animal. Kids always do well with pets. I'm glad you brought him with you."

Willet chuckled. "There's a lot to know about Smoke. He's not a 'pet', he's like a spirit animal, *my* spirit animal. He turned into a cougar and saved me from being shot. Later he turned into a bobcat. He's a shape-shifting spirit animal, Thomas. He saved my life."

TJ put his arms around her shoulders and searched her eyes for signs of insanity.

"That's not even the most amazing part, Thomas," she said, wondering how much he could process of what she was about to tell him. "When the shooting happened, I got trapped in a web of emotions coming from everyone in a big Swap Meet in Fontana. It felt like hot wires squeezing the life out of me. I couldn't get free."

"Lars Lake. He seemed like an ok guy, but he can be rude and pig-headed."

"Lars is usually pretty sharp, though he can be opinionated. What'd he do now?"

"He delivered a load of the black sand to a school. A school! Can you believe it?"

"Yeah. That's bad." TJ rubbed his wet hair with a towel and then stopped. "Will, you've been dealing with a lot, and I haven't been there for you. I'm sorry."

She dropped onto the bed. Her shoulders sagged. She suddenly felt so tired. "This Guardian gig is kicking my rear end. I'm definitely not the right person for it. You had to take care of Jonah. I understand."

He sat next to her on the bed and pulled her against his chest in a deep hug. "It's not ok." He rested his cheek on the top of her head. "I love you. You're priority one. Don't forget that."

She needed to hear those words. "I love you too. When I can't talk to you, it makes me crazy."

"There's nothing more important to me than you, than us."

"You've spent a lot of time with Evelyn lately."

"Evelyn hasn't exactly been present. I haven't talked to her since she went in the hospital. Besides, it doesn't matter what she wants. I just want you."

They leaned back on the bed, wrapped in each other's arms, and exchanged kisses, so tender they brought tears to her eyes. A knot of anxiety unraveled in her chest, and she was able to take a deep breath. She couldn't resist spreading open his bathrobe to kiss his clean skin. Beads of water glistened on his sculpted chest and six-pack abs. Her thoughts became jangled. *Could this beautiful man really be mine?*

He reached for her and pushed her back on the bed. His green eyes sparkled with that seductive smile that never failed to excite her.

"You're not taking the situation seriously," she said, running her hands up his chest.

"I will take it very seriously in a little while." Warm lips pressed to her cheek and then to her lips. "Right now, I'm taking you."

"There's a young boy in the kitchen. What if he walks in?"

"He's busy with the cat." TJ rose up and straddled her.

"With all that's going on, is this really the best time?"

"There's never a *best* time for us these days. We have to take the time when we can..."

Her shirt and underwear came off so fast she barely noticed them gone. His tongue was in her mouth. She opened to him in all ways, and he filled her completely. Stress and worry melted away as his strong arms pulled her close. She felt devoured by his kisses on her neck, his tongue across her nipples. A gasp escaped her. Her hips rose to meet his. Their bodies rocked together.

After the crest passed, he rolled to the side and whispered in her ear. "I'm not used to having a kid around. I guess we should be more careful."

"Too late now. I hope Jonah didn't hear us."

"Would it have stopped us?"

"It should have, but no." They lay in contented silence, holding hands with eyes closed.

"Life doesn't work without you, Will," he said. "Not anymore. I'd do anything for you."

"Don't ever stop."

They rolled into each other's arms and hugged like they were one being with a single beating heart. She wished it could last all day, but some things couldn't wait. "I have to venture out again," she whispered in his ear. "The Guardian of L.A. can't hide from her city. Not when something is growing in the black sand. I can feel it, and I don't think it will end until it reaches full size. Other breaches can open in the city too, in places I'm not looking. I need to find them before the Underworld attacks us from multiple directions."

His lips brushed hers. "I'll take Jonah back to the hospital, but when I get back, we'll figure out what to do next. Promise. Let me know when you're at Hope Place. I'll come find you."

She took a long stretch. "That will get me through the day."

TJ got up from bed and then stopped, looking down. "There were blood stains on this rug after Evelyn used the gun. Where'd they go?"

"I tried to clean them when I got here last night. They were glaring at me. I did the best I could. You'll need a professional to get out the shadow stain."

He leaned over and kissed her forehead. "You're amazing." He went into the bathroom.

She closed her eyes, feeling so tired. Maybe she could just sleep through the morning. Her phone buzzed. It was Lars again. "Lars. You hung up on me."

"Sorry, but I thought you should know. I got a call from another customer. She walked out on the new patio we poured for her yesterday and got second degree burns on the bottoms of her feet. She'll sue me for sure. I'm sending a truck to remove the sand from the school grounds."

"Make sure you sweep up every grain. Don't leave any sand there."

"Yes ma'am."

"And Lars, don't touch the crystal boulders around the sand mountain. They are the only things keeping the sand under control."

"How do they control sand? Why does sand need control?"

The explanations kept getting trickier, but she couldn't stop now. "The crystal digests the dangerous energy I told you about. little by little. The more it digests, the bigger the boulders get. Eventually, they'll be enormous, but the danger from the sand will be kept in check."

Lars gave a short laugh. "Another explanation I don't understand and can't tell anyone. I'm giving up a small fortune, woman. I hope you appreciate that. Two people who want to buy the boulders are coming over today to inspect them. I don't look forward to giving them the bad news that they're not for sale."

"I appreciate your change of heart, Lars. I really do. Would it help if I was there to explain it to them? They can think I'm the crazy person instead of you."

"Maybe it would help. I wouldn't mind seeing you again either."

"This is serious, not for fun."

"Would a little fun be so bad?"

"I'm in a relationship, Lars."

"Oh. No fun, then."

"No, but I'll be there."

Chapter 20

After TJ and Jonah left for the hospital, Willet had time to practice her new barrier-building abilities. The black sand would gain power as time went on, and she would confront it again soon. She needed to know what she could do with her new ability to forge solid materials, hopefully something stronger than glass. Not for the first time, she sorely missed Dean. He knew fundamental physics and could explain things so well. For now, she had to rely on her own education and information gathering.

She sat on a barstool at the kitchen island, opened her laptop and fired up her favorite AI tools, searching for information on everything she saw in the air - energy waves, atomic particles and whatever those flashing lights might be. There were many pages of information. Her eyes began to swim, but she found an explanation of the Standard Model of Particle Physics with a good graphic. Atoms were made up of subatomic particles, and those were made of quantum particles. That took her to a table of quarks, leptons and bosons along with their anti-particles. They produced the rigid structure of matter and its forces. Atoms fused into heavier atoms under extreme heat, and then into molecules. Molecules in the air could be the building blocks of the barriers she needed. Philendra said she could generate her own heat, but she had her doubts

What about the tiny flashing lights she saw? Showers of neutrinos fell constantly from the sun. Could it be them? Each neutrino was one millionth the size of an electron. It passed right through solid objects and disappeared into the earth. Even astrophysicists had a hard time seeing them. With so little mass, neutrinos wouldn't be useful for building a barrier, but they sure bothered her eyes.

She found another graphic that showed the full spectrum of electromagnetic waves, ranging from slow to fast waves, some visible to the human eye, some not. Waves outside the visible spectrum were now visible to her. She needed to distinguish the different types of waveforms by their shapes and speeds. Gamma rays, x-rays, and ultraviolet rays were fast and choppy. Infrared, microwaves, and radio waves undulated slowly. They cut through the air on their own trajectories. Transverse sound waves pushed through the air like slinkies, clumping and expanding at a slower pace. The gammas were crazy fast. X-rays were barely perceptible streaks. UV was steady. Could she use any of them? The UV light of the sun was hot. How hot were gamma rays or X-rays? She'd have to experiment.

There was also chemistry to consider. The periodic table of the elements – she knew about it from home schooling. Hydrogen, helium, and oxygen were the lightest elements. The air was full of those, along with nitrogen, carbon, and water. The lightest elements fused into heavier elements, like cobalt, tin, lead and iron. Making iron would require a lot of heat. Armed with this meager trove of information, she went out to the patio beside the house to see if she could create something solid. TJ had landscaped his property beautifully. Orange birds of paradise and white calla lilies bordered the sunny patio, with a variety of green succulents tucked in between. Paving tiles of green and gray cement, flecked with pieces of quartz, sparkled on the ground. If she squinted into the white-bright sunlight, it prismed into a full rainbow of colors, all wavelengths in the visible spectrum. Sparkling neutrinos fell like rain and disappeared into the hardscape. She tried to touch them. Other than a slight tingle which might have been her imagination, they passed right through her hands.

According to Philendra, she had the gravity and heat of a planet. She tried to picture herself as a planet exerting gravitational pull on particles in the air around her. It felt ludicrous, but she hummed a HU song to focus her attention on light and sound instead of her own doubts. *I could be like Venus.* Hot, scorching Venus, the planet second closest to the sun. It was the hottest planet in the solar system with ninety percent of the earth's gravity. She imagined the ashen pearl planet spinning slowly in space and tried to project herself into that vision. Her body flushed uncomfortably warm. Atoms of carbon, silicon, water, salts, and grains of cement flew at her, and condensed in a cloud of material in front of her. The cloud grew denser and hotter and began to spin. It sizzled and roiled. She felt like a mad scientist with a beaker of bubbling potion. She tried to control the cloud, but her legs felt as heavy as stone pillars. She struggled with the cloud, trying to hold herself upright, and drew the cloud closer until she could almost grab it between her hands. It rolled out of reach and fell apart into a sprinkling of dust.

Her gravity must not be strong enough. She tried to feel it in her torso and limbs, drawing every floating particle to herself. A diffuse cloud formed again and circled her like a satellite. When the cloud passed in front of her, she grabbed it between her hands and compressed it to the size of a ping pong ball. Her body shuddered. The pressure on her chest was so heavy, it felt like her ribs might crack. She said 'glass' and quickly released the ball. It dissipated into nothing. *That worked at the beach. What's the problem?*

She reestablished her focus on Venus and tried again. Another swirling cloud condensed. She was drawing molecules of quartz and granite from the paving stones and stucco dust from the walls of the house, along with all the other lighter atoms. She said 'Block' and compressed the cloud between her hands until it burst. Some kind of liquid splashed in front of her and hardened quickly into an amalgam similar to cement. It was a barrier that could protect her, but it wasn't perfect. Gamma rays and x-rays streamed right through it. She didn't want to be hit by radiation. *Have to stop the rays.* She dropped her creation and tried again. "Lead," she commanded. She thought that word should work for sure, but no barrier formed. She gathered another swirling cloud, compressed it and said, "Diffract." The cloud inflated in what she now recognized was the prelude to manifestation. A hard barrier formed and fast-moving rays bounced off it at all angles. That was better, but still a problem. If innocent bystanders stood near her, they would get a concentrated hit of the rays. Couldn't let that happen. There had to be a better solution. She tried again. "Absorb," she said. This time, gammas and x-rays stopped dead when they hit her barrier. It had the shielding capability of lead without any dispersion and felt firm, but sort of rubbery. It wasn't like any substance she'd ever touched. *Will I be able to create this again if I don't know what it is?*

She tried other words, like 'Brick', 'Steel', and 'Concrete'. Those words did not produce barriers. Verbs seemed to work best. She fetched a pad of paper and a pen from the house and jotted down a list of verbs that worked for her, along with their results. This would be her Guardian lexicon. She would memorize it. Finally some progress. *Wait till I show Thomas. He'll freak.* Would it work in a real life or death situation? No way to tell for sure until someone attacked her, or she met a radiation monster. Also, there was a price to pay. Exerting that much heat and attraction left her sore and dehydrated. Her muscles ached like she'd been dead-lifting blocks of iron. It. All she wanted to do was chug a gallon of water and soak in a salt bath. She'd need to build up her muscle strength if she was going to act like a planet.

Chapter 21

**** Dean ****

Lucius took Silas by the elbow and hurried him through the market, reprimanding him as they walked. Silas stumbled along, hanging his head. They veered onto a side street leading to a row of mudbrick buildings across a courtyard and crossed to an open door. They entered what turned out to be a training hall. Sunlight poured over the floor from windows high in the walls that caught the afternoon breezes. Soldiers engaged in boxing and sword play. The clink of swords echoed through the large room. Some were lifting giant rocks and wooden logs, grunting with the strain of the weights. Others wrestled, wearing nothing but loin cloths. Their bodies glistened with sweat.

When Lucius entered the hall, all the soldiers turned to him and stood at attention. As commanding officer, he wielded considerable authority. From humble beginnings as a foot soldier, he had developed his strength and skill as a fighter, excelled in battle in Galatea and Histria, and worked his way up the ranks until he became First Centurion of this cohort of 360 soldiers. These memories belonged to Lucius. Now Dean remembered them too, as if they happened yesterday.

Lucius turned Silas by the shoulders and pointed him toward the workout area. "Attend to your training. Make better use of your time. You will swab the floor of the room when the day is done." He gave Silas a nudge in the back. The young soldier stomped off with a sullen expression on his face.

With that, Lucius walked out of the building in full control of their physical body. *Where are we going now?* They hurried through the streets again, this time arriving at another two-story building made of red mudbricks. Lucius entered a door on the ground floor It was his living quarters. The main room contained a couch with a sheep skin thrown across it, a small table and two wooden chairs. Wooden shutters covered a rectangular window cut out of the wall. Lucius folded the shutters back. The dark interior flooded with light. He stripped off his heavy leather uniform, weapons and tunic and replaced them with a light cotton shirt that hung over one chair. "Now that feels better," Dean thought as all the weight was removed. Lucius picked up an earthenware bowl of cold wheat porridge from the table. Dean thought it looked disgusting, but Lucius was eating for sustenance, not for pleasure. He finished off the morning porridge with his fingers, licked them clean and gave a satisfied sigh, then lay down on the couch and closed his eyes. Their physical body was soon snoring, and their dreams began.

Lucius looks at a village on a hill above the bluest of blue waters. Calabria, in the southernmost part of Italy. An old woman with long gray hair and kind eyes in a wrinkled face wearing a brown sack dress and sandals walks slowly toward him along a rocky path on the crest of the hill. The sky is as blue as the water below, and the sun is bright. The woman waves. A whisper of recognition rises in Lucius. "Mama". A small child with sparse black curls walks beside the old woman, wearing nothing at all. She holds him by the hand. Lucius whispers, "Enzo, my son". He reaches his arms out to the boy, and the boy smiles. The woman and child are connected to the core of his being. Ocean water below the cliffs laps at the rocks. The heat of the sun bakes the ground.

Dean watches as if he is standing beside them. He feels the same happy anticipation that Lucius does. These are his own memories of Calabria. *My mother, my son, Enzo. I never wanted to leave them. The Roman army took me away. I yearned to go back.* He wants to lift his boy in his arms and press him to his chest, but Lucius is falling into a deeper sleep, and the dream is lost. Dean feels himself floating backward. The last thing he sees before the dream fades are the wide brown eyes of his son watching him go.

He falls away into darkness, ripped out of a life that used to be. His heart aches for it, but he lands in another dream, this one at TJ's club in West Hollywood. He and his band, Shock Value, play there often. He becomes lucid in the moment, walks up onstage and sits perched on a stool behind his monster Ludwig drum set of black and chrome tubs and Zildjian cymbals, looking out at the crowd. Stage lights strobe into his eyes. Fire ignites in his being. He kicks the bass drum, beats on the tom-toms, and crashes the cymbals in a frenzy of energy. Banks of speakers on either side of the stage vibrate with a sonic onslaught. He roars at the top of his lungs. "Mamba samba rock and roll ma baby all night long." Electric guitars blast the crowd on either side of the stage. Everyone roars. It's rock and roll ecstasy. Dean's spirits soar, but the dream fades as before. He feels himself drop heavily into the body lying on the couch.

Lucius bolted out of sleep and groaned, his body trembling. "What hellish dream is this?" he murmured, sitting up and holding his hands over his ears. He staggered out of bed, barely able to keep his feet and began to pace. Sweat beaded on his forehead. He went into the other small room and splashed water on his face from a stone basin. They were both awake now. Dean's memories of his life in a modern world were incomprehensible to Lucius, who thought he had been cursed by the gods. "I will go to the temple and make an offering to Venus. She will ease my affliction."

Lucius dressed quickly in his toga, wrapped the belt of his leather pouch around his waist, and strode out of the apartment. They trudged through the twists and turns of Rome's narrow back streets, where the masses of Romans lived. The buildings made of red mudbrick were three and four stories. Gaping holes in the walls served as windows. The streets were filthy. People hung out of the windows, yelling down to pedestrians, and dumping their dishwater and chamber pots out on the street. The lives of these Romans were nasty and brutish and usually cut short by disease. Dean tried to suggest to Lucius that he cover his nose and mouth, but Lucius didn't listen. He was accustomed to the horrible smell.

They emerged from the back streets to the Roman Forum and turned right along the avenue running on the east side. Romans came to the Forum for news and comraderies. It was briskly busy with people, mostly men, strolling and chatting in small groups. At one end, a man stood on a stage wearing a red toga over a white tunic, loudly addressing a small crowd that had gathered before him. This was where an elite Roman could have his say. The extent of free speech depended on the emperor in power. Slander was punishable by death, and political discussion was reserved for the Senate. The current emperor, Marcus Aurelius, was more tolerant than most.

Lucius kept walking and came to a massive gray stone temple situated on the Velian Hill, a stone's throw from the Colosseum. It was fronted by two rows of ten Corinthian columns, with broad bases and ornately carved crowns. Long covered porticos ran along the sides, held up by more columns. A flight of side stairs took them up into the shade of the portico roof. They walked around the huge building to the east side to a pair of heavy oak doors. Lucius pulled one of the doors open and walked inside the cool space.

The walls were covered in large squares of brilliant red and white marble alternating with alcoves containing white marble statues framed in red. The marble tiles on the floor were arranged in geometric patterns. Under a high half-dome, an enormous white marble statue of a woman draped in a white sheet sat on a throne holding a spear and a cupid. Her hair curled around her head, and her smooth lips smiled benevolently from her high perch. Venus, the Roman Goddess of Love. Flowers were strewn at her feet. Dean had to admit the statue of the Goddess was impressive. She had the loving, beatific face of an angel. No wonder Romans came to her for help.

Lucius fell to one knee and bowed his head. "Goddess, help me, cure me of my affliction," his voice echoed in the hushed quiet of the temple. "I am beset with terrifying visions." He pulled out his leather pouch and removed a shell and a coin from it. He laid both on the ground before the statue. "Accept this humble offering of my heart. Heal me!"

Dean felt bad for Lucius. There was nothing Venus could do for him. Dean tried to ease his worries. "Lucius," he whispered into their shared mind, "have no fear. All is well. The visions will not harm you."

The soldier's head shot up, and he gazed at the statue in wonder. "Goddess," he said. "You are kindness itself. Thanks be to you. I will sing your praises across Rome." He rose from his knee and backed away from the statue, bowing his way through the columns, and walked out into the sun with a spring in his step. It was time for a bath.

Uh oh. The Baths. Dean didn't relish the idea of sitting in a tub of water with a bunch of naked men. He'd have to figure out a way of exerting more control over decisions made in their shared body. If the Traveler returned, Dean didn't want to run away from her a second time, and he really didn't want to take a bath, but Lucius seemed set on it.

**** Audrey ****

To get over her guilt about Nick Hardman and the horrible way he died, Audrey would have to face him. The memory of finding him suspended in Georgina the Spider's web played over and over in her mind's eye. The sticky silk threads of the web had wrapped tightly around his head and body and trapped him like a fly. He either had a heart attack or was suffocated. Every time she pictured his glassy eyes and open mouth, it broke her heart all over again.

If she could find him, she could at least apologize. Maybe there was something she could do to help him, but she had no idea where he was in all the infinite worlds that existed. If she couldn't picture his location, she wouldn't be able to get there. So, she pictured his face as it looked when she first met him, when he and Jain were trying to carjack Dean's car in a desperate attempt to escape the Wall of Unknowing in L.A. At the time, Audrey's body was emitting a bright green glow from an unhealthy amount of crystal energy she absorbed in Bart Johnson's crystal field. It amped her own energy to a dramatic level. She remembered the solicitous way Nick had spoken to her when they first met. He received an electric shock when he touched her shoulder. It wasn't on purpose, but she felt guilty about that too. Nick was so concerned about her health that he and Jain offered to take her to the hospital. It was the kindest and most respectful carjacking possible. Instead, they all ended up at Griffith Park. The lives of Nick and Jain were on a collision course with the Circle of Augustus from that point forward. There was no turning back for them.

She held the memory of Nick's face in her mind. Her guilt connected her to him through time and space. The rock grotto faded away, and a new place came into view. She was standing in front of a tall iron gate. A man in a green uniform with silver pins on the collar and colored bars across the chest stood at attention in front of it. His eyes focused straight ahead.

She wondered if he would speak to her. "Excuse me. What is this place?"

The man shifted his eyes to her. "It is the Realm of Heroes. Only those who give their lives for the sake of others may enter."

"I'm looking for Nick Hardman," she said.

"Who may I say is calling?"

"Audrey Du Place." She hadn't expect the soldier to recognize Nick's name so readily without looking it up on some kind of list. The Realm of Heroes must not be that big.

"Yes," the soldier said with a nod, opening the gate. "Please come in."

She hesitated. "I thought only heroes could come in."

"You are that, miss," he said and gave her a short bow. "I see it in your light."

"There must be some mistake. I was never in the military."

"You gave up your physical life to save others."

Audrey was speechless for a moment. Technically, she had done what the soldier said, but still didn't feel she fit the definition. "I'm in the Circle of Augustus. It was my responsibility."

A glimmer of a smile played on the soldier's lips. "That's what all heroes say." He swung the gate open wider and waved her in.

She wasn't about to argue, so she floated through the gate into the most beautiful park she'd ever seen. Tulips, hyacinths, and paper-white narcissus were massed in beds of blue, gold, pink, white and red winding under shade trees, scenting the air with a heavenly perfume. Jewel-colored birds flew from branch to branch, chirping and singing. She heard the soft music of woodwinds. She drifted along a path following the contours of the flower beds. Her fingers brushed the soft petals of the flowers. The light felt like warm butter. The beauty of the place made her heart sing with joy. *Where am I going? Do I even care?* She looked back to the gate. It had already closed. She floated on through the flower-filled park until she emerged onto a straight, wide road running between broad green fields dotted with trees. Her feet touched down on the road. Soldiers in uniform lined each side of the road, standing at attention. Someone was walking down the road toward her from the opposite direction. As he got closer, she recognized it was Nick.

When Nick reached her, he looked so strong and happy, without a trace of the anxiety and PTSD that had plagued him in life. "Audrey," he said with a smile. "Welcome." He walked to her side and took her arm. "Walk with me." They proceeded down the long road, chatting as they walked between the rows of soldiers. Each soldier raised his or her hand in salute as they passed.

"Are they always here to salute you?" Audrey murmured. "That's so formal."

"It's you they're saluting, Audrey," Nick said and patted her hand. "A new hero in our midst. Will you be staying with us or just visiting?"

"I work for the Circle of Augustus. My sister needs me. Evil is afoot in Los Angeles."

"Spoken like a true hero. Now tell me what I can do for you."

"I, uh, came to apologize, for not saving you. From the Spider. I'm so sorry I didn't find you in time. I know that's too little too late, but I wanted you to know."

His eyes harbored no resentment. "Please don't think like that. It wasn't your fault. I took a lot of medicine for PTSD, some that wasn't so good for me. I was susceptible to heart failure. Lots of things could have triggered it. Just happened to be a giant spider."

"You must have been terrified," she whispered. "That Spider was awful."

"I was in war, Audrey. I saw many terrifying things. It was my destiny to face those experiences. My deep regret is not protecting Jonah. He was too young for that kind of trauma."

"TJ and Willet are taking good care of him. You don't have to worry about him, but JJ kind of lost it after your death. I don't know how he's doing now."

A shadow passed over Nick's face, cooling the happiness that was there before. "I've worried about J. He tries to be the man in every situation, but he's got a tender heart. He'll lay it on the line for his friends, just like my brothers in the Army. I really miss him."

"Will you go back? To physical life?"

"Sure, eventually. For now, there's a lot in me that has to heal and no better place than this to do it. Can you tell JJ I love him? In case he forgets?"

Audrey had to think about that. "You can tell him, Nick. Just think of him and say the words. He'll hear you."

Nick smiled, and Audrey felt a circle closing. There *was* something she could do for Nick. The aching guilt that had plagued her eased, and that beautiful land started to fade away. Nick waved at her until she could no longer see him. Her next movement was almost instantaneous. It brought her to another place, not as beautiful, but familiar. She had work to do.

Chapter 22

Smoke was already in the Jeep when Willet got in. "How do you do that, cat? I just left you in the kitchen." She wouldn't be going anywhere without her spirit animal, it seemed, so she resigned herself and started the engine. The white-knuckle drive from the Hollywood Hills to downtown L.A. triggered her anxiety but she handled it better this time. Hugging the slow lane, she let any other driver cut in front of her if they were so inclined. When she arrived at Hope Place, she parked a block away. "Wait for me here, please," she told Smoke, then reconsidered this request. "Unless I need your special assistance, of course." Smoke meowed. Willet climbed out of the Jeep and walked down the block, then crept to the corner of a building on the square and peeked around at the black sand mountain before it noticed her, if that was even possible. It was packing a lot of power, even more than yesterday. Red lights flashed out so brightly she could barely look at it, and dark shapes slithered in and out of the sand. The mountain looked like it might erupt. She slipped on a pair of sunglasses.

Lars was standing in front of the sand with two men who were inspecting the crystal boulders. Red lights from the sand bombarded them. She came out from behind the corner and walked across the courtyard to join them. The rumbling voice from the sand still spoke in that foreign tongue, and the mountain's heartbeat still pounded. The men seemed oblivious to the dark energy seething just a couple of yards away.

Lars introduced the shorter man as 'Thaddeus Moon', the artist who wanted crystal for his art projects. He wore a black tunic, black leggings, and black leather sandals. Sparse strands of black hair crossed the pale scalp on top of his head. The rest of his hair hung from the sides of his head in thin black braids anchored at the ends with onyx beads. Wire rim glasses with amber tinted lenses covered heavy-lidded eyes rimmed in kohl. He had the bored look of the tragically hip, but the spiky red color of his aura conflicted with that look.

Lars introduced the other man as 'Lionel Degner', deeply tanned skin and salt-and-paper hair with neatly trimmed mustache. His starched white shirt and crisply pressed black trousers over polished black loafers looked professional and expensive. The dark gray aura around him made it seem like he was shrouded in shadow. Lars said Degner was an agent representing an interested buyer from out of town.

"Deep pockets," Degner mumbled. "Very private. Prefers to remain anonymous."

He had a mild accent Willet couldn't place. Despite the mumbling, his alert dark eyes darted left and right, then came to rest on her face and gave her a bold stare. A black wire sprouted from his forehead, sprang out and pierced her third eye like an arrow. The light-filled space between her eyebrows flooded with inky darkness. A sense of desolation rushed through her. She swayed on her feet. It was a total assault, and they had just met. If Degner intended to weaken her, he succeeded.

Thaddeus Moon didn't meet her eyes. His emotions were hard to read. Red wires sprouted from his forehead and twisted languidly in the air before wrapping around her waist. *What does this guy want?* Degner's black wire delved deeper into her forehead. She lost focus for a moment, shook herself, and got mad. *Get your wires off me, you creeps.* She had to cut these guys off now or Smoke would come running into the courtyard in some big cat form, which would be difficult to explain. She gathered her wits. Ripping away the wires and using her hands to compress a cloud of matter and energy would look pretty weird. Maybe she could create a barrier with less overt movement. She said, "Reflect," under her breath and just imagined a cloud gathering in front of her, then clenched her fists. The cloud appeared and compressed into a swirling hot mass, spread out in front of her and hardened into a mirror that reflected the men.

Thaddeus Moon glimpsed his own reflection and looked startled, then smiled. His odd red wires snapped back to him. However, Degner's eyes glinted as if suspicions he had were confirmed. His black wire retracted. It was a relief to have that wire out of her head. *Who do you work for, Mr. Degner? I wonder…* She held her mirror long enough to be sure they were done attacking her, then let it drop.

"Mr. Moon has some interesting art concepts he's pursuing," Lars was saying, unaware of what was going on. "He'd like to use crystal as a part of the project. Mr. Degner hasn't said what the buyer's objectives are."

"Can't say," Degner said with a cough. "Not at liberty."

After what she just experienced, Willet wasn't willing to give either man any part of the crystal, but she had to have a plausible reason. Directing an innocent stare at Lars, she said "We can't let the crystal go without knowing how or where it will be used, can we Lars?"

The conversational ball had been passed to Lars, but he wasn't sure what to do with it. "Yes," he said clearing his throat. "Uh, we need to consider all aspects of the transaction…" His voice trailed off and he stared uncertainly at Willet.

"Yes, all aspects," she said. "Such as, where will the crystal boulders be taken?" What would Degner's reaction be to that question?

"Who are you, young woman?" Degner said pointedly. "What is your interest here?"

She plunged in with the first thoughts she had. "I represent the Natural Resources Office of Los Angeles County. These are rare examples of prehistoric crystal formation from this area and must be protected. By law." Lars was overcome by a cough.

"Really," Degner said with a skeptical tone. "I've never heard of such an office."

"We need to know the location to which the crystals would be transported, as a matter of protection for the artifacts." She was really reaching here. "They must be preserved as is."

"I told you. The buyer was very specific about anonymity. As for preserving them 'as is', I cannot attest to that."

"We don't have to know *who* the buyer is, Mr. Degner, if you can tell us *where* the objects will be installed. For our records." She smiled.

Degner snorted. "If you must know, the buyer has a large property in the Mount Wilson area. That is the destination."

A wave of nausea hit her, and she gulped. "Mount Wilson. I see." The first time the Circle of Augustus actually encountered Jat the Deceiver was at Mount Wilson. She herself had been thrown into an underground mine and almost died there. This couldn't be a coincidence.

"As I said, we would need to inspect the crystal periodically, to guarantee its preservation. If you cannot agree to that, I'm afraid the sale cannot be completed."

For the sake of form, she turned to Thaddeus Moon for his destination plans, though she wasn't as concerned.

"My, uh, studio is in, uh, Brentwood," the pale artist slurred with a wave of his hand. "I want to reflect light from overhead windows through colored prisms into a maze of translucent cylinders." He scratched his balding pate. "The design isn't finalized."

"Fascinating," she said briskly. "A single crystal boulder is very large. Would your project require so much?"

He gave her a vague shrug of his shoulders and muttered something about future projects.

Mr. Moon wasn't the threat that Degner was. "Gentlemen, thank you for your time. We'll be in touch when our office reaches a decision."

Thaddeus Moon wandered off, looking flustered. Degner fumed "You got me all the way over here for this? I expected to make a deal. My buyer wants those boulders ASAP..."

Degner continued blustering when Willet took Lars by the elbow and steered him across the courtyard. "Keep walking, Lars," she whispered as she ushered him along. "You and I need to talk." They walked out of the courtyard to the street before Lars stopped and turned on her, red-faced. "What do you think you're doing? There were two legitimate offers made! I think Degner was prepared to pay twice what Moon could offer."

"No doubt. I have a bad feeling about who Degner's buyer is. If I'm right, we absolutely do not want to sell the crystal to him. The boulders need to stay where they are, at least until we figure out a safe way to dispose of the sand. Until that point, please, work with me, Lars. I'm begging you. Shut down this job site."

Lars gave a frustrated huff and ran his fingers through his hair. "I don't understand how you got so involved in my business. I just met you yesterday. Now you're trying to dictate my financial decisions. Are you some kind of con artist?"

She turned away from him and swept her eyes across the courtyard. The space around the sand was alive with waves of energy traveling at different speeds. Subatomic particles went in and out of existence and electrons jumped between energy states as atoms decayed, giving off flashes of light. Red lights shot across the courtyard as before, but there was something she hadn't noticed before, something that wasn't on any of the graphics she had studied. An oily-looking black substance oozed out of the sand and swirled around the crystal boulders. The boulders soaked it up. It dispersed through the crystalline structure until all traces of blackness faded in the depths. That's why the boulders were there, to neutralize negative energy. If they weren't in place, the black energy would quickly fill the courtyard and spill out to the streets. How could she explain any of this to Lars in a way he could accept?

She remembered what the knitting girl, Carla, had said, and turned back to him. "I see what others don't, Lars. You have to trust me."

"Willet, you seem like a nice person, but I'm beginning to question your sanity. I can't base a significant business decision on this kind of explanation."

"I'm trying to protect you and your crew! If you remove the boulders, people will be hurt by the energies coming from that sand. Eventually, the whole city will be affected. By then it will be impossible to avoid serious consequences."

"What kind of consequences?"

She wasn't sure exactly what they would be and didn't want to claim insight she didn't yet have. "That is TBD, but it'll be bad. Guaranteed."

He studied her for a long second and shook his head. "I'll keep that in mind. Now, if you'll excuse me, I have to get back to work." He walked away from her once again, into a conflux of energies he wasn't aware of. A red beam tracked him like a laser focused gun before hitting him in the chest.

"Oh Lars," she murmured. "I wish I could explain it better, before it's too late."

Chapter 23

TJ sat in a chair by Evelyn's bedside, waiting for her to wake up. Jonah perched on the side of the bed holding his mother's hand. It was past noon, and they had been there since early morning. TJ listened to the soft intermittent beep of the cardiac monitor and watched the blips of the heartbeat trace scroll across the screen. He felt the need to keep it together for Jonah's sake. He closed his eyes briefly, just to rest them, and chanted a soft HU under his breath. His chin dropped to his chest, and he dozed off.

He was sitting on the edge of a cliff looking down into a deep flat valley. A ribbon of blue water ran through it, reflecting the cloudless sky. His legs dangled off the edge of the cliff. He wondered if he could fly. A small black bug buzzed in his face. He swatted it away.. The slow-moving bug returned to his eyes and nose again. He batted it away more forcefully. His arms flailed at the bug, and he came close to falling off the edge. Suddenly he recognized Evelyn's face on the bug, her blue eyes wide and her arms reaching for him. "Tom," she said. "When will we be a family?"

"Go away, Evelyn." He slapped her away. She dropped out of sight into the valley.

Jonah's frantic wail broke through his reverie. "Mr. Tom! Something's happening to Mom!"

When his eyes opened, a doctor was bent over Evelyn's bed pushing the heel of his hand against her chest. A nurse was injecting something into the drip bag that hung on a pole beside them. A loud tone blared from the cardiac monitor. The heartbeat trace had flatlined.

Evelyn seemed to float on a cloud of white bed sheets and pillows, her skin gray against the sheets. Her wispy red hair spread in a halo around her bandaged head. Her blue eyes were open and staring at the ceiling. Two nurses barged into the room pushing a crash cart. The doctor picked up two paddles from the cart, rubbed them together, and pressed them against Evelyn's exposed chest. Her body arched off the bed at the abrupt shock and then fell. Jonah cried out. The doctor shocked her again. And again. Everyone in the room held their breath, waiting for her heart to restart. A faint intermittent beep started up on the monitor, and a jagged trace ran across the screen, settling into a weak but regular pattern. The doctor listened to her heart with a stethoscope and checked her vital signs. Nurses rubbed her hands and feet to get blood flowing. The crash cart was pulled out of the way to make room for another nurse carrying a tray of syringes and medical tools.

Jonah came to TJ's side and buried his face against his waist. TJ wrapped an arm around the boy's shaking shoulders. As the staff worked, he watched the monitor, hoping and praying that the line on the screen would not go flat again.

Chapter 24

Willet was barely aware of the drive back to the Hollywood Hills. She was so lost in thoughts about how to get Lars away from the sand that she had to remind herself periodically that her hands were on the wheel. *One day in L.A. traffic and you're over the speed limit. Audrey would laugh.* Fortunately, traffic was light. By the time she pulled into the driveway at TJ's house, it was late afternoon. She went in the house and turned on the air conditioning, then headed into the shower. She let hot water pour over the bunched muscles in her shoulders and focused the spray on the back of her neck. With any luck, she'd avoid a migraine. By the time she finished, she heard TJ and Jonah in the kitchen. Their voices murmured and dishes clinked.

She dressed quickly in black leggings and a concert tee in faded black and green, brushed the knots out of her hair and gathered it into a blue scrunchie, leaving a ponytail down her back, then walked briskly into the kitchen. "How is Evelyn? Better, I hope."

Jonah sat at the kitchen table with Smoke in his arms. He pressed his forehead against the soft fur of the cat's head and closed his eyes. He didn't answer.

"We had a close call. Evelyn's heart stopped, but the doctor was able to resuscitate her. We're just here to grab a quick bite and shower. Don't want to leave her too long…" He gave Willet a raised eyebrow that said, Just in case.

Jonah looked up. There were dark circles under his eyes. "Mom looked at me," he said, stroking Smoke's back. "She smiled too. That's good, right?" A residue of tears remained in his haunted eyes.

Willet walked to him and wrapped him in a hug. "Yes, that's good," she said. After she let him go, she sniffed the air. "What are you making, Chef Tomaso? I should be cooking for you so you can rest a while. You two must be exhausted."

"Nachos," he said. "Nothing to it." He pulled a plate out of the microwave. Tortilla chips were dripping with cheese and heaped with sliced jalapenos. He spooned salsa on top. "Let it cool first." He lifted a chip from the plate and touched it with his tongue.

Willet and Jonah were soon crunching away on the chips. Jonah would need more than just an appetizer growing boy that he was. His arms were skinny. She could see his ribs through his shirt.

"Let's order pizza," she said, "to round out the meal. I'll make a salad too. You need ruffage."

"Sounds good," TJ said. "Thanks, babe." He gave her a weary smile.

She sensed there was something on his mind that he didn't want to discuss in front of Jonah. "A shower would feel good, Jonah," she said. "Why don't you go into the guest bathroom. There are clean towels on the rack. By the time you're done, pizza will be here."

Jonah put Smoke on the floor, wolfed down as many chips as he could stuff in his mouth and then nodded. "OK, Miss Willet." He snarfed another couple of chips and then walked down the hall to the guest room. They heard the door close.

"OK, what's up?" she said when they were alone.

"Waddya mean?"

"I know you, Thomas. You look worried. What happened? Beside the medical emergency."

TJ scooped the last of the cheese off the nacho plate and put it in the sink. "Before things hit the fan, I was sitting by Evelyn's bed and sort of dozed off. l had a dream about her. She was a bug, talking about us being a family. Same old song."

"Sounds familiar."

"She flew in my face. I swatted her with my hand, and she fell into a valley. When I woke up, she was in cardiac arrest. Could I have caused that?"

She went to him and looked in his eyes. "Evelyn had a serious injury which she caused herself. You can't take responsibility for what is happening to her now."

"I could have been kinder about it." He shook his head.

"You protected your space in the dream. That's your right. What's going to happen when she checks out of the hospital?"

"I'll offer to take her to her old apartment. That place scared her after the Wall of Unknowing rolled through her neighborhood, so she probably wouldn't want to go there. If so, I'll try to find a place for her and Jonah in one of my properties or a condo somewhere. She won't be up to much after what she just went through."

"What about Jonah? He won't want to be separated from you."

"I don't think I can just leave him in his mother's care. She's so unstable. You were right."

"So, he'll live with us?"

"We've had this conversation before. Evelyn *is* his mother. She has legal custody unless we try to pursue it in court. I wouldn't do that to Jonah. The best we can do for now is offer him a safe place if he needs one. Beyond that, I'm not sure. Maybe a summer internship with us?"

Willet decided not to press the issue. There were other things she needed to discuss with him that couldn't wait. She went to the frig, took out butter leaf lettuce and tomato and began washing them for a salad. "We'll figure something out. Right now, I need your help with some skills I've been practicing. Gaia Philendra suggested I try them. They'll be helpful to both of us."

"Who is she again?"

"She's in charge of all Guardians on this continent. An unfathomably ancient being. She travels with her spirit animal, Olanthe. It landed on the beach, right in front of me. She stepped out of its chest, if you can picture that! She said she knew I was worried and came to help."

"Do you trust her?"

"Of course, I trust her! She's the Guardian of North America. She scares the bejezus out of me, but I trust what she tells me. She said I could create walls to protect myself by imagining I was a planet and had the heat of a star. I imagined it and created a glass wall out of sand at the beach. With my own hands. That's an oversimplification, but... it actually worked!"

"Are you sure it wasn't her doing?"

"I was able to create different walls in your driveway. I also created a mirror today when I was with Lars. All by myself."

A hint of accusation flickered in his eyes. "You were with Lars? Again?"

"Let's focus on the important point here. I created a mirror right in front of me."

"I like to know when you're in the city. What if something happened?"

"I told you I was going to the city. I had to go. Two different people were trying to buy the boulders and remove them from Hope Place. You know I couldn't let that happen!"

"Did it happen?"

"For now, no, but I don't know how long Lars can restrain himself from being the capitalist he is and selling them off. I think he's having second thoughts about using the sand for his building projects, though. That's progress."

"Wait, get back to the other thing. You created a mirror?"

"The two men with Lars were poking me with wires coming out of their foreheads. One of them tried to hurt me. His wires went right into my third eye. I almost blacked out."

"What? I'd like to meet that guy and show him where he can stick his wires. What did you do?"

"I did what Philendra told me to do. I pulled particles out of the air and created a mirror, but it happened much faster than before. The two men saw their reflections, and it messed with their heads so much that their wires retracted. I think the one guy, Lionel Degner, could be a front man for Jat. He seemed to know about me, that I'm a Guardian. He wants to take a crystal boulder to some unnamed buyer up at Mount Wilson. If that doesn't ring alarms in your head, I don't know what would."

Neither one of them could forget the frantic car ride the Circle took out of the mountains under a hail of rocks and boulders.

"Yeah. Bad memory. What's the plan?"

"The thing I have to do is make sure my defensive skills are strong enough that I can approach the sand without being skewered by red lights or rendered helpless in some way. I need to know what kind of barriers I can create. You can help me practice."

"What do you need from me?"

"You have to throw things at me."

He frowned. "What kind of things?"

"Start with small stuff, work up to big, heavy things, end with something sharp."

"You actually expect me to throw something sharp at you."

"As hard as you can."

"I can't do that, Will. I might hurt you."

"Let's start with small things and see where we go from there." She moved through the kitchen gathering wadded up aluminum foil, sponges, an empty plastic spray bottle, and some utensils, then headed out to the patio. TJ followed her. Willet moved several steps away from him. "Ok, throw the foil at me when I say." A cloud formed in her hands. She pictured a non-specific barrier, and said, 'Stop'. A wall formed from the stucco dust in the air. "Go ahead. This wall won't last long."

TJ took the ball of foil in hand and tossed it at her. It bounced off the stucco and fell to the ground. He stared at the foil with a perplexed look on his face.

She let the flimsy wall drop. "I'm trying for a variety of materials. When I tell you to, throw the sponge." She said 'stick' and raised a sticky wall of a glue-like substance. "OK. Throw it. Harder this time."

He picked up the green dish sponge and threw it. The sponge hit the wall of glue and stuck to it, suspended in midair.

"You're doing something, that's for sure. How are you doing this?"

"I draw on the atoms of whatever's in the air around me. The cement paving stones, the stucco of your house, the wood trellises, anything metal, like the fences and door handle. I melt it all together, picture what I want to make and then say a forming word." She let the sticky wall disappear and the sponge dropped on the ground. "It takes a lot of heat, which bakes me. My body aches afterward, so I don't know how many walls I could create in a row."

He digested that tidbit for a moment and shook his head. "A new Guardian power. Wow."

"New for me. The details are fuzzy, but the results are indisputable. I've created materials that no chemical company has invented to my knowledge. Let's get back to it." With a deep inhale, she gathered a cloud and said, "Block". The cloud condensed to a small, tight ball in her hands, then exploded. A cement wall formed in front of her. She tapped it to make sure it was hard.

"Now throw a rock. Hurl it."

"I'm not comfortable with this."

"Just do it, please. I'll be fine."

He looked around the garden for a rock, found one and tossed it in her direction. It hit the barrier with a sharp knock and fell. "OK, you're doing good. Can we stop now?"

Her head ached like someone had punched her, but she decided to get more creative. She condensed a cloud of particles and pictured a layer of rubber. When she said the word 'Bounce', the air in front of her thickened. "Now throw something sharp. Do you have the knife? Scissors would be even better."

He picked up a butter knife and tossed it. The knife bounced harmlessly off the rubber and clanked on the ground.

"That's a bunny throw," she chided him. "You have to throw it with force. I won't know how well this stuff holds up otherwise."

"I was a baseball pitcher all the way through college. I throw pretty hard."

She lifted her chin and met his eyes. "Show me what you got, big guy."

He picked up a steak knife and threw it. The knife bounced off the rubber.

"Again, harder."

He swore as he picked up the steak knife and flung it overhand with some muscle behind it. The knife rolled through the air end over end and hit the barrier. When it came to a stop, a silver spear was wedged into the rubber in its place with the point sticking through, ending two inches from Willet's face.

"Whoa." She let the rubber wall drop. The silver spear fell to the ground with a clink. It was a foot long and slender, gleaming in the sun. The point looked wicked sharp. It disappeared before their eyes and left the steak knife lying on the ground.

TJ picked up the knife. "What the ...?" He examined it as if it might speak.

Willet nodded at him. "You can manifest a silver spear."

"No way."

"Yeah way. That might be what Gem meant when she called you the Silver Warrior."

"I never understood why she called me that. Always wished she'd explained it."

"I think this is the explanation. Want to try it again?"

"Yes. Please put up something harder than rubber. The whole thing makes me nervous."

She pictured concrete and said, "Stop". A concrete barrier formed in front of her. "OK, go."

He wound up and hurled the steak knife in her direction with the full strength in his arm. It turned into a silver spear in mid-air, hit the wall and fell, leaving the steak knife on the ground. It had cracked into two pieces. "Does that count? The spear kind of came and went."

"It counts," she grinned. "Welcome back to the Circle of Augustus, Silver Warrior, and not a moment too soon. I'll need this kind of help. Seriously."

He stared at the broken knife. "I can't believe it."

"It'll take both of us at full strength if we're going to deal with the sand and whatever's inside. Not to mention Mount Wilson."

He groaned. "Not that place again."

"It depends on what Lionel Stegner has up his sleeve, but first, you and I pay a visit to the sand mountain. You need to see it in person as it is now. It'll make your skin crawl."

"Sounds uncomfortable."

"It's definitely creepy. We have to be prepared, so let's work on your speed and accuracy. Try the throw again, this time with scissors."

Chapter 25

After she left the Land of Heroes, Audrey found herself in a small pocket park in downtown Los Angeles. She flew slowly over the green grass and through the trees, searching for James Jain, until she spotted his close-shaved head. The man himself sat on a wooden bench staring up at the sky. Circles of amber surrounding the pupils of his brown eyes reflected the sun, and the dark chocolate skin of his face was covered in a light sheen of perspiration. He wore black jeans and a black leather jacket over a black tee shirt. He lifted a small silver pipe to his lips, closed his eyes, and inhaled deeply, then exhaled a cloud of smoke with a long sigh. His shoulders curled forward, and his head drooped down. The swagger and confidence he once exuded were replaced with a look of defeat.

It hurt her heart to see the sorrow and regret swirling around him. "JJ. Can you hear me?"

He stared straight ahead, eyes glazed, with no reaction.

She would have to do something he would notice. She spun a small ring of energy on her index finger and dropped it on his knee. The gold ring glowed and sparkled. Would he feel it? He looked down, and his eyes went wide. He tried to touch the ring with one tentative finger, but it blinked out of existence. "Audrey," he whispered. "Hah." He took another drag on his pipe and stared straight ahead again. His brow furrowed. He resisted memories of rings, the Circle, and what happened to Nick, but Audrey made it impossible to ignore. She spun up a stream of small gold rings and dropped them on the grass at his feet, spelling out the word 'Hope'. Jain's nickname was 'Boulevard', because he claimed to know every street in L.A. Would he take the hint before the rings disappeared?

Jain stared at the glowing circles on the grass. "Hope Place," he mumbled. "Yeah. I know that damn place." The rings winked out. What he was thinking was impossible to deduce from the look on his face, but after a couple of minutes, he stood up and tapped the smoking material out of his pipe onto the gravel below the bench, then walked off through the park and disappeared between the trees.

Audrey could only hope her message got him moving in the right direction. It was time to deal with her own phantom existence. Waiting for Dean was driving her crazy. She had to let that go. As for Matt Gregg, her role in his death was self-defense. She had to convince herself deep down. She tried to imagine weights lifting from her, leaving her lighter, but she felt herself fading away, back to the in-between world. She'd drift there like a zombie without a purpose unless she figured out a way to join her sister and help her with the sand.

Chapter 26

TJ and Jonah went back to the hospital, and Willet got ready to go on a lookout drive, searching for breaches in the Gate as she had seen Gem do so many times. She wasn't sure where to look for them in a city as big as L.A, but she had to try. From the Hollywood Hills, she planned to head south, stop at Griffith Park for an overview of the city, and then turn east for a long drive before doubling back. She would look in on the sand mountain on her way home.

Smoke was already in the Jeep when she got in. No way would he allow her to leave him behind. She backed the Jeep out of the driveway and headed down the hill. It wasn't five minutes before she got a call. "Lars, what's up?"

He sounded breathless and distraught, unlike his usual confident demeanor. "One of the crystal boulders is gone, the big one that was right in front of the mountain. Lights are coming out of the sand. People are getting hit and falling down. Three of my workers were electrocuted. I don't know what's going on. It's a madhouse here. I need some of that help you offered."

"I'm on the road. Be right there." So much for plans. She leaned heavily on the gas. *Who could take a boulder that size? The artist? He didn't seem like the type to exert that much energy. Heavy machinery or supernatural intervention would be needed to move it. My money's on Degner. If anyone had the means to do it, he would. Or maybe there's another player...*

Out on the freeway, the speedometer rose to 95mph. *Concentrate, Will. You're no race car driver.* When she exited into downtown, she bobbed and weaved through midday traffic, trying to gain seconds. Every time she had to slow for a light or a traffic jam, it made her want to wail in frustration. Without the big crystal boulder in place, more of the black energy would leak into the courtyard. Her heart pounded painfully. She dreaded what she would find when she got to Hope Place.

Ambulances were racing through the heart of downtown with sirens blaring. Not hard to guess where they were going. Police had the streets around Hope Place barricaded. She jammed the Jeep into a small parking space. "Stay here unless absolutely necessary, Smoke. I mean it." She got out and ran toward the crowd of people gathered at a barricade. They stared up at the giant mountain of black sand, rubbernecking and yelling at the streams of red light spitting out in all directions, unaware of the danger they were in if one of those streams hit them. Even worse, the emotional quagmire of fear, fascination, curiosity, and horror created by the hysterical crowd shot out in wires that aimed right at her. They came fast and tried to wrap her up. She ripped them away with both hands and elbowed her way to the front. On the other side of the barricade, ambulances were parked, and paramedics tended to bodies on the ground.

"I need to get in there," she said to the nearest policeman, yanking a red wire from around her neck. "Lake Construction called me. I can help."

The policeman raised the visor of his helmet and gave her a fish-eyed look. She was grappling with a stubborn black wire around her waist. He probably thought she was crazy. "Sorry, lady," he said, "no one goes in. People are getting hit by some kind of light. We can't get close enough to pull 'em out." As he spoke, streaks of red light flew past his helmet. He flipped the visor down and ducked. She hoped he was wearing body protection too.

The black sand mountain sparkled red in the sun. The sand had come alive without the biggest crystal boulder to restrain it. The heartbeat from inside the mountain drummed loud enough to rattle her brain, and the deep voice inside it ranted in words she didn't understand, but she felt their meaning. Her stomach twisted. She had to get closer. When the officer's head turned, she squeezed around the barricade and took off running toward the sand pile. Police yelled behind her, but she wasn't going to stop. Inside the courtyard, she came to a skidding stop. Bodies lay on the ground twitching as if they had been tazed. Water in the pond in the middle of the courtyard was boiling. Soon the mountain would recognize her presence and turn its blasts on her. She needed to have her barrier defenses in place before that moment came. If only she felt as confident about that as she had in practice. She let the sense of gravity build inside her. A cloud condensed from the chaotic flux around her, full of cement dust, leaf debris, water molecules, and of course, sand. She caught it between her palms and squeezed until the cloud was hot enough to burn her skin off. "Reflect," she said. The cloud spread out before her into a large mirror. She stood behind it and walked slowly toward the mountain, which immediately recognized the presence of the Guardian. All the red-hot blasts turned toward her. They reflected off her mirror and ricocheted back on the sand. Small fires started on the surface of the mountain. It made her smile. She walked closer. *How do you like the feel of your own fire, eh?*

Hot lights flew back and forth between mirror and sand, strafing each other relentlessly. It looked like the whole mountain might go up in flames, but suddenly the fire snuffed out, and the red blasts stopped, silencing the crowd. An eerie quiet fell. For the moment, the sand had given up. She turned to the injured people on the ground and counted ten. Some were men from Lars' construction crew wearing hardhats and reflective vests. She saw Lars lying at the edge of the courtyard in front of the low concrete wall. She let her mirror drop and ran to him. "Lars! Get up!' she yelled, shaking his shoulder. "You and your men have to take cover before the sand starts shooting again." There was nowhere to hide inside the courtyard. With the sand mountain temporarily quiet, the paramedics had a small window of time to pull bodies to safety. She went back out to Hope Street and jogged from ambulance to ambulance, urging them to enter the courtyard. Paramedics looked hesitant, but they jumped out of the ambulances with stretchers, sprinted into the courtyard and started picking up those who were down. One paramedic went with her to help Lars. They managed to lift his big body to standing, half-dragged him back to an ambulance, and laid him down on the ground. The paramedic put an oxygen mask over his mouth. When she saw his chest rise and fall, her tension eased out in a long breath.

Lars regained consciousness. His blue eyes opened, round with shock. After a moment he pulled the mask away from his mouth. "Willet. My guys are hurt." He got winded after those few words and started to hyperventilate. The paramedic pressed the mask over his mouth again. Panic shot out from Lars in red-orange spikes. They wrapped her shoulders and shook her.

She hadn't known Lars long, but she figured he didn't panic easily. She took his hand between her two hands, leaned in and whispered in his ear. "Don't try to talk, Lars. It'll be ok." The wires melted from her shoulders. To the paramedic, she said, "Everyone needs to stay behind the cover of an ambulance. I don't know how long before the sand mountain starts shooting again."

The paramedic gave her an odd stare. "What do you mean?"

"The only thing protecting you from the red blasts coming from the sand is this ambulance. Don't go out in the open." She pointed at a man on a stretcher next to an ambulance a few yards away. He was twitching and shaking. Willet nodded at the paramedic. "That's what can happen to anyone hit by the red lights. Tell everyone."

The paramedic stood and went to the side door of the ambulance, leaving her in charge of Lars' oxygen tank. She placed Lars' hand over his mask and pressed it against his mouth. The paramedic emerged from the ambulance wearing a padded vest and thick rubber-soled shoes. He yelled at the other paramedics to do the same before they went out to retrieve more bodies from the courtyard.

She wasn't sure a padded vest and shoes would protect them from the kind of lights the sand was shooting, but it couldn't hurt. She shook off more of Lars' panicked emotional wires so she could think. *What do I do now?* She called TJ. To her surprise, he picked up on the first ring.

Chapter 27

"Thomas. We have big problems."

"Tell me."

Just hearing his voice made her feel better. "One of the crystal boulders is gone. The sands going crazy, and people are down. I need backup."

"Just got home from the hospital. I'll be there as soon as I can. There are some complications…"

"What complications?"

TJ lowered his voice. "Evelyn was released from the hospital, and I had to bring her home with me. There was nowhere else for her to go."

"She's at your house again?" Willet couldn't keep the chagrin out of her voice.

"I had to do it for Jonah. She's fragile right now. I'll get her settled, and he'll look after her. Then I can leave."

Willet felt like she was always second on his priority list. It was a childish thought, but it irritated her like a scratchy sweater. "Are Evelyn's needs more important than mine? I have a mountain of sand trying to kill me. Where does that rate in your priorities?"

"I'll be there ASAP, I promise. Just hang tight."

"You hang tight," she said, and hung up. It was petty, but she couldn't help it. She turned her attention back to the sand to avoid thinking about it.

Lars' workers who had been downed by the red blasts were receiving medical attention at the ambulances. One man was dead, apparently of a heart attack. Lars was so distraught, it affected his breathing. "This is my fault," he gasped. "Simon was my foreman. Five years. I didn't know he had a heart condition. How can I face his family?"

A person with a weak heart could easily be pushed into cardiac arrest by the amount of energy in the red blasts. The sight of the mountain alone could scare a person to death. Lars himself was on the verge of losing it. She felt his pain, but what could she offer by way of comfort? "I'm so sorry." She hugged him, feeling completely at a loss. "I wish I could be of more help."

"You tried to help, Willet," he said, struggling with his own failure. "You told me. I *didn't listen!*"

"It does no good to berate yourself. This situation is hard to understand. Anyone would have had difficulty believing it. I don't always know what's real, and I've been dealing with stuff like this for a while."

Lars closed his eyes. "I feel like running out there and letting the lights hit me again."

"Please don't think like that, Lars. It solves nothing. That sand is dangerous, and there are other people who depend on you. You know what the danger is now. We need to keep people out of the way."

He couldn't let it go. "I'm an idiot. What help could I be? My chest is aching, and I can hardly breathe."

She didn't want to stress him any further. "Do you want me to take you home?"

His breath rose and fell in a deep sigh. "Maybe that would help. I don't want to be another problem for the paramedics to deal with."

Chapter 28

James Jain avoided the crowds at the Hope Street side of the courtyard. Instead, he climbed to the top of the Bunker Hill Steps and entered Hope Place from the other side. When he saw what was going on, he immediately questioned the wisdom of his decision to come. The mountain of black sand looming above the courtyard brought back awful memories. The tall man in the black suit who carried the inert body of his best friend, Nick Hardman; the horrors of the Dragon Head Building; and the giant spider inside it. Here he was again in the same courtyard with no backup and no way to protect himself. A smell of ozone permeated the air as if lightning had struck. This was a bad place. He felt it in his bones, but he settled the black leather jacket on his shoulders, flipped his aviator shades down over his eyes and walked to the fountain. Standing behind the narrow pedestal with the statue on it, as if such a small thing could protect him, he studied the sand from close up. Tiny red currents were running through it. They looked like blood vessels, as if the sand was alive. He backed away with a shudder and headed to where ambulances were lined up at the curb. Paramedics hurried back and forth carrying stretchers and medical equipment. His gaze swept over the scene, searching for someone who could tell him what he was supposed to do next.

Jain knew the Circle of Augustus was involved. He deplored the day he got mixed up with those people, but when he recognized Willet Du Place kneeling next to one of the ambulances, he felt relieved. Willet would explain what was going on. She had tried to comfort him during the memorial service for Nick. He appreciated her effort. Her presence here only confirmed his suspicions. If the Circle was involved, there would be more weirdness. More danger. And the possibility of death.

He was supposed to assist the Circle somehow. That was the message of the gold rings. He could walk away right now, refuse to get involved. *Yeah, that's the smart thing to do, J.* Somehow, he knew if he did that, nothing would change for him. Since Nick died, he spent his days in the park smoking his hash pipe. Loaded. Numb. He felt impotent. The tall man in the black suit gave Nick to the spider and sacrificed his life. Jain wanted to deliver payback. The Circle could make that happen. Just thinking about revenge gave him an energy boost he hadn't felt since he beat the spider to death in the Dragon Head Building. He walked toward Willet.

Willet looked up and did a doubletake. "James, what are you doing here? This isn't a good place to be right now."

Jain crouched down beside the ambulance, trying to verbalize how he got there. "I got a message to come."

She frowned. "A message from whom?"

"Gold rings. They spelled out Hope Place. I thought it was from your sister. So, I came." He knew it sounded crazy, but this was Willet he was talking to. She understood crazy.

Willet stared at him. It did sound like something Audrey would do. Why? "The black sand is electrocuting people with red lights. At least one man is dead. It's quiet right now, but the lights could start firing again any minute. You have to stay out of the way. After all that happened, do you really want to get involved again?"

"Don't really want to, but it seems right. Sounds like you got some messed up stuff goin' on."

"That's an understatement. You went above and beyond helping us with the spider. You don't need to expose yourself to this. There's nothing for you to prove."

Jain took off his shades and met her eyes. His shoulders rose and fell with a deep sigh. "Nick is dead. My mother passed last month. My apartment building collapsed in a pile of dust when the crystal broke out of the ground underneath it. Everything I owned was destroyed or buried, including my wheels. I'm crashin' on my sister's couch 'cuz I got nowhere else to go except the street. Not sure where I'll end up."

The way he hung his head, Willet could see how much he was hurting. She sat on the ground to ease the ache in her knees.

"I'm so sorry, JJ. Is there a way I can help?"

"Why am I alive? Can you answer that? If there's no reason for to me being here, I might as well end it."

There it was, the question Gaia Philendra told her to think about when they first met in the Guardian Enclave. Willet hadn't given it much thought since then, but this was a cry for help. She wanted to offer something.

"Why are any of us alive? To love and be loved. To help each other. Especially at times like these."

His eyes rolled. "Yeah, that's what my sister always says. But why? What's the point?"

She thought her own life and all the things she had done that she never would have thought possible. "I think... each of us chooses to be here in this life. For a purpose. Figuring out what our purpose is and then fulfilling it is the point. If you don't, the lifetime is wasted. You'll just come back to try again."

"But why does it matter what I do? Who cares?"

"The fabric of existence is made of love. It depends on the strength of every thread in it. Gem taught me that. Sometimes it's really hard to fulfill one's purpose. I can attest to that from experience. There are no guarantees, but it's why we were created. That's my take."

He was staring at her. Then he closed his eyes. "I've probably screwed it up already."

"You're strong, JJ. I've seen you be strong and brave, and you know how to love. You have something unique to contribute. Each of us is here to contribute our unique thing to life." She felt a little guilty saying it after being miffed at TJ and resentful of Evelyn, but her words felt true when she said them.

"What can I do, like, right now?" he murmured. "To not feel useless."

"If you want to help us out, you have to be ready for whatever breaks loose from the sand, because I don't know what it will be. The mountain is full of destructive energy. It might be worse than the Dragon Head Building if that's possible. Can you commit to fighting something so potentially dangerous?"

He hesitated. Willet watched thoughts flash across his eyes, questions, and memories of very bad experiences. He finally nodded. "I'm in."

Jain knew the kinds of weirdness the Circle dealt with. At least he wouldn't be shocked. "Good. Right now, we're hiding beside this ambulance to stay out of range of the red lights. TJ is on his way. He's manifesting silver spears from stones these days. Long story. Audrey is lurking beyond the veil in an in-between space, and Dean is reliving a past life. In ancient Rome, no less. I don't know when or even if he'll be back. Is that weird enough for you?"

It was a new level of weird, he had to admit. "What's the plan?"

"The ultimate plan is to get rid of the sand. The short-term plan is to protect people from it until we can figure out the ultimate plan. That's all I got right now."

"Are we gonna knock off the tall guy in the black suit who took Nick?"

"You mean Jat?" Willet shook her head. "He's not killable, J. We sent him back to the Underworld. There's not much else we can do to him. There's a breach in the Gate to the Underworld hidden inside the sand. Demon Souls can use it to sneak back to our world. I don't know what kind or how many, but we have to be ready for anything - Red Souls, Needle Men, or whatever comes through. Jat is always involved in some way. You may get another crack at him."

Jain nodded. "What do you want me to do, like, right this minute?"

"We've got to help these people who are down on the ground, so they don't get hit by the lights again, like this man here. This is Lars Lake. Lars, this is James Jain, a good friend."

Lars and Jain lightly bumped fists. "What happened to you, man?" Jain asked.

Lars cleared his throat. He sounded hoarse. "A red light shot me in the throat, another in the thigh. I collapsed, passed out. Probably would have been toast if Willet hadn't got me out of that courtyard."

Jain nodded. "If you got a member of the Circle lookin' out for ya, that's good luck."

"Circle?"

Jain looked at Willet and caught the 'Be quiet' signal she was giving him. "It's Willet scene," he said with a shrug. "She can fill in the deets."

Willet slipped a hand under Lars' arm. Jain took the other arm, and they hoisted him to his feet. "My Jeep is down the street. I can give you a lift. There's a cat in the car, by the way, so don't be surprised."

Lars gave a weary chuckle. "That would be the least surprising thing that's happened today."

Chapter 29

She left Jain at the ambulance in case TJ actually showed up and led Lars to the Jeep. He seemed steadier, more like his robust self once he got moving. "I can take you home or to your car," she said, looking up at him. His blue eyes were on her with an intensity she couldn't interpret.

"Willet." He said her name with quiet urgency. "I don't understand what happened. Are you going to explain it to me?"

"You endured a shock, Lars. The sand hit you with blasts of energy. It has that ability. I'm not sure what the long-term effects are, other than... well, I don't know, but you should stay away from here and get some rest."

"I don't want to rest now."

He put his hands on her shoulders and pulled her into his broad chest. The warmth of his body was confusing. She couldn't help feeling abandoned after she talked to TJ, but her concern rose when Lars laid his cheek against the top of her head. This was getting way too intimate. She tilted her head back to look up at him. Before she knew it, he was kissing her. His lips were insistent. Hungry. She pulled away and stepped back.

"You have to stop that, Lars."

He didn't seem to hear her. "I wanted to do that the first time I met you," he murmured and moved closer.

She was nervous now. "I'm in a relationship. A serious one."

His smile became more of a leer. "Couldn't be that serious. It didn't stop you from kissing me."

"*You* were kissing *me*. Let's be clear on that."

Lars shook his head slowly. "You're saying you weren't in control of yourself? That's not a worthy excuse for someone like you." He moved in until he towered over her and then backed her against the Jeep.

She was looking directly into his eyes. Red lights flickered in the depths of his pupils. *Uh oh. Not good.* The red blasts he endured had penetrated deep into him. She saw it happen to Dean after Red Souls attacked him. "You may not be in control of yourself either. The blast you took from the sand could affect your feelings and behavior. Make you do things you wouldn't naturally do. I've seen it happen." She pushed against his chest, but he didn't budge.

"Oh, I'm in control," he said, his voice a low rumble. "This is me being natural." He grabbed her shoulders and kissed her. It wasn't gentle. His tongue was in her mouth and his groin pressed against her. She could feel his hardness.

What if Thomas drives up?! A sharp sting of energy flowed from his tongue to hers. It shocked her into action. She pushed against him as hard as she could, but his feet were planted, demanding what she couldn't and wouldn't give him.

Just then, a growl came from the back seat of the Jeep that made the car shake. Lars' head snapped up. "What the hell is that?" He stared into the back window. What he saw made him jump back. "Holy s__t!"

Willet looked over her shoulder. A large spotted feline with slitted gold eyes stared out through the back window, lips pulled back in a snarl, exposing a mouth full of sharp white teeth. Smoke looked like he was ready to rip Lars apart. "Oh. Yeah, that's my cat. He's very protective."

Now Lars was the one to look flustered. "That's not a cat. What is it?"

"Hmm. He looks like a leopard."

"You drive around with a leopard in your back seat?"

"The sand is affecting both of us, Lars. We have to remember who we are. You're a gentleman."

"I'm a gentleman," he repeated in a monotone and swayed unsteadily on his feet.

"Yes, you are. Let me drive you to your ride before you fall down. Where are you parked?

Lars stared at the Jeep and squinted like he was just waking up. He took another look at the big spotted animal in the window. "I'm not getting in there. I can walk." He turned away and walked off down the street without a word or backward glance.

She didn't try to stop him. Instead, she opened the back door of the Jeep and looked inside at the fluffy gray cat sitting on the back seat. "A leopard, huh? You're full of surprises." Smoke meowed. He was the picture of innocence.

Chapter 30

*** Dean ***

Lucius was dead set on taking a bath. He steered them to the Baths built by Emperor Trajan, the same bath house Dean peeked into when he first became conscious of Rome, but now the experience was physical. The air inside felt humid, scented with clove and cinnamon, jasmine oil, and sage. Not terrible, but rather clammy. They went to a changing room and found clean sheets stacked on a stone bench. Lucius hung his tunic on a wooden hook, wrapped himself in a sheet and walked into the warm bathing area. He went to the middle tub, dropped the sheet, and stepped into the heated water. It was pretty hot, not scalding, but it did put a sting on the skin. His body eased down into the water on the stone seat beneath the surface. After the initial sting of heat, relaxation followed. *Ahhhhhh.* Tight neck and calf muscles went soft. Shoulders rolled forward. Lucius tipped his head back to rest it on the ledge. Dean had to admit – it felt pretty good. His thoughts drifted, not worrying about the other naked men around them. He'd have to find a hot tub to go to if he ever got back to his modern life.

Thoughts about Amisi rose in Lucius' mind. Of the amorous kind. Soon, Lucius and Amisi were deep into lovemaking. *I do NOT want to watch this.* Dean tried to divert his own attention to something else. Audrey. Yes, that was a pleasing thought. He pictured her and tried to recapture the essence of her honey scent. He pictured her talking to him with those soft red lips pursed in a smile. He wanted to kiss them so much. He imagined it, stepping to her, pressing a lingering kiss on her lips. After a few sweet moments, he pulled back and saw he was kissing Amisi. He scrambled to re-imagine Audrey but couldn't quite grasp her. *Stay out of my daydreams, Lucius!* Then he heard Lucius talking in their shared mind. *Who are you, woman? Where is Amisi?* Lucius found himself kissing Audrey. He was mumbling to himself. *I do not know this woman with the gold hair. She is not from this land. Why is she in my thoughts? She is comely indeed. I could enjoy her. She seems willing...* Fortunately, before Dean was forced to witness Lucius taking pleasure with Audrey, Lucius' thoughts wandered, and he dozed off. Dean was free to think about Audrey in peace.

After a fifteen-minute soak, Lucius roused himself, stepped out of the bath, and walked naked into the next room where the cold pools waited. He dipped into one and shivered. The shocking cold really cleared out the cobwebs in their brain and closed the pores on their skin. Bathing in cold water had become popular since the Emperor Augustus Caesar had supposedly cured his painful liver abscess by bathing in the cold springs of Chiusi. The emperor was so grateful to the doctor who suggested it, that he had a public statue erected in his likeness, and the practice of cold bathing was adopted throughout Rome.

Across from the cold pool, workers were cleaning out an empty pool with rags smelling of rosemary and a tinge of urine. *Urine? So that's what they're using for disinfectant.* Urine had astringent properties. It made sense, though the aesthetics were unappealing. The Romans were not the first to figure that out, or the last. Dean thought fondly of the better alternatives available in modern times.

Lucius dressed in his tunic and leather sandals and steered their body outside. The odor of the streets was a shock after the relative cleanliness of the bath. Foul stench hit Dean's olfactory sense and turned their stomach. This confused Lucius, but Dean would never get used to it. There was no sanitation system in Rome. Trash and waste were dumped on the streets and left wherever they landed. The air was filled with swarms of flies that fed on the waste and spread contamination to whatever they touched. Food and water were often unhealthy, and disease was common. Acquired immunity went only so far. People didn't live long in these times.

Dean would have liked to leave the streets and go back to Lucius' apartment, but Lucius headed to the training hall to check on Silas. When they arrived, the young man was not there. This was insubordination, and Lucius could not let it stand. He questioned some of the centurions working out. They told him Silas went to the market. So off to the market Lucius went. He retraced the steps they had taken earlier. Silas was not in the fighting ring or at the table of the drum seller. They found him in front of Amisi's table of fruits, leaning towards her with a big leering smile and flirting for all he was worth.

Amisi saw Lucius approach and blushed pink under her golden skin. "Lucius!" she said brightly. "You have returned for a pomegranate?"

Silas spun around and glared at Lucius. "Do you follow me?"

"I am your commanding officer!" Lucius said loudly. "It is my duty to know your whereabouts. You are not in the place you should be. I insist you return with me to the barracks where you will be consigned to a cell until such time as a suitable punishment can be delivered."

Silas gave Lucius a killing look. He was embarrassed in front of a woman and every shopper around them. His eyes smoldered with hatred. "You think to jail me? My father is a member of the Senate, a confidante of the emperor. He will have you whipped."

"I am within my rights as the leader of your cohort. The emperor will support my decision." Lucius grabbed the neck of Silas' tunic and yanked. "Come with me, or I will dispatch you here and now." Lucius out ranked him, and he was stronger. Silas acquiesced with a scowl and no deference. Lucius took his arm and pulled him into the crowd. Silas shrugged him off to walk on his own.

Dean observed this scene with a growing sense of déjà vu. Somewhere in his memories was a snapshot of this moment and those that followed. It felt as inevitable as a boulder rolling down the side of a mountain toward a cliff. He recognized that feeling. It was the inevitability of a final confrontation. There would be no escape from it in this life.

Chapter 31

After Lars left her standing in the street, Willet returned to the ambulances. Jain was holding a fluid bag above a man's head while a paramedic administered CPR to one of Lars' workers. Standing beside him was TJ. She felt overjoyed to see him and guilty at the same time. The feeling of Lars' kisses lingered on her lips. She wiped any telltale signs away with the back of her hand in case they could be detected. "So, you made it," she said when she reached him.

"Of course, I made it." He gave her a curious look. "Did you think I wouldn't come?"

That made her feel worse. She knew he'd come. "I didn't know how long it would take to get Evelyn 'settled'." She knew her tone was peevish but couldn't help it.

"Can we talk about this somewhere else?" He took her hand and led her down the street away from the ambulances. "What's going on, Will? You seem upset with me."

She felt even more embarrassed. What right did she have to be angry with him when another man was just kissing her? "You and Evelyn, I'm sorry, it's just...I don't know why I'm reacting this way, but I don't like it."

"There is no 'me and Evelyn'. There's only you and me. And then there's a delusional woman recovering from head trauma in my guest room. Temporarily. What else do you think it is?"

"She despises me, Thomas. To the point of doing me bodily harm. The idea of her being at your house makes me uncomfortable and a little angry."

"A little angry?"

"Maybe a lot angry. I'm not proud of it. If a Guardian is supposed to be perfect, then I would have flunked the entrance exam."

TJ searched her face with a helpless look. "I'm here. I don't know what else you want me to do."

"I need to stay at Pine Siskin House for a while. Until you move her somewhere else."

"That won't work. How are we supposed to coordinate on the sand problem if we're on opposite sides of L.A.? Besides, if you leave me alone with her, she'll get ideas about us playing house. I don't want her to get ideas."

It was a persuasive point, and they did need to coordinate closely. Why cede the field to Evelyn? OK, that was a childish way to think. It was the way Evelyn would think, and she didn't want to think like her. TJ was in a difficult spot, and she wasn't helping. She threw her arms around his neck. "I'm sorry," she said and kissed him on each cheek. "What happened in the courtyard really threw me. It's the first time I used my blocking ability in a real fight. I was scared it wouldn't work."

He hugged her and planted a kiss on her forehead. "What did happen? Can you tell me?"

"It's better if we go take a look at the sand. It might be easier to explain."

They walked back to Hope Place. She put up a brick-hard wall, and TJ walked behind her as they entered the courtyard, coming to a stop next to the fountain. He got a good look at the sand, and the sight was alarming. The mountain smoked. Tiny currents of red light ran through the black sand like little arterioles full of blood. "The sand shot hot red lights at me. I put up a mirror and reflected the lights back on the sand. Little fires started on it. That'll tell you how hot those lights are. The fires were getting bigger, but then they went out for no apparent reason, like the sand decided to stop fighting. As for all the little red currents, I have no clue."

He scanned the mountain up and down. "Looks almost like a living thing, with a blood supply."

"That's not the half of it. A voice from the sand has been speaking to me in a language I don't understand. Jat usually talks to us in English. I think someone else is in there."

They backed away, keeping their eyes on the mountain as they exited the courtyard. Willet let her brick wall drop. "I'm burnt out," she whispered. "Not sure how many more walls I can raise."

"You need a rest." TJ put an arm around her. "Let me take you back to my place, just for a little while."

"Do we dare leave? What if the sand starts shooting again? And what about JJ? He's here helping the paramedics. He wants to work with us"

"Like you said, you're burnt out. What are you going to do if you can't raise a wall? Jain is occupied with a job for the moment. We can tell him we'll be right back. The Zinger can get us back to the Hills super quick. You'll recharge your batteries, and then we'll come back here just as quickly. We both need to be at full strength."

The thought of resting sounded too good for Willet to say no. She was ready to fall sleep on her feet, so she put her hand in his and let him lead her away to the aforementioned Zinger, the big hunk of white metal with large tires and two black racing stripes down the hood. TJ pulled out onto the street and drove over to the Jeep to pick up Smoke. Willet hauled the cat out of the back seat and brought him with her into the Zinger. He nestled into her lap without a fuss. TJ made a U-turn with a squeal of rubber and headed for the freeway. The Zinger *was* super-fast. She had no sooner tilted her head back to close her eyes for a moment when they were pulling up into TJ's driveway.

"Here we are," TJ said, giving her shoulder a squeeze. "Let's get you in the house. You can relax, and I'll rustle up some food."

They went in through the front door and found Jonah in the kitchen. Evelyn was sitting on the living room couch bundled up in a green blanket with a big white bandage wrapped around her head. Her eyes were closed. When she heard them come in, she threw off the blanket and stood up. She was wearing a white bathrobe that billowed around her like a cloud and covered her to the ankles. Willet recognized the bathrobe as one of TJ's. That didn't sit well.

Evelyn was bleary-eyed and wobbled on her feet, but she managed to stumble into the kitchen. Jonah helped her to sit up on one of the barstools at the center island. She gave Willet a half-lidded squint. "Tom, you brought a guest," she said with a sour smile. "And a cat too. You should have told me. I would have bought kitty litter."

"Willet is not a guest, Evelyn," TJ said evenly as he ushered Willet through the kitchen. "She's the lady of the house. We've had this conversation before. Let's not have it again." Jonah pulled a bowl out of a cupboard, filled it with water, and put it on the floor for Smoke, who sidled up to it and lapped happily. "Smoke's house trained, Mom," the boy said. The troubled look on his face gave way to a smile as he watched the cat.

Evelyn's blue eyes turned icy cold. She gave a long-suffering sigh. "Very well. I should dress. Jonah, put that animal outside. It looks dirty," she sniffed.

Willet bristled at this. "Smoke isn't dirty."

"All animals are dirty. They shouldn't be inside people's houses."

TJ put up his hand. "Enough, Evelyn, please. Smoke is welcome here. I'm tired, and Willet is tired. We're going in to take showers and rest." They went on down the hallway to the master bedroom. The door closed behind them.

Jonah picked Smoke up in his arms and nestled his cheek against the cat's silky head. "He's not dirty. He's a good kitty." Smoke purred softly. Jonah left the kitchen with Smoke and went out to the porch. Evelyn was left in the kitchen by herself. Fuming.

Chapter 32

After a night of welcome rest, Willet and TJ returned to Hope
Place the next morning, and not a moment too soon. The sand
mountain looked about to explode. Its black surface bubbled
and bulged into irregular shapes that broke off and turned
into large black crows. Ten crows, twenty, and then thirty flew
into the air and circled the courtyard with claws out and beaks
open, squawking loudly. Fire burned in their yellow eyes. A
murder of crows descended and attacked them, pecking at
exposed flesh, leaving trickles of blood, but hands and arms
were not the real target.

Willet covered her head with her arms. "They're aiming for
our eyes!"

TJ ducked down, covering his own head. "Now would be a
good time for a wall."

The king of all sand piles was right in front of them, but it was probably dangerous to use that sand for defense. She had to gather different materials. "Protect!" Willet declared and tried to draw other molecules from the air. A mixture of cement dust, tire rubber, metals, carbon, and plant materials came together in her hands. She compressed the cloud into a hot liquid, threw it up, and let it pour down in front of her. A barrier formed. She wasn't sure what substance she made. It felt solid but pliable. She spread it over them in a convex shield. The crows screeched and scraped at the shield, hitting it and bouncing off before attacking again. They tried to wiggle underneath it. Willet stretched the material to the ground.

"Nice work, Guardian," TJ said, "but we can't allow these birds to leave the courtyard. They'll terrorize and hurt people wherever they go."

"How do you suggest we stop them?"

TJ reached in the pockets of his jeans and pulled out some small stones. He held them out on his palms. "Cover me. Let's see what the Silver Warrior can do."

She tilted the shield forward so he could stand up. He hurled a stone at the crows with each hand. The stones turned into silver spears in the air and skewered two crows right through the breast. He ducked down behind the shield. The remaining birds dive-bombed the shield in a frenzy. He pulled handfuls of stones from his pockets. She waited for the moment when the birds swooped away, then tipped the shield forward again. He stood and threw stones one after another. The stones turned to silver spears and hit their targets with accuracy. One by one, birds plummeted in a fluster of flapping wings with spears in their chests. All thirty crows disappeared in puffs of smoke as they hit the cement. The spears disappeared with them, leaving stones clattering to the ground. She dropped the shield, and he retrieved the stones to reload his supply.

"That was awesome!" Willet marveled. "What made you think to bring stones?"

"They seemed to work when we were practicing. I thought I should come prepared." He gave her a wink and smiled.

A pleasant shiver ran through her. *My hero.* She wanted to kiss him right there, but the black sand mountain was in a state of continuous manifestation. Some odd shapes emerged in blebs and burbles, seeming unsure of what form they should take. The sand quickly absorbed them, but more crows bubbled off the surface.

Willet raised her shield, and TJ speared the crows as fast as they appeared. Most dropped to the ground. Some flew away. When the sand went quiet, she dropped the shield, he collected his stones, and they backed up to the edge of the courtyard to seek cover behind the low wall. Willet needed to conserve energy. She sat on the ground and stretched her legs out in front of her. "I could use some food, but I don't want to take my eyes off that monstrosity."

"Maybe JJ could get us something," TJ said. "Be right back." He stood and stretched and then headed toward the ambulances.

Willet got up on her knees and peeked over the wall at the sand. A stream of red light burst out of the sand so fast she couldn't react and hit her squarely between the eyes. Searing pain shot through her head. She listed to the side, unable to support her own weight. The voice from the sand roared a series of sounds that may have been words in a language not of the modern world. Her mind blanked, and then she was standing in her Light body looking down on her own physical body slumped on the ground. The pale crumpled form seemed sort of pathetic. That body wasn't her. She was Light. *Do I really have to go back to it? I could just leave it here and move on. There are other worlds to explore.*

A different voice sang in long, open-mouthed tones. The voice was full of yearning. Without any words, it implored her to understand something important, so deep, she tried to grasp it, but its meaning eluded her. An image slipped into her consciousness, and she realized why she couldn't abandon her physical self. Thomas. She couldn't do that to him. And she had Guardian responsibilities. How could she turn her back on the city when the mountain of sand was there, threatening to do-- what? She didn't know.

She turned to face the sand, but she wasn't in the courtyard anymore. She was standing at the entrance to the great granite cave of the Guardian Enclave. The cave blazed with light just as she remembered it. Guardians stood in the entrance, looking at her as if they expected her arrival. Their voices rang out. "Welcome, Guardian of Los Angeles and esteemed Listener, we heard the call of your heart. How may we assist you?"

It took a moment to gather her thoughts. *The call of my heart? I don't remember making a call.* She had wished for a sandwich. That couldn't be it. She also wished for information about the crows. Who better to ask than the Guardian Enclave? When she spoke, her words chimed. "There's a mountain of black sand in my city, full of destructive energy. Crows are flying out of it. Why is this happening? How can I stop it? I need help. Please."

The Guardians turned to each other and conversed quietly in low murmurs. After a few minutes, the Guardian of Atlanta, Sebastian Ibbis, stepped forward. "Come into the sanctum. We will deliberate."

Willet followed the glowing Light bodies of the Guardians into the cave. This time, the air inside was scented with roses. Invisible violins played a heartbreakingly beautiful tune.

Sebastian Ibbis turned to her with a look of concern. "Now then. A mountain of sand, you say?"

Words tumbled out of her. "Yes. The sand shoots red energy at people. It shot me in the head and knocked me out of my physical body. And crows are flying out of the sand. They tried to peck out our eyes. I think they will hurt many people. The Circle of Augustus lost two members, and I don't know how to fight without them. How do I stop the crows?"

A wave of HU song rolled through the room. The sound lifted her and tossed her on an invisible sea. She almost forgot her purpose for being there. When the HU stopped, she stood once again in front of Sebastian Ibbis.

"What sound do the crows make?" he asked.

"Well... they caw. Like crows."

"Do they say Ka by chance?"

"Well, sure. That's like caw, isn't it?"

"Could it be O-Ka? Do you hear that?"

She concentrated and tried to bring the sounds of the birds back to immediate memory. When she replayed the sounds in her mind, she couldn't come to a definite conclusion. "It's hard to tell with so many birds making noise. They just sound like crows. It could be O-Ka, I guess." The Guardian of Atlanta looked concerned. "What?" she asked, her unease growing by the moment. "What is it?"

"If O-Ka has inhabited the sand, the crows do his bidding, feed his appetites. That is a dire situation for your city."

"What is O-Ka? Who is it?"

"O-Ka the Fallen is an ancient Soul, one of the earliest Homo Sapiens on earth to be condemned to the Underworld. He lived fifty thousand years ago in the land now called Ethiopia. His mate was Niha. They had an infant son, O-do. O-Ka found Niha with another man of their tribe. He experienced jealousy, an emotion not common at that time as it is today. It drove him insane. In a frenzy, he butchered their son and ate him alive. His taste for human flesh grew, and he turned on other children of the tribe. The men of the tribe killed him and burned his body. He has roamed the Underworld since his death, terrorizing other Souls there. He is violent beyond imagining and completely unrepentant."

"How can he be in the sand?"

"O-Ka last appeared in the physical world ten thousand years ago. A serious breach in the Gate between Worlds allowed him to escape the Underworld at that time. It seems this has happened again in the sand. When he appears, he comes in shadow. If he emerges from the sand, he will haunt the streets of your city looking for victims. People will die, of fear if nothing else."

"But what does he want?"

"Human flesh."

A sense of dread made her Light body flicker. "This is so beyond what I'm prepared for."

"If O-Ka has escaped the Underworld, the Guardian of California must be informed immediately if she is not already aware. You will need her assistance."

Before she could ask another question, Willet woke in the courtyard where TJ was shaking her shoulder and calling her name. "Will! What happened?" he said when her eyes opened. He helped her sit up against the concrete wall and crouched close to her with his arm around her shoulders. "Are you hurt?"

"I went to the Guardian Enclave. They told me what is going on in the sand."

"What'd they say?"

Willet shuddered. Her voice quivered. "There's a cannibal in there."

Chapter 33

*** Dean ***

That night after the scene with Silas, Lucius retired to his apartment and tried to sleep. He tossed and turned. Dean was beset by nightmares in which a woman cried, her shoulders shaking under a black shawl. He couldn't see her face, but he knew it was Lucius' mother. There was no one in the dream to help her. In the morning, Lucius awoke and did not feel refreshed by his sleep. He got up and threw water on his face from the basin in his room. There was a loud knock at the door. It was too early for a visitor. He went to the oak door and threw it open with an irritated sniff.

A junior centurion stood on the doorstep. "Primus, forgive the intrusion, but the Praefectus requests your presence in his meeting room. He said not to delay." The young centurion stepped off with a deferential bow of his head.

"Very well," Lucius said, the gruffness of sleep still in his voice, and closed the door. Dean was curious what this meant. A summons from a superior was never boded well. Lucius dressed and armed himself and headed out the door in the direction of the main barracks several blocks away, winding through the same narrow, dirty streets and crowded squalor of working-class Rome they traveled through the previous day. He entered the main barracks through a side entrance in the mud brick wall. The meeting room was empty except for a square wooden table and four wooden chairs in the middle. Rectangular windows high on the walls were covered by iron grates.

The Praefectus was already there, watching the doorway. The man was in a ready stance with his right hand on the long sword hanging from a leather belt around his waist.

Praefectus Liberius stood five foot five, built of solid muscle. He had a plain square face with a long scar down his left cheek and a sun-bronzed bald head. The red tunic he wore over brown leggings was stretched tight over his broad chest. His biceps bulged. As a war-hardened veteran, he was third in command of the entire Roman Legion. Nothing would take him unawares, especially not in his own barracks. His tough persona was legendary among the soldiers. No one wanted to be on the receiving end of the squint-eyed stare from his dark eyes that Lucius was receiving now..

Lucius clapped his right arm across his chest in salute. His right hand rattled the metal of the chest plate over his heart. "Lucius Avitus at your command, Praefectus."

Liberius was a man of few words and no pleasantries. Those he did share were dry as gravel and just as gritty. "Primus, I received a missive from Senator Magnus Fabius complaining that his son has been subjected to unfair treatment under your hand. Is there any truth to this?"

Lucius knew that cowering before Praefectus Liberius would win him no favors, so he returned a level look. "Silas engaged in a fist fight with a free citizen in the marketplace, causing the man harm. When I gave him duties to perform in the training room, he left his post. I had to seek him out in the market and bring him back to the barracks, which he resisted. I did not employ any methods of discipline that would not have been used with any other soldier. Sir."

Liberius gave him an expressionless look and nodded. "I understand the explanation, Lucius Avitus, but I cannot dismiss an inquiry from a Senator. You understand."

"Yes, sir. What would you have me do? I must maintain order in my barracks. If one soldier ignores my direction, it will give the others leave to do so."

"Use a method of discipline that is less – public. Give the boy a way to maintain his pride in front of his fellows. He is not one we can simply remove from the ranks."

This was good advice if it could be followed. Lucius was not about to argue. "I will find a way, Praefectus. Thank you for your counsel." He gave a short bow and another cross-body salute, then stepped back. Liberius waved him out the door of the meeting room. Back on the street, Lucius fumed at the trouble that pampered pipsqueak, Silus Fabius, was causing him. He walked back to his barracks at a fast clip, wracking his brain for a suitable solution to the problem.

Dean had watched the exchange with Liberius silently, not wanting to agitate Lucius any more than he already was. He tried to think of something he could suggest to his old self that might help in dealing with Silas. He came up with a few whispered words: *Think of an activity you can share with Silas. If he sees you working on something right beside him, he won't feel singled out for punishment.* Dean felt the exact moment when his words reached Lucius' consciousness. Lucius walked back to the training hall in search of Silas.

Chapter 34

If O-Ka was really in the sand, he might be able to hear what they were saying. Willet didn't want to attract his attention. She whispered into TJ's ear. "The Guardians told me he's a man from very ancient times who eats people. Now he's an Underworld demon who eats people. He's here to feed. Gem needs to know."

No sooner had the words left her lips, than a flash of gold turned into a nimbus of bright light in the center of the courtyard. The Guardian of California herself stepped out of the center of it. Gem wore her long purple print skirt and white ruffled blouse, the clothes she usually wore when fighting demon attacks. Dora, Gem's faithful companion, stood resolutely beside her. Dora's ears flicked in all directions, and her eyes scanned the courtyard, alert to signs of danger. "I wondered when you would call, Guardian," Gem said with a small smile. "You do not have to solve every problem by yourself."

Willet's surprise turned to overwhelming relief at seeing her beloved teacher and guide standing with her like old times. Tears came to her eyes. She jumped up, ran to her and threw her arms around Gem.

"I am here, baby girl," Gem said, patting Willet's back. She turned to the sand pile and looked it over, then frowned. "How long has the sand been this way?"

TJ couldn't hide his own relief at seeing Gem. "We got here this morning, and crows were flying everywhere. They flew out of the sand faster than I could kill them. Anyone who enters this courtyard will be attacked if they start flying again."

"Crows." Gem's eyes narrowed as she watched the unsettled surface of the sand roll and bubble. "A harbinger of ill intent."

"I went to the Enclave. The Guardians told me to expect O-Ka."

Gem's glowing brown skin flushed a pale undertone. A look of alarm flashed in her eyes. "This is an unusual danger," she said. "We must prepare accordingly."

Willet had never seen Gem look so disturbed before. "What do you know about O-Ka? Anything that could help us?"

Gem was silent for a minute. "The sand holds him for now," she said slowly. "That gives us time, we do not know how much. If he escapes the sand, he will move through the streets in smoke and shadows, difficult to detect, especially at night. His body is large and misshapen, but very strong. Other Souls from the Underworld may accompany him. We may have to fight an army."

"Could you freeze it?" Willet said. "The sand, I mean."

"Sand itself cannot be frozen. The substance was probably chosen with that in mind. If it were doused with water, I might freeze it. A mountain of that size would require an enormous amount of water, and it would be only a temporary solution. Jat would melt the ice with his fire. We must find a more permanent solution."

"We don't have the full Circle!" Willet said. Her anxiety spiked all over again. "Not Audrey's rings or Dean's golden-hearted strength. I feel like I'm working without all my body parts."

TJ tried to think of something positive to add. "We've got my silver spears, Gem's ice, and your walls." He turned to Gem. "Will it be enough to fight a cannibal?"

Gem's shrug did not look encouraging. "We will use all that we have," she said solemnly. "To do otherwise would admit defeat."

Chapter 35

*** Dean***

The training room was stuffy from all the sweating bodies of soldiers in various states of exercise. The air rumbled with the sounds of exertion. Silas was lounging in a corner, talking with another soldier. Lucius felt his ire rise and took a deep breath to control himself. He walked around the perimeter of the room to where Silas stood. "Come with me," he said pleasantly. "We will spar together. I need to warm my muscles. So do you. Step into the private training room with me."

Silas gave him an ugly glare and then smirked. "Are you afraid of an audience? I might punch your face, old man. Does that not worry you?"

"Not at all," scoffed Lucius, barely holding his temper. Dean felt every muscle of their shared body tense, and Lucius' thoughts toward Silas were cold. A reckoning was coming. The soldier Silas had been talking to looked uncomfortable and walked away, leaving Silas and Lucius trying to stare each other down.

"Enough talk," Lucius said. "If you prefer an audience, meet me in the circle. Let us box."

They moved to the center of the training room and wrapped their fists in rags. The other soldiers cleared out of the way and took positions around the room to watch the fight. Lucius and Silas faced each other, two feet apart, and then Silas moved in to throw the first punch, a roundhouse throw of his right arm that jarred Lucius' chin. *That kind of hurt.* Silas laughed and danced away. The other soldiers murmured. Lucius stepped forward and threw a flurry of punches with both hands that had Silas backing up. Silas was a trained fighter and light on his feet. Lucius was both trained and experienced, heavier, and more focused. His fists were hard as rock with muscles behind them in his forearms like bands of iron. When he landed a punch, his opponent felt real pain..

Silas felt the weight of Lucius' fists hitting his shoulders over and over. It weakened his arms and made him angry. He came forward with a series of quick punches. Lucius dodged them easily, then threw a punch that landed squarely on Silas' nose. The whole room heard the crunch of bone. Silas stepped back holding his nose and groaning in pain. Blood started to flow. He would have two black eyes by the afternoon. The young man looked around and grabbed a broadsword from a nearby rack. The stakes were raised.

Lucius chuckled. "Do you really want to resort to swords, Silas?" he said reasonably. "It is a dangerous choice for you. Your arms are already too weak to lift your fists."

"It will be dangerous for *you*, old man," Silas growled, the skin around his eyes already turning an ugly red. "I will cut off the hand that struck me."

"Bold words for one too young to have seen any actual battle."

Yeah. My money's on Lucius.

Lucius beckoned for a broadsword, and a soldier handed one to him. He raised the sword and invited Silas to meet his blade. Silas charged in with his sword raised. The blades crossed in a ringing clank of metal. The swings were flat and wide, then chopping, then slicing. If one of the thrusts landed on flesh, it would do major damage. Lucius easily swung the heavy broadsword in both hands. He had fought with such a weapon for years. Oxygen surged through his blood, and his thick, strong muscles sang with energy. He would not tire before Silas' arms gave out.

Dean relished the heady, powerful experience. *This is what a body in fighting shape feels like.* He would remember that feeling.

Silas was too immature to realize his disadvantage. After five minutes of blade work, the younger man's arms were visibly weakened. The heavy sword drooped in his hands, and Lucius moved in. Before Silas could raise his sword, Lucius' blade was at his throat. "Yield now," ordered Lucius.

Blood flowed from Silas' nose and splattered down the front of his gray tunic. "My father will have your head for this," he snarled.

"Not before I have yours," Lucius said quietly. "Now attend to your injury and then resume your duties. You are not yet ready for battle." He turned to the soldiers standing by the walls. "All of you. Get back to your training. This is no time for loafing."

There was a mumble among the soldiers, but they quickly obeyed the order. The outcome of the fight was never really in doubt, though Dean doubted it was truly a victory. Lucius couldn't have risen up the ranks to first centurion without making a few enemies. Now he had an enemy whose father was in the Roman Senate. What was supposed to be a private session between Lucius and Silas had become a public beat down. Silas would not let this embarrassment pass without a face-saving rebuttal.

Chapter 36

The drama in the courtyard had stopped for the moment. Crowds thinned out on the streets around Hope Place. The police moved their yellow tape and barriers farther back from the courtyard entrance and pushed onlookers back with them. Paramedics loaded the remaining victims onto stretchers, and the ambulances left for the hospital.

Gem, Willet, and TJ sat on the low concrete wall that bordered the courtyard, keeping an eye on the silent pile of black sand. Jain arrived with his arms full of bottled water, turkey sandwiches, and bags of corn chips, and handed them out. Willet finally got her wish for a sandwich. "Thanks, JJ. For the food. And for sticking around." She didn't like it that Jain was so exposed to the sand, but she did appreciate his help. "I'm concerned about you being here, though. It's not safe."

"You said you needed help. I'm helping."

"You're right, we do need help but things may get hinky. If crows start to fly, seek cover. I can't guarantee we'll be able to protect you."

Jain gave her a funny look. "You think I can't handle myself?" It wasn't even a question. The image of Jain on the back of the enormous spider in the Dragon Head Building, bludgeoning its shell to a pulp with his bare fists, was burned into her memory. "Your bravery is beyond question. But it's a different situation now. We don't understand the threat or how it works, and we don't have a full Circle. I'm not sure what it will take to defeat the crows or whatever else comes out of the sand."

"Yeah, J. A lot of crows. They aim for the eyes." TJ tore into a bag of corn chips and stuffed a handful into his mouth. After he chewed and swallowed them, he downed another handful of chips, followed it with a gulp of water and then reached in for more chips.

Willet eyed him. "You must be really hungry."

"Sure I am. Aren't you?"

"I'm famished," she said and tore the wrapper off her sandwich. She took a big bite, relishing every morsel.

"Thomas is right, JJ. The crows will go for your eyes. You have to be careful."

"I'll take my chances," Jain said, and squared his shoulders. "I'm not afraid of crows."

"These aren't normal crows. We think they're announcing the arrival of a demon presence in the sand. One that eats human flesh."

That sent Jain back a step. If he took off running in the opposite direction, no one would have been surprised, but he stood his ground, though a light sheen of perspiration broke out on his forehead.

 TJ watched the black sand bubble as he ate, then stood up suddenly, almost choking on his chips. "Look. More crows coming. Get ready."

Crows started breaking out of the sand. There had to be two hundred of them, their flapping wings cracking like lightning. Willet quickly raised a barrier, taller and wider than before. She, TJ, and Gem crouched behind it. Willet pulled Jain down beside her before the crows dive-bombed them with claws out and beaks open. Gem stood and blew a long blast of frigid air that sent crows careening backward, colliding and screaming. TJ stood up and took advantage of the confusion, hurling stones into the swirling mass of black feathered bodies like his arms were windmills. The stones turned into silver spears as soon as they left his hands and multiplied. Each stone produced five or six spears, taking out as many crows. Maybe the presence of the Guardian of California amplified his power. The birds plummeted to the ground all around, popping out of existence in puffs of black smoke.

Gem sent blast after blast of her cold breath at the sky. The remaining crows froze solid and dropped to the ground like rocks. It got quiet again when all the crows they could see had been dispatched. TJ gave Gem a short bow. "Thank you. We've missed you."

"I am always as near as a thought, Silver Warrior," she said with a smile. Dora trotted to Gem's side. The big black dog had taken down her share of crows too, catching them in her jaws and shaking them until they went limp. Gem stroked her head appreciatively. "My brave girl," she murmured.

Jain was hunkered down behind the barrier with his arms over his head. He peeked up. Sweat beaded on his forehead and dripped down his temples. His expression was not as confident as before. "I've never seen crows attack like that, except in the movies." He tapped Willet's wall with the tips of his fingers. "And what *is* this?"

"It's a shield. Don't ask what it's made of. Even I'm not sure The next time the crows act up, you might want to be elsewhere. It could get worse."

Jain stood up, now convinced. "Yeah, ok. I'll go hang out with the paramedics," he said and started for the street. He looked back over his shoulder. "Yell if you need me. I mean that."

Willet ached in every muscle. If another wall had to be raised, it might be impossible. She stretched, trying to get circulation back into her shoulders and arms, and then folded forward to ease her aching back before another question came to mind. "Gem, how is O-Ka different from Jat? Are they both Lords of the Underworld?"

"O-Ka is nothing like Jat," Gem said. "Despite his efforts to deceive and conquer, Jat is a member of the spiritual hierarchy. His job is to challenge Souls with threats and illusions, so they develop strength and work out their own survival. O-Ka is just a demented bully, intent on indulging his own appetites. He is treacherous in a totally different way. There is no reasoning behind his actions."

"Does that mean he's easier to defeat?" TJ asked.

"O-Ka is hot-headed and ruthless, a terror in the Underworld, whereas Jat is shrewd and devious. He left a giant hole in the Gate inside the Dragon Head Building for a purpose. Jat will let O-Ka terrorize the people of this city into submission."

Gem shuddered slightly. "Then he will step in."

"Have you ever seen O-Ka?"

"I have never seen him myself. He is not easy to see."

TJ had other issues. "How long do we camp out here? I know Willet is spent. She should rest eventually."

"Perhaps a bit of rest could be taken," Gem replied. "We cannot leave the sand mountain completely unattended, however."

Willet nodded in agreement but couldn't suppress a yawn. "If I could grab a nap for just a little while, it would really help. Thomas isn't saying so, but I know he's tired too. How about you, Gem?"

An amused smile played on Gem's lips. She appeared as fresh as ever. "As Guardian of California, I need little rest. Let me keep watch while you both refresh yourselves. If trouble arises, I will contact you."

"How?" Willet asked.

"Do not fear. You will hear my voice."

Willet and TJ gratefully took her at her word. TJ walked Willet to the Jeep. "You don't have to sleep in the car," he said. "We could do what we did last time. Zip home in the Zinger, take a rest, then be back in no time."

It sounded so easy, but she didn't feel right about it. "What if there's a traffic jam? Or a flat tire? I don't like leaving Gem on her own in front of that awful sand..."

TJ chuckled. "You're talking about the Guardian of California, right? She could probably handle the sand without us. I filled the tires this morning, and as for traffic, that's what the shoulders are for. We'll make good time."

Willet was so tired, her resistance to persuasion was low. She grabbed Smoke out of the back seat. "OK, let's go. We can't be gone too long. And please don't drive on the shoulders. It's illegal."

Chapter 37

*** Dean ***

I am Primus, the First Centurion. That boy cannot threaten me. His father will understand the need for discipline in the ranks. He will take my side. Despite this optimistic thinking, Lucius felt Dean's worries about the fight with Silas. Who knew what a powerful father would do on behalf of his pouting, injured son? With this in mind, Lucius began to make plans. He gathered what coin he had available into a leather pouch and laid it beside a leather sheath containing his preferred long dagger along with a couple of shorter blades to hide on his person. He laid out a set of nondescript clothing – brown tunic and brown trousers, plebian garb. If he had to leave quickly, he'd be ready. His plan would be to escape back to Calabria, visit his son, and then continue on to the coast. He could board a shipping vessel and head across the Mare Nostrum, out of immediate reach of the Roman Guards. He'd hunker down for a while in Sicily and think what to do next. It was a desperate plan, leaving behind all he had built and achieved in Rome. He hoped it wouldn't be necessary.

Dean felt sorrow for his old self. If Senator Magnus Fabius turned against him, it would be a great injustice. Lucius was an exemplary leader and devoted soldier of Rome. It seemed politics was the same in every time and place, driven by personal agendas and inside dealings. Merit was too easily overshadowed.

Lucius washed himself, lay down on his bed, and dozed. He was awakened later by a loud whisper in his window. "Primus, the Praefectus comes for you. He brings soldiers. Leave now while you can." So that was how long it took for the Senator to side with his son. Less than an hour. The punishment could be harsh. Lucius jumped up, threw on the clothes, strapped on his belt and sword, and gathered up his coin pouch and short blades. He was out the door and into the alley behind his apartment within sixty seconds. He knew the back streets of Rome far better than the Praefectus. They would not find him.

He headed for Amisi's apartment on the outskirts of the city, hoping to rest there before he started on his long journey. She might have relatives in Sicily he could call upon for assistance. It was late in the afternoon. Shadows cut across the narrow streets, giving him good cover. He walked with no particular haste that would attract attention, head down, dodging other pedestrians as well as the spatter of whatever was dumped out of apartment windows. A bit of soil on his otherwise clean clothes might authenticate his disguise, but he didn't want to bring anything foul into Amisi's rooms. Then, he spotted a small group of soldiers farther down the street, marching in his direction. These soldiers may or may not be looking for him, but Lucius would take no chances. He slipped into a side street, turned a corner quickly and ran right into – Augustus. The older man bounced back on impact and hit the wall. "Ho, citizen, you are in a great hurry," Augustus said as he righted himself with his walking stick. "Such haste can be unwise." Dean knew who it was, but Lucius did not. Why was Augustus there? It couldn't be a coincidence. "I am seeing a woman, sir," Lucius explained. "You understand. I must be off." Lucius was about to continue his run down the alley, but Augustus put a hand on his shoulder."

"A woman can ease the mind of pressing matters. Or cloud it… Be cautious, my son."

Such a cryptic statement made Lucius stop short and give the older man a closer look. "What do you mean, Wise One?" Augustus gazed into his eyes. His voice was low and urgent. "The world is full of dangers. They come from unexpected corners. Take nothing for granted."

That kind of advice could be given at any time. Lucius nodded respectfully. He didn't have time for further questions and took off running, ready to dismiss Augustus' words from his memory, but Dean knew Augustus had conveyed a message that should be heeded. Dean's worry confused Lucius, who wasn't sure why he suddenly felt hesitant to proceed, but he shrugged it off, picked up his pace and kept to the darkest edges of the streets, alert to any signs of pursuit or sounds of marching feet pounding the ground. Women carrying baskets of food on their heads or babies in their arms ambled past him. Men made their way down the street or stepped into doorways. Lucius adopted their pace, just a working man on his way home from a job. Nothing to see there. He eventually came to a cross street that led to the edge of Rome where Amisi lived. He walked steadily, eyes shifting left and right, alert to the presence of military. It seemed he was in the clear, but he wouldn't feel at ease until he reached her doorway. After an hour of evasive movements through the outskirts of Rome in gathering dark, Lucius reached Amisi's apartment. He gave a quiet knock on the heavy pine door and waited. After a minute, the door cracked open.

Amisi's sister, Banafrit, peeked out at him. "Lucius!" she whispered. "We did not expect you."

The door didn't open to him any further. This wasn't the reception Lucius usually received. Dean's suspicious thoughts floated through his mind. "Is Amisi within?" Lucius whispered back. "I need a place to rest before a journey. Tell her I am here."

The door slid shut. After a moment, it opened again, wider this time, and Amisi's sister allowed Lucius to enter. She put her hands on his chest. "Soldier, I hope I can entertain you until my sister is available. I have missed you," she said with a suggestive smile. She tried to press herself against him.

Lucius was not there to see Banafrit. "Bani my sweet," he said, pushing her gently backwards and pulling her hands off his chest. "I must speak to Amisi. Does she know I am waiting?" Banafrit disappeared down a short hallway, knocked on a closed door, and disappeared inside. Then she returned to Lucius and nodded in the affirmative. She asked him to wait.

After a few minutes more, impatience got the better of Lucius. He marched down the hall to the bedroom door and knocked twice. Murmurs and scuffling could be heard from inside the room. He pushed the door open and entered. Amisi stood in the middle of the room in her bed shirt, her long black hair in disarray. She turned wide eyes to him. "Lucius! I was just about to come to you. Give me a moment."

Lucius went to her and pulled her to him. "We only have a few moments to share, Amisi. I am on my way back to Calabria."

She drew back and looked into his eyes. "How long will you be away?"

"That is uncertain. For now, let us enjoy our time together." He pushed her toward the unmade bed, grabbing her shoulders and kissing her lips insistently. As he bent her backwards, he heard a soft sound behind him and turned to look. Silas stood there with a knife in his hand and a furious look in his eyes. He leaped over the short distance between them and plunged the knife into the side of Lucius' neck with a snarl. Amisi's screams cut through the air. Lucius tried to pull the knife out of his neck but fell to the floor in shock, losing too much blood. The carotid had been cut.

Soul soon withdrew from the failing physical shell and rose above the scene of death. Lucius and Dean watched events unfold like a dream in slow motion. Amisi stared at Lucius' dying body but did nothing to help him. Silas stood over Lucius with the bloody knife in his hand and a triumphant smirk on his lips. Lucius had given him an unexpected opportunity for revenge. Amisi may not have held the knife, but she was as complicit in the betrayal as if she had.

The faces of Silas and Amisi blurred and became those of TJ and Audrey. TJ held the knife and Audrey looked on with regret in her eyes. The shock of realization hit Dean. His closest friends had killed him. These were the last images Dean held in memory before he receded from that ancient time and place and returned to the time track where the Traveler waited for him, tall and regal in dark red robes.

"Warrior,", she said, "that was not an ideal way to leave a past life, but it was effective. Have you seen what you came to see?"

"I was murdered by my friends," Dean's voice shook. "How can I look them in the eyes again without thinking of it?"

"Much time has passed to bring you to where you are in present day. Consider what may have transpired over that time to resolve things between you."

Dean couldn't get past the act of violence he had just endured. "I don't want to go back to the present. Not sure what I'll do when I see them."

"This is not a decision I can make. I will bring you to Augustus. You can discuss your future with him."

Chapter 38

TJ pushed the Zinger into sharp turns and sped through the narrow downtown streets. Willet wrapped an arm around Smoke and held on to her seat belt. "Do we have to go so fast? I hear police sirens. Maybe they're coming after us."

TJ hit the brakes and then sped onto a one-way street. "We're being followed."

"What? By whom?"

"See that black truck behind us? It's been tracking us since we left 5th Street."

The Zinger maneuvered through traffic as they left the city center. Once they were on the freeway, racing towards the Hollywood Hills, TJ cleared his throat and looked at her.

"Sorry, babe. The sun is setting. It will be difficult to spot that truck in the dark. I'd rather be clear of him and well on our way home by then."

Willet turned and peered over the back of her seat. Sure enough, the truck in question was right behind them. "What makes you think it's following us?"

"I took every side street and made every crazy turn I could to shake him in the city. He never left us. Now that we're on the freeway, I hope the Zinger can leave him in the dust." With that, TJ punched the gas and sped into the left-hand lanes, zig-zagged between lanes and used larger vehicles for cover, trying to ditch the black truck. After several minutes of evasive driving, TJ sat back in his seat with a satisfied smile on his face. "I think we lost him."

"Why would someone want to follow us? I don't like this, Thomas. The driver probably knows who we are and wants to stop us from fighting the sand." She pulled Smoke closer to her chest. "Did you see a license plate?"

"No plate on the front. I don't see him now. We'll keep eyes peeled, but don't worry. Me and the Zinger got this."

"It's literally my job to worry."

They reached the road leading to TJ's neighborhood and turned up the hill. The next thing they knew, the black truck appeared out of a side street, heading right for them, aiming for the passenger door. TJ yanked the steering wheel to the left, turning the Zinger out of the direct line of collision. The truck slammed the brakes with a screech and backed up, then aimed again at the Zinger and accelerated. It slammed into the back end and pushed the heavy car over the side of the hill. The Zinger careened down the slope hitting every rock along the way and came to a thudding stop in the ravine below with the engine still running and the airbags deployed.

Willet and TJ sat in shocked silence. Smoke whined softly. He was buried in the balloon of silky material in Willet's lap. Her hands found him under the airbag and stroked his head. "It's ok, Smokey," she murmured to him. "It's ok. We're ok."

"Are we ok?" TJ asked, staring at the airbag in his face.

"I'm very glad we were wearing seat belts." Her voice sounded breathy and faint.

TJ shook himself into action and turned off the engine. "We need to get out of this car, in case it catches fire."

They quickly unhitched their seatbelts, slid out the doors, and scrambled halfway up the side of the ravine. From a distance, they surveyed the damage to the Zinger. No smoke came from under the hood. The body didn't look bent or crumpled. The sturdy hunk of metal seemed surprisingly unaffected. It was too soon to tell if the tires would go flat. "We know for sure now that the truck was following us," TJ said.

After a few minutes without an explosion, TJ walked back down to take a closer look. He lifted the hood, sniffed, and jiggled the hoses. "No leaks around the engine." He bent down and looked underneath. "Don't see anything leaking. It would take more than a slide down a short hill to hurt this car. It really is a tank. I'll fire it up and see if I can back it to the top." He got in the Zinger and started the engine. It started right up. He put it in reverse and tried to back up. The wheels just spun, digging into the loose dirt. He soon turned off the engine and got out. "That's a losing cause. We need a tow." He climbed up the side of the ravine, picking through bushes and brambles until he reached Willet.

Smoke wiggled in Willet's arms, trying to get down. She let him go, and he disappeared behind a scrubby bush to do his business. When he came back, he leaped into her arms. She caught him in mid-flight and followed TJ. "What if the truck is up there, waiting for us?" she said, stroking the cat's fur.

"If he is, we run back down into the ravine. Then we call the police. And the tow company."

Near the top, they peeked over the edge to see if the black truck was waiting. "He could be hiding like before," TJ said quietly. "Let me go first." He stepped up and scanned the street. "I don't see him, but that doesn't mean he's gone. Let's move. Keep to the side of the road so we can drop into the ravine if we have to."

They walked up the hill toward TJ's house. At the top, the road turned sharply to the right, and there, idling in the curve, was the black truck. Willet caught a glimpse of the driver. "It's that artist, Thaddeus Moon!" Willet said. "I can't believe it!" The truck revved with a snarl and accelerated right at them. Smoke screeched and jumped out of Willet's arms. She tried to grab him before he hit the ground, but he bounded away, straight for the truck. "Smoke, no!" Smoke made a flying leap onto the hood, gaining size in mid-flight. He was a much bigger cat by the time he landed and started clawing at the front windshield. A shriek came from the driver, and the truck swerved into a crazy S-curve.

Willet was shaking so hard she could barely get words out, but she had to do something before the truck hit them. She drew every kind of particle floating in the air, the street and the ravine. A hot amalgam of dirt, rock and cement formed in her hands. She threw it into the air. "Stop." In the moments before the truck was about to hit them, a solid wall rose in front of her. A moment later, the truck hit the wall at full speed, and the front end smashed. In the silence that followed, they heard a high-pitched voice cursing, and then, with a squeal of tires, the truck backed up and rattled off down the hill with steam coming out of the radiator and something metal dragging on the ground underneath it.

"He's gone now, I think. Unless he doubles back," TJ wrapped his arms around her. He can't drive far with that kind of damage."

The sound of the truck's engine faded out of earshot. Willet let her wall drop. "Moon didn't seem like the type to be so aggressive," she said in a raspy whisper.

"Why would he do something like this?"

"No idea. I blocked his effort to buy the crystal for his 'art project'. Would he really want to kill me for that?"

"People have killed for less. I have to keep a better eye on you, Will. We'll be joined at the hip from now on. You don't make a move without me by your side."

"I'm not sure I *can* move right now. Raising that wall so fast took it out of me. My arms feel like lead weights."

"You're trembling,' he said. "I'd like to strangle that guy for upsetting you like this. Let's get inside before he circles back." Willet took TJ's right arm with her left, and then realized Smoke wasn't with her. "Where's Smoke? Smoke! Where are you? Smoke!" She spun in a circle, searching all directions. "He was on the hood of the truck. If anything happened to him I'll strangle the guy myself." The furry gray creature ran up and stopped at her feet, looking at her with his blue eyes wide and innocent. "Smokey!" With a plaintive 'meow', he jumped into her arms. She clutched his warm body to her chest and nuzzled her cheek against his head. "Crazy kitty! Don't scare me like that. What were you trying to do?"

TJ put his arms around both of them. If something had happened to Smoke, Willet would have been a wreck. She wobbled on her feet and leaned closer to him for balance. With Smoke's return, her voice gained strength. "It seems like my new ability is changing. The barriers are forming faster than when we first practiced. I pulled the materials in and compressed them in seconds. The wall went up almost by itself. It was just – there."

"The faster the better. You said that guy had a studio in Brentwood, right? I'll have to pay a visit to Mr. Moon. Maybe I'll introduce him to my silver spears."

"You know you can't do that, Thomas. He's not an Underworld demon, at least as far as we know. Hurting humans is not what the spears are for. Anyway, I'm about to fall asleep on my feet. Can we go home now?"

TJ took Smoke out of Willet's arms and carried him the rest of the way to the house. "I hope Evelyn doesn't give us any static," he muttered. "I'm in no mood."

Chapter 39

Dean

Dean and the Traveler returned to Samhasa in the twinkling of an eye. Dean found himself once again standing in front of the big glass desk in Augustus' office. The white-haired Guardian of all Guardians stood with hands clasped behind his back, rocking heel to toe on his feet. "Welcome back," he said with a small smile. "Did you enjoy your past life visit?"

"It was illuminating. Not in the way I expected," Dean grimaced. "Someone I trusted betrayed me, and someone else I trusted stabbed me in the neck and killed me." He softened his tone. "And I ran into you. That was cool. You warned me not to trust a woman, but I didn't listen."

"Hmmm," Augustus said, smoothing the right edge of his mustache, "viewing a past life can be an uncomfortable experience. Perhaps that is why few choose to do it."

"I don't know what to do now." Dean looked down at his feet and shook his head. "I don't think I can ever face TJ and Audrey again. And they're my best friends!"

"The Ring Thrower has been waiting for you between worlds, expecting your return as you promised her. The rest of your Circle is in the midst of a battle, with more serious challenges to come. Will you abandon them?"

"They killed me while I watched, Augustus! How am I supposed to get that memory out of my head?"

"People change over time, Warrior. They have grown, and you have too." Augustus gestured at a thick book with a white cover that lay on his desk. "This book will tell us how it happened."

Words embossed in gold on the title page read: *Dean Simmons Book of Lives*. Dean was incredulous. "Is that book supposed to be about me? Where did it come from?"

Augustus stepped around to the back of his desk and flipped the cover open. "This book is on loan from the Library of Lifetimes in the World of Cause. Every Soul ever incarnated in a physical body has a book there that details the history of their incarnations. Including you."

"But... who wrote it?"

"The Keepers of the Karmic Records compile these books and keep them up to date. They are very detailed. Let us see if we can give you a broader view of your history." He slowly turned pages, reading whatever was on them, and then stopped. "We can start here."

A sparkling hologram rose above the book and figures moved inside it. Dean recognized Amisi. She held a baby in her arms. Augustus read from that page. "After the passing of Lucius Avitus, Amisi married a Sicilian shipping merchant two years later. She gave birth to a baby boy, whom she named 'Lucius'. The baby was you, returned to the physical world for another lifetime. Amisi, who you know as an early incarnation of Audrey, died soon after from complications of childbirth. You went on to become a Roman Senator in that life." The hologram dissolved into mist, and Augustus turned several pages before he stopped. Another hologram rose over the page showing another woman with a child. "Here in 752 A.D, in Calabria, you married a woman named Amelia, another incarnation of Audrey. She bore you two children, one of whom was your friend, Thomas Barlow. You abandoned her and the children for a tavern maid and moved to Napoli. Your children never saw you again, and your family was reduced to abject poverty." Augustus continued turning pages until a new hologram rose over the book. In its sparkling lights was a wooden masted ship under full sail on an angry sea. "In 1206, you and your friend, Thomas, were slaves on a Spanish ship bound for the Far East. The ship caught fire. As slaves, you were chained to oars and could not escape. Thomas broke his hand to free himself and then freed you. Your leg was broken in the escape. He helped you jump into the water in time to avoid a fiery death and held your head above the water until you both were picked up by fishermen who brought you to Sicily. There, Thomas sold you into slavery. You later escaped and cut his throat when you found him."

Dean stared at the holograms, momentarily speechless. The accounts were so vivid, he could remember living those lives. "OK. I get it. We have a long history." Conflicting emotions threatened to tear him apart. His Light body dimmed to a pale beige.

Augustus gave him a reproachful look. "If your light gets any darker, you might disappear from Samhasa altogether."

Dean tried to get his emotions under control. "Do I have to see more?"

"One or two more will suffice." Augustus continued to flip pages. "Not all the lifetimes are so dramatic. In 1648, Thomas was your father and Audrey was your sister. In 1837, you were the father to Thomas and Audrey, who were your children." He turned another few pages. "Here is a significant one." A hologram appeared over the page in which Dean recognized both himself and TJ in turn of the century suits and top hats, sporting handlebar mustaches. They stood on a cobblestone street in front of a two-story brownstone building. Stairs leading up to a landing in front of a door were lined on each side with stone bannisters.

"I recognize those stairs." Dean gazed in wonder at the hologram. "They used to be called 'stoops'. Neighbors would sit on them and watch people go by. Can't believe I remember that."

August continued with his litany. "At this time in 1910, you and Thomas were partners in a business venture selling bicycles in New York City. After it became a success, you swindled him and left him penniless. He committed suicide, leaving his wife, Abigail, to beg on the streets to support their two daughters, one of whom was named Willomena. Abigail was an incarnation of Audrey, of course, and the little girl was an incarnation of Willet." The hologram dissipated to mist and blew away. Augustus closed the book and gave Dean a level look. "As is sometimes said in the modern world, what goes around comes around. Have the scales not been balanced?"

Dean felt his righteous anger drain away, replaced by red-faced embarrassment. There was a bit of lingering resentment, but his outrage had cooled. A smile dawned on his face as a realization hit. "I was afraid I'd have to stop loving them. That's what hurt most of all. We've been friends so long, me and TJ. I felt awful thinking we couldn't be friends any more. And Audrey. I'm pretty sure I love her." His light brightened even more. "Now I can just forgive myself and them. We'll go on being friends, like always. Right?"

"Maybe better than before," Augustus nodded and smiled that beatific smile that never failed to open the heart. "That is why you are the Golden-Hearted Warrior, my boy."

Dean met Augustus' eyes and straightened his shoulders with new resolve. "Where can I find Audrey?"

"The Ring Thrower is as close as your thoughts."

"Can I get my old body back? How does that work?"

"As a member of the Circle of Augustus, you have earned the right to manifest a new physical body for your work in the Circle. They need your heart and courage more than ever. The body will materialize for you when you demonstrate your commitment."

Encouraging words. The 'how' of it was fuzzy. For now, he pictured Audrey, just as he had seen her in his dreams in Rome. Augustus' office disappeared in a dizzying swirl of light and sound, and Dean found himself in deep space dotted with distant stars and pierced with the tails of comets. Just ahead, Audrey floated, eyes closed, her head thrown back and arms spread wide. Just drifting.

He moved closer. "I'm here," he whispered into the exquisite quiet.

Audrey opened her eyes and looked at him. "I thought you forgot me," she said and started to fall.

Dean caught her in his arms before the darkness of space swallowed her. "Never," he said before he kissed her.

In the next moment, they hovered above the courtyard at Hope Place, watching the chaotic scene. Crows were pouring out of the sand mountain with shrill caws, diving at people on the ground with claws out. The black sand boiled. It looked like hell would break out of it. In the midst of it all, Gem was blasting crows with her Freezing Breath and bringing them down in large numbers, but more kept flying out of the sand.

"Are you ready for this?" he said.

"I don't feel the hot energy in my fingers," she said. "Maybe I was inert too long in the nether world. It may take me a while to get going."

"Do what you can, Ring Thrower. We're needed."

Ready or not, their Light bodies dropped into the fray.

Chapter 40

Evelyn was sleeping when TJ and Willet tiptoed in the front door, so another confrontation was avoided. Jonah took Smoke to the kitchen to feed him, and Willet went in the master bedroom for a quick shower while TJ called for a tow. When he went to the bedroom, she was already asleep and snoring. Just as well. TJ had plans. He took a shower too, and by the time he was done, the tow truck operator was knocking at the door. He wore gray overalls with a name patch that said 'Dave' and a brimmed cap that said, 'Taylor Towing.' TJ walked down the hill with him and showed him where the Zinger was stranded in the ravine. Dave attached a pully from the truck to the car's back bumper and hauled the car up to the road in short order. He lowered the back end of the car to the ground with a light thud.

TJ got in the Zinger, started the engine, and let it idle, then did a turn around the hill and tried the brakes before driving back. He got out and looked under the chassis again and checked under the hood. Still no leaks.

"You got a solid vehicle there," Dave observed. "After a dive into a ditch there's usually something needs fixing. Let's tow you to the station."

"Thanks, but I've got somewhere to go right now. I'll take it in for a thorough checkup after I get back."

Dave looked dubious. "What are you gonna do about the airbags?"

"I'll have to live with them for now."

"Suit yourself."

With the bill paid, the tow truck took off, and TJ checked his phone to find the address of Moon Gallery in Brentwood. They were supposedly open until 8PM. He set the GPS and stuffed the airbag down between his legs. It was 5PM and the sun hovered in the sky above the ocean, soon to take its nightly dip. Rush hour in the city was always tricky and slow, but traffic would be coming into the Hills, not out. He hoped he'd catch a break, so he set out for Brentwood.

Avoiding the 101 Freeway and taking surface streets proved to be a good choice. He maneuvered the Zinger through not-so-heavy congestion, came to a full stop at some points, but managed to make it to Brentwood in less than an hour. The Moon Gallery was located near the Getty Museum. He pulled up on the side street and looked in the large gallery window. The space inside was bathed in a cool gray light coming from recessed fixtures in the ceiling. *Like moonlight*, he thought. *Clever.* He didn't see anyone inside.

The first objective was to see if the black truck with the bashed-in front end was parked anywhere nearby. He drove down the street to the back of the gallery. There were three parking spaces behind it. A silver Beemer was parked in one of them. He continued around the block. Down a side street he caught sight of the battered black truck parked next to a small office building. *Gotcha.* He parked and sprinted over. Nothing in the front seat from what he could see. Nothing in the flatbed in back. The front windshield was scratched on the driver's side. Could Smoke's claws really do that?

He returned to the front of the gallery, parked, and went to the front door. The Gallery was open. He walked inside. The light jingle of a bell announced his arrival. Colored glass art objects and wood sculptures on white pedestals were arranged in the center of the room. Framed art hung on the white walls, large pieces done in strokes of black, red, and yellow with traces of green. He walked up to one particularly dark picture and stared at it. The label beside it said, 'Terra Incognita" by Thaddeus Moon'. Someone entered the room. He turned to see a smallish, thin man dressed in black standing next to a white desk. "Can I help you?" he said.

"Are you Thaddeus Moon?"

"I am."

"What is this?" TJ asked, pointing to the painting. "What is it supposed to mean?"

The artist walked over and stood in front of the painting. The braids hanging around his head were tied at the ends by small white bones shaped like finger bones. They clicked together with his movement. He gazed up at the painting with a dreamy look on his face. "The complexities of thought and emotion keep us from our heart's desire," he said, "like tethers around our necks. It's a reflective piece." He turned to TJ with a pensive expression. "What does it say to you?"

TJ looked at the painting again. The slashes and swirls of color were ambiguous, evocative, but the artist's question seemed earnest, so he tried to give some honest feedback. "It feels troubled."

"Hmm," Thaddeus said, nodding his head slowly as he studied the painting. "Are you a collector?"

TJ didn't want to waste time pretending to be something he wasn't. He drew a business card from his shirt pocket and handed it to Moon. "Thomas J. Barlow. I'm here to find out about a car accident in the Hollywood Hills. A hit and run."

Thaddeus Moon looked at the card and frowned. "Attorney at law? Why would I need to talk to an attorney?"

"Were you driving in the Hills today, Mr. Moon? In a black truck?"

"I drive a BMW," he said with a slight shrug of his shoulder. "It's parked out back. I've never had an accident. Why would you think I was involved in one?"

"Someone at the scene thought they saw you driving a black truck."

The artist fell back a step, and the pitch of his voice went up half an octave. "Who would say such a thing?" A flustered look washed over his eyes followed by confusion. "I've been in the gallery all day."

TJ was almost convinced. *This guy is either the best actor in L.A. or he really doesn't know about what happened in the Hills. Could Willet have been mistaken?*

A scuffling sound came from the back of the gallery at that moment, and a second man dressed in black shirt and pants entered the room. A mass of curly black hair framed his light bronze face, sharp cheek bones, and coal black eyes. A thick tuft of black hair was growing out of his chin. When he saw them standing by the painting, he walked over to Thaddeus, put an arm around the artist's shoulders and gave TJ an appraising stare. "Who is this, darling?"

The man stood four inches taller than Thaddeus, who leaned into him as if needing help to stay on his feet. "Kagan, this is Thomas Barlow," Thaddeus said. "He's a lawyer. Mr. Barlow, this is my husband, Kagan Moon. Mr. Barlow is inquiring about a car accident. He's wondering if I was involved."

Kagan Moon turned horrified eyes on Thaddeus. "Not in the Moon Beem!" he said breathlessly. "That can't be. I just saw it in the back. It looks fine."

"He's asking about a black truck. I don't know about a black truck, do you?"

Kagan gave TJ a sharp glare. "Why would you think we were involved in an accident? We don't know a thing about it, and we have our own legal representation. You can talk to our lawyer. The gallery is about to close, so if you'll excuse us…"

TJ would not be brushed off. "There's a black truck parked a block from here that was in an accident. The front end is totaled. A witness said she saw Thaddeus driving the vehicle in the Hollywood Hills. The truck ran into a brick wall and almost hit a woman. Have either of you been up there recently?"

"No!" Thaddeus exclaimed. "We haven't!"

Kagan's glare turned hostile. "You can't come into our establishment and question us this way. You're making false accusations. We don't answer questions without our lawyer present. Leave now or we'll call the police and have you arrested for harassment.

There was heat in Kagan's tone, and even a flash of teeth. Thaddeus looked dazed. TJ decided he'd seen enough "I didn't mean to harass you. I'm just following up for a friend. If you recognize the truck or hear anything about the incident, you have my number." He took his leave and exited the gallery. As he walked back to the Zinger, the exchange ran through his mind. Thaddeus seemed genuinely surprised. Kagan got angry, which was often the reaction of a guilty person. Could Willet have mistaken Kagan for Thaddeus? They dressed alike, but their hairstyles would certainly distinguish them. Thaddeus met Willet before and was turned down by her when he tried to buy one of the crystal boulders. That could be considered motive. And then there was the presence of the truck in their neighborhood. That was a smoking gun, but was it their gun? If it wasn't, why was the truck in Brentwood? It was too big a coincidence to ignore. He needed to go home and get some sleep before he thought any more about it. He got in the Zinger, pushed the airbags out of the way, and let the big car carry him off into the night.

Chapter 41

TJ got home well before 10PM from his trip to Brentwood. It had been a long day. He crawled gratefully into bed beside Willet and fell into a dreamless sleep as soon as his head hit the pillow. At 2AM, he felt someone poking his shoulder repeatedly and calling his name. Willet. He opened one eye and mumbled. "Wha?"

"Thomas! Wake up. Gem is calling for us. We need to get downtown. There's another bird attack."

He turned over with a groan. "You're kidding. What time is it?"

"2 AM. Sorry, sweetie. She wouldn't summon us if it weren't urgent. I got an image of the birds dive-bombing a homeless woman."

TJ cleared his head, then tossed the covers back and planted his feet on the floor. "I'm up. I'm up." He was in pants and shirt within seconds. Willet was in the bathroom splashing her face with water. He needed that too. It would take plenty of cold water before the cobwebs cleared. In under ten minutes, they were dressed in their fighting clothes – t-shirts, jeans, and gray hoodies. They slipped out the door as quietly as they could without waking Evelyn and Jonah. TJ rolled the Zinger away from the curb, and they were speeding out of the Hills when they heard a mew from the back seat. "Is the cat back there?" TJ muttered. "I thought he was asleep in our bed." "No way Smoke will let me leave without him," Willet said. She turned to look. Of course, Smoke was curled in the back seat, giving her a big-eyed stare. "Smoke won't let me go to the sand alone. He's here to protect me. We have to accept that."

TJ snorted and switched on satellite radio. Had the events at Hope Place hit the news? Sure enough, the airwaves were on fire. "Unexplained bird attacks in downtown Los Angeles," a news voice reported. "Large flocks of black birds are flying through the city, attacking anyone exposed on the streets. The homeless encampments have been especially hard hit. The following is graphic information and not appropriate for younger listeners." The voice paused. "People injured have had one or both eyes pecked out by the birds. All available paramedic, police and fire personnel are actively working in the area to find and treat the injured. You are advised to stay clear of the downtown area and remain in your homes." TJ and Willet looked at each other with the same thought. "It's worse than we imagined."

At that hour, traffic was as light on the freeway as traffic ever got in Los Angeles. The Zinger practically flew. When they arrived downtown, TJ headed for the Bunker Hill Steps and came to a squealing stop. Sirens were blaring and red lights flashed everywhere. So much wave and particle distortion streamed through the air, Willet could barely see the street. She was reluctant to get out of the car, but there was no help for it. They jumped out and hit the stairs running, not waiting for permission from the police who were yelling at them. At the top of the long staircase, they skidded into the courtyard, ready for whatever was happening, and stopped short. It was chaos.

A hundred crows swarmed around Gem. Their frantic screech was ear-splitting. In the darkness of night, it was hard to tell where Gem was in the swirl of black feathers, but they could see her Freezing Breath. Her wind and ice swept through the murderous crows and drove them back towards the sand. Frozen crows dropped to the ground in bunches. Dora was there, protecting the Guardian of California. She growled and jumped up into the thick of them, bringing down two and three birds at a time in her jaws. Crows still poured out of the black sand faster than Gem and Dora could dispatch them.

There were people in the courtyard trying unsuccessfully to dodge the crows. Some had fallen, some were bleeding. "What in the world are they doing here at this hour?" Willet shouted. "Get them out." She and TJ pulled people to their feet. They herded them out through the courtyard entrance as fast as they could, pointing them toward the street. "Go. Run fast!" TJ instructed them. The people who could, ran. The rest hobbled, fell down and started crawling away.

With the courtyard cleared of stragglers, Willet and TJ returned to the fight. The field of battle had changed. Bright lights shined in the middle of the bird scrum. It was Dean and Audrey in their Light bodies, glowing like stars. Dean held a long sword in his right hand and sliced it back and forth through the mass of birds, cutting many of them in half. Feathers turned to dust and blew away. Audrey stood beside Dean with light rings spinning around her fingers. Willet wanted to run to her sister and hug her, but the immediate chaos demanded attention, and something was wrong with the Ring Thrower.

"Audrey!" Willet cried. "What are you waiting for? Throw the rings!"

Audrey watched the rings spin on her fingers, but didn't throw them. She looked up and stared at Willet as if frozen.

TJ pulled stones out of his pockets and started hurling them as hard and fast as he could. Each stone multiplied into seven silver spears, piercing the bodies of as many crows. It was still not enough. There were too many of them. They would be overrun without protection.

Willet felt her inner forces of gravity and heat waiting for her command. *Brick is too heavy. Glass is too brittle. What about metal? Light weight. Strong. Yes.* 'Clang,' she commanded. With that word spoken, the air compressed into a mass so tight it sucked the breath out of her lungs. Energy turned to heat and ignited matter, and the mass exploded. A sheet of liquid metal poured down. She stepped in front of TJ and curved the bendable metal at the sides before it hardened into a shield. They moved together slowly behind the shield. A hundred beaks and claws pecked and scratched against the metal. It sounded like hail hitting a tin roof. Willet and TJ moved as close to Gem as they could without blocking her storm breath. Willet slid the shield sideways until it fronted all three of them.

The vibration of her eardrums was out of control from all the bird screeching. She was dangerously close to a migraine, but she had to focus on maintaining the barrier. If they couldn't stop the continuous stream of crows coming out of the mountain, they'd be overcome and pecked to death.

"Audrey!" she called out to her sister again, unsure whether Audrey could hear her. "We need fire. Torch the sand." Audrey was looking uncertainly at her rings. Had the Ring Thrower forgotten what to do with them? Willet tried shouting at Dean. "Dean. help her." Would he catch her point? Thankfully, he did. Dean laid the tip of his sword on Audrey's shoulder as if he were knighting her. The blade flashed gold, and Audrey startled as if she just woke up. She tossed the rings of light above her head. They merged into a single glowing ring of fire. She grabbed the ring and spun it into the sand mountain like a frisbee. Several new light rings formed on her fingers almost immediately. She merged them and hurled an even bigger one with force. The ring sliced into the sand and burst into flame. Fire swept over the surface of the sand and started to rise. It was heading for the peak of the mountain, but the sand would not allow itself to be consumed. As Willet had witnessed before, the fire abruptly snuffed out. Not a total loss. The barrage of crows had stopped.

Between Gem and TJ, crows remaining in the air were dispatched with freezing wind and silver spears. Bird bodies hit the ground and disappeared in puffs of smoke. When the madness of the crows was gone, the quiet of night returned. Willet let her shield drop. Her shoulders ached and her head pounded. She stood up and stretched, then crouched down and wrapped her arms around her knees to stretch her lower back. A wide yawn escaped her. She looked sheepishly at Gem. "I didn't get enough sleep last night."

Gem's expression contained no judgement. "The vigils of a Guardian can be long indeed."

"I never saw *you* sleep, Gem. Did you need to?"

"Any Soul inhabiting a physical form needs rest. Guardians need less than others, but still... I took what you would call cat naps to refresh myself."

TJ stretched too, moving his shoulders, and shaking his legs. "We have company. Not a moment too soon."

The Light bodies of Dean and Audrey floated toward them like celestial visions.

"I can't believe this," Willet said, blown away by the awesome and unexpected sight. "I want to kiss you both! Is the Circle of Augustus re-forming?"

Dean's voice vibrated like an echo coming from another world. "Augustus said we need to serve the Circle to get our physical bodies back. The battle isn't over, is it?"

"Hardly," Gem said. "Crows have flown out across the city. They wreak havoc and must be brought down."

Everyone looked at Willet. "What do you think we should do, Guardian?"

They were waiting for her to give them some direction. *You're the Guardian, Willet. Say something.* She took a deep breath. "Follow those birds."

Chapter 42

*** James Jain ***

Jain volunteered to help the paramedics. Under the chaotic circumstances, they gratefully accepted it, and he rode along with them as they looked for victims. There were bodies on the streets throughout downtown and not nearly enough emergency workers to respond to all of them. Jain carried stretchers, moved equipment and managed traffic while the paramedics did their life-saving work. He did it happily. The flow of ambulances into hospitals overwhelmed surface streets. He stood out on the street in a hazard vest and directed traffic with flashing lights so the ambulances could get through. Whatever they needed, he did it.

It felt good not to think, to just respond to the crisis of the moment and know he was actually doing something useful. *Could I do this for a living? Take paramedic training. Help people. What's happening now isn't normal. It's a Circle thing, and I know about Circle things. I could help the paramedics deal with that kind of weirdness.* He thought about Hope Place and wondered if he should return. *Audrey said I should help the Circle. This is helping, isn't it?* He let the rhythm of paramedic duty carry him on: Cruise the streets. Spot a body. Jump out with a stretcher. Alive or dead, lift the body onto the stretcher. Carry it to the ambulance. Head for the hospital with sirens blaring. Spot another body on the way. Stop and make room for it. Head for the hospital.

Eventually, the paramedics were so stretched that they asked him to drive the ambulance while the techs administered aid and oxygen in the back. 'Boulevard' Jain was back in action.

If a victim lost one eye, there was a chance of survival. With two eyes lost, there was little chance. The shock and pain could kill a person. *Could I really do this every day, see the gross things these paramedics see?* Memories of empty, bleeding eye sockets would haunt his dreams for years, taking their place in his memory next to the truck-size spider that killed Nick. He hadn't slept well since Nick died. Now there were new images to mess with his head, but he couldn't think about that right now. He helped unload stretchers at the hospital, then drove the ambulance back out to the streets.

The ambulance dispatcher directed them to the Skid Row District to pick up victims. When they arrived, it was bedlam. Hundreds of crows flew above the streets, swooping and attacking. People ran in all directions, colliding with each other in their panic to flee from the crows. They tried to hide in the many tents lining the sidewalks. Those offered no protection. The crows tore apart the thin tent material and drove people to the ground. If a person fell face down, he had a chance of crawling away. If he fell face up, the crows were on his face immediately. Those clever birds worked together to get a person to trip and fall backward by diving at his face and nipping at the backs of his knees at the same time. Jain watched the maneuver happen over and over. The diabolical intention and execution by the crows chilled him to shivers.

There were three additional ambulances dispatched to Skid Row, but it was still a struggle. Crows didn't hesitate to attack the paramedics while they worked and tried to claw the protective glasses off their eyes to get at them. The paramedics swatted them away as they loaded the wounded onto stretchers. Their hands got scratched and bitten while they struggled to hold on to the handles of the stretchers to keep from dropping them. With their heads down, they ran as fast as they could to the safety of the ambulances. Jain helped carry a stretcher to a victim – a middle-aged woman, heavy-set, gray-haired, not breathing. He tried not to stare into the two bloody eye sockets, but his stomach lurched. There was no hope for her.

Out of the corner of his eye, he saw something that almost made him drop the stretcher. In the midst of the crows, Dean floated in a bright light like an avenging angel, swinging a long, flashing sword and cutting through large swaths of birds, turning them to dust. Jain dared another glance up. There was Audrey in her own bright light, spinning her rings and throwing them over bunches of crows descending on the street. The rings encircled the crows and incinerated them.

Audrey and Dean gained the upper hand and reduced the flocks to almost nothing. The remaining birds flew off to find easier prey. Jain peeked at the other paramedics. If they were aware of what was going on above their heads, they gave no indication. It didn't seem like the time to mention it.

Chapter 43

"How are we supposed to follow flying birds?" TJ said. "Run down the street flapping our arms? Drive? The streets are blocked by emergency vehicles, and the birds could have flown anywhere. Did I mention they're in the air?"

"We might be able to follow them," Dean said in that vibrating voice he now had. "Me and Audrey, I mean. We might be able to chase them in the air. There could be a problem, though."

"Not another problem," Willet said.

"Yes, what problem?" Audrey said. "Now that my rings are working, I'm ready to throw."

Dean hesitated. "I think I'm on the verge of turning solid," he said, choosing his words carefully, "like, manifesting a physical body. At least that's how it feels. That's the problem. You might be too, Audrey."

"What does 'turning solid' feel like?" Audrey said. "I feel weird and disconnected, but I've felt that way for a while. That can't be it."

"It's like my atoms are slowing down. It feels like they're clumping, binding into molecules. If I'm in the air fighting birds when my physical body forms, I'll plummet to the ground like dead weight."

"Yeah," TJ nodded. "That *is* a problem."

Audrey scrutinized her own form. "I don't think it's happening to me yet. What if I do the flying, and you fight on the ground? Just in case you start to solidify."

Dean shook his head. "No way I'm gonna let you go up there among the crows alone." He looked at Gem. "Does what I said make sense?"

"It is a valid concern," Gem said with a nod.

"How does it feel when a physical body forms?"

"The more a person transitions between physical and non-physical, the quicker the transition happens. You will have more control of it. I have manifested physical bodies for more than a century, so the change feels natural to me. I can remember how it was, however."

"I shouldn't let Audrey fly alone, should I?"

"That is the Ring Thrower's decision. And of course, the Guardian's."

Another reminder that she, Willet Du Place, was now Guardian of the Gate in Los Angeles. It was her call. With her sister's life at stake, she felt the full weight of that responsibility. "Of course, Audrey and Dean must make their own decisions." It seemed like the only reasonable guidance she could give. She knew she had the support of the Circle, but what could she offer them to make their tasks easier? "I hear the birds. I know where they went. If you want to fly, I can point you in the right direction. Hopefully there are ways to minimize the risk."

"What if we don't fly too high or too long?" Audrey looked at Dean for confirmation. "The crows will come down to the streets eventually. That's where the people are. We'll fight them there. If it feels like we're still light-bodied, we go higher to chase the flying flocks. If we start to feel heavier, we drop back to the street."

Dean couldn't argue with the logic, but he still looked uncertain. "That might work, I guess..." He turned to Gem again. "If I return to a physical body, will I lose my sword?" He brandished the long gold blade in his hand.

"Yeah, where did you get that sword, Deano?" TJ asked. "You never had one before."

"It was a big part of my lifetime in ancient Rome. I was a soldier and pretty skilled with it, turns out. Not sure why it made the trip back to the present with me. I hope I can keep it." Dean gave the sword a flourishing swipe through the air. "It's pretty kick-ass."

TJ watched as Dean swished the sword. "Finally. Something about Rome. Tell us more."

"It's a long story."

"No time for telling travel stories, guys," Willet said. "Get back to the crows. Are you going after them? It not, we'll have to drive or call the Traveler."

Dean and Audrey exchanged thoughts and glances that brought them into agreement. "We'll fly low enough not to break bones if we fall," Dean said. "A lot of people will be hurt if we don't get those birds."

Willet gave them directions. "I hear screaming in the streets just southeast of here. That's Skid Row. Another flock is flying due south toward Pershing Square, and one more flying east in the direction of Little Tokyo. Go after the southeast contingent first. They're already attacking people on the ground. That needs to be stopped right away. And please, please, don't fall."

Dean looked at Audrey. "Let's jump."

They jumped. Their Light bodies shot into the air and disappeared in seconds, leaving Gem, TJ and Willet standing with Dora.

"That settles the flying question," TJ said. "What are *we* going to do? Twiddle our thumbs until they come back? We could follow them to Skid Row…"

"Someone needs to keep an eye on the sand," Willet said. She wouldn't presume to give any kind of order to Gem, but Gem was the most likely candidate to stand guard, because she had defense plus offense. She didn't need to ask.

"I will stay here with Dora to face the sand," Gem said. "If you wish, Guardian."

"We can't leave you here without protection, a barrier of some kind."

"I'll manage, baby girl," Gem said with a sweet smile.

Shadows were falling over the courtyard again as crows returned to the sand mountain. This time they made no attempt to attack. Each crow carried a small, round object carefully in its beak, flew directly into the sand and disappeared, leaving the object embedded in the sand like a Christmas tree ornament. The objects were eyes. Human eyes. More and more crows swooped in and planted their awful treasures. By the time the last crow placed an eye and disappeared, there had to be three hundred bloodshot eyes staring blankly out of the sand.

Willet's dreams about crows and visions of eyes in the mirror suddenly came together in her mind. They were premonitions of this very moment. She had been warned and didn't realize it. The number of victims and what they must have suffered was so hideous, it could hardly be contemplated. "Those poor people. I should have done something sooner. Why is this happening?"

They soon found out. Thin red currents appeared in the sand and connected the eyes. Willet had seen the currents before and thought they looked like small arteries with blood flowing through them. Now she suspected a neural net of some kind, connecting the eyes in a communications grid. Lights flashed through the grid, and the eyes became alert. They stared in different directions, searching the sky and out to the streets. Straggler crows arrived with more eyeballs and pressed them into the sand. The new eyes quickly joined the network and became aware, watching, searching. Many eyes looked down on the Circle and glared.

"They can see us now," TJ muttered. "Great." He felt his phone vibrate in his back pocket and pulled it out. Someone was calling from his home phone. "Jonah? This really isn't a good time. What's going on?" TJ nodded and murmured into the phone. "Put your mother on, please." His foot tapped rapidly. "Evelyn, for God's sake, what are you doing? You don't need to cook. Order a pizza." He listened and spoke again. "Let me talk to Jonah." After a few seconds, "Jonah? There's a menu from Adamo's Pizza in the drawer next to the sink. Just order pizza and charge it to my account. They'll deliver. Don't let your mother use the stove, OK? And open some windows to let the smoke out. Thanks, kid. I have to go." He clicked off and shoved the phone back in his pocket. "Evelyn was trying to cook something and started a fire in the oven. The smoke alarms went off. She's gonna burn the house down. I hope Jonah can distract her long enough to get a pizza."

The mention of Evelyn's name exasperated Willet. "That's so Evelyn. Does she know we're dealing with a potential catastrophe here?"

"You're kidding, right? All Evelyn knows is, she wants to play house. We could go home to a smoking ruin."

Willet stifled a chuckle. This was no time for humor.

Gem spoke up, out of the blue. "Guidance comes to us in the events of everyday life. Even those that seem wrong or inconsequential. Something is coming. We must be ready." The Guardian of California was sometimes cryptic, but her comments could never be ignored.

"What is it, Gem?" Willet asked. "Something coming from the sand?"

"Something's coming alright," TJ said, pointing to the courtyard entrance. "Look."

Chapter 44

The crows that ravaged victims on Skid Row flew off to join
another flock. The dark mass of feathered bodies moved
through the sky like a storm cloud, flying fast, but Audrey
and Dean flew at the speed of thought. They were waiting for
the crows when they arrived over Little Tokyo. The Ring
Thrower attacked the flock with a barrage of sizzling hot
rings. The Golden-hearted Warrior wielded his blazing sword
like a scythe, taking crows out in mid-flight and reducing
them to smoke. They had only made a dent in the enormous
flock. Crows began to dive to the streets to attack whoever
was there.

Audrey trapped as many of the diving birds in her rings as she could, but Dean was laboring. The sword felt heavier in his hand and harder to lift. It was a most inopportune time to turn physical. He was flying too high. Audrey noticed him start to drop toward the ground. Too sudden. Too fast. "Dean," she called to him. "Slow down." Dean felt his body weight increasing. The ground loomed closer and closer as gravity pulled him down. If he hit at this speed, he'd break every bone in his body.

Audrey followed him down to the street. She felt her own body growing heavier as she turned into solid matter and descended. Her feet touched the ground moments before he did. She moved beneath him and held her arms out, trying to break his fall, caught his full weight and fell backwards. They both ended up on their behinds in front of a dry cleaner. Their lungs expanded immediately. They gulped air and stared at each other with shocked faces.

Dean checked himself for injuries. Nothing seemed broken. "I think we're back, girl," he murmured. "Are you ok?"

"I might be bruised," Audrey said, rubbing her elbow. "You're heavy." Her tailbone was already getting sore, a bruise was certain, but she could actually feel the asphalt beneath her. She put her palms down flat and felt its knobby texture. It was solid and warmed by the rising sun. It was a wonderful sensation to be physical again.

Dean got to his feet and wobbled, getting used to the feeling of the earth's gravity again like an astronaut returning from a long journey in space. Astronauts experienced muscle wasting without the pull of gravity on their bodies, but Dean and Audrey didn't have to worry about that. The bodies they wore now were newly made, even though they looked like the old ones. He held out a hand to help her up. She scrambled to her feet. "We have to get back to the Circle. They'll wonder what happened to us."

"Where are we?" he said. Without a phone or map, they had to look up at the tall gray buildings all around, trying to find a landmark they recognized. "I don't know this area of the city."

"Maybe we can ask a policeman," she suggested. "Hopefully, we won't sound like lunatics."

Dean took her arm. "Wait a minute." He leaned in and whispered in her ear. "How are your rings? Still got 'em?"

She spun a small one on each index finger and then extinguished them. "I'm good to go. How about the sword?" He looked at his hands, wiggled his fingers, and shook his hands. Nothing.

"Try the swoosh," she said. "That's how you made it work before."

"The swoosh. Yeah." He swept his arm through the air like he was swinging a sword, and there it was, the long sword glittering gold in his hand. He pulled it in quickly and glanced around to see if anyone else was watching. With the sky suddenly clear of crows, a few people were hurrying by with their heads down before another bird attack. No one looked their way. "OK. We have weapons. How do we get back to Hope Place without money?" Their new physical bodies were clothed, but they didn't manifest with money in their pockets. Audrey looked up and down the street. "If we can get a cab, then we take it and hope TJ or Willet has some cash on them when we get there. What choice do we have? Do a song and dance? Beg for coin?"

"Audrey. Ever the financial planner."

They walked into little Tokyo. It had the festive look of a tourist area. Red and white paper lanterns hung on wires strung between the trees. Some structures were topped by pagoda-shaped roofs, their long-armed corners turned gracefully to the sky. Souvenir shops sold paper parasols for people to carry on their shoulders. There were people on the streets, strolling past the cafes and tea rooms, as if there were nothing to fear in the city.

Suddenly, shadows darkened the street. In seconds, the crows descended with loud caws. People screamed, covering their heads, and ran. Those who fell were trampled under the crush of stampeding feet. The crows were on them in seconds, tearing at any exposed flesh. There was no choice except to step in and fight. Dean's sword flashed out from his hand, and Audrey's rings started spinning. They marched into the fray, slashing and burning their way through the attacking crows, turning them to dust. The more crows they killed, the more seemed to arrive overhead.

A young Asian woman with straight shoulder-length black hair, wearing black pants and shirt with a red beret perched on her head, stumbled on the sidewalk and fell. She broke her fall with her arms and landed with her beret tipped off her head. A crow flew down on her to rip at the side of her face. She shrieked and covered her face with her hand. The crow pecked at her hand until she cried in pain and tried to brush the bird away, exposing her pale porcelain cheek. The bird pecked her cheek and forehead, trying to dislodge her eye. A jagged wound opened on her temple near the corner of her eye. Blood dripped down the side of her face onto the sidewalk and soaked into her hat. Blood and beret were the same violent color red.

Audrey ran to the fallen girl and stood over her, driving the crow away with a hot ring. Another mass of crows circled overhead, waiting for an opportunity to descend on the girl. Audrey caught the crows in a large ring and cooked them until they sizzled. She followed up with a barrage of rings that drove the rest of the birds away. "Get up now," she said, shaking the girl's shoulder. The girl struggled to her feet, sobbing. Blood streamed down her cheek. "Take cover. There's a café right over there. Go inside and stay there." The girl grabbed her beret off the ground and tried to wipe her cheek with it. It left a smear of blood. She took off running, leaving a trail of blood spatter behind. Audrey watched her until she reached the safety of the café, then turned her attention back to the skies.

Crows strafed the street relentlessly, dive-bombing people and driving them to the ground. Dean was slashing through them, taking out large swathes with each sweep of his sword. An older man fell to the sidewalk nearby, clutching his chest. He curled forward and covered his head with his hands. Crows descended on him, pecking at his hands. The man fell forward, groaning.

Dean ran to him with his sword raised and sliced through the black feathered bodies until the flames reduced them to dust. He put a hand under the man's arm and helped him stand. The man was shaking uncontrollably and blood flowed from his hands. It looked like his knees might buckle. "Can you walk?" Dean asked. The man's voice was weak. "You can't stay here. Go into that café," Dean pointed down the street. "Hurry." The man took a few steps, started to wobble, and then fell. Dean lifted him to his feet and walked with him into the café. Patrons and staff inside were huddled at the windows, watching the catastrophe taking place. Dean helped the man to a seat. It was all the help he could give. He had to get back outside quickly,

Another murder of crows was already descending on the street. The flock hovered in the air and some began to dive. Audrey threw ring after ring, incinerating crows before they could attack. Then she threw a very large ring into the air and trapped most of the flock in the ring's burning circumference. They couldn't escape it. The ring cooked them, and their bodies fell, turning to smoke before they hit the ground. The remaining few crows took off, and the sky cleared.

When Dean returned her side, she was a bit miffed. "Where have you been? There were a ton of crows here. I had to take all of them out by myself. My arms are aching!"

"Sorry. A man needed help." He took her by the elbow. "People are watching us," he whispered. "Let's get out of here."

People on the street had witnessed Dean and Audrey's inexplicable abilities to dispatch the crows. They were staring with slack jaws and befuddled expressions. Phones were out and pointed at the Circle warriors. Videos had probably been taken. Not good. The rings and sword wouldn't be visible in videos. They would show Dean and Audrey waving their arms around for no apparent reason. What *would* show up were the smoking bodies of the crows falling to the ground and disappearing all around them. Inevitably, the photos and videos would find their way to social media. The Circle didn't need that kind of attention. Dean and Audrey started running, reached the corner, and made a quick turn left out of the line of sight of the cameras. A cab was idling at a cab stand a block down the street. They made a mad dash. When they reached the cab, they didn't bother to ask if it was available. They just opened the door and jumped in. "Hope Place on 5th. How fast can you get there?"

Chapter 45

People were walking into the Hope Place courtyard like
zombies. Men and women stared straight ahead, approaching
the sand mountain with sluggish steps and robotic focus.
Flames burned in the depths of their eyes. More and more of
them came and gathered at the foot of the mountain. The eyes
in the sand focused down on them with an intent stare.

"I guess this is why O-Ka wanted eyes," Willet said.

"What are they doing here?" TJ said as the parade of people
continued.

Willet recognized some of the men from Lar's Lake's crew.
Lars himself walked into the courtyard with the same
mechanical stride, staring straight ahead. "Lars!" She waved
her arms at him. "Stop!"

He walked right past as if he didn't notice her.

Thaddeus Moon came skipping into the courtyard and danced around the fountain, a cartoonish figure waving his arms and hopping. His black braids bobbed around his head, and his skinny legs in black leggings and pointed toe black boots made him look like a crazy elf. He gave a high, cackling laugh. "I had a feeling that little punk was lying," TJ grumbled. "He drove the truck at us, I'd bet anything."

Willet pulled her attention away from Lars Lake. "Thaddeus," she called to him. "This is not a safe place for you."

If Moon heard, he ignored her and continued his dance with eyes closed. She went to him and poked his shoulder hard to get his attention. He stopped and raised his drooping eyelids. His eyes were unfocused, with the same flames in them as the other people entering the courtyard. He lurched on his feet, close to falling over, then righted himself and giggled. Willet backed up a step and TJ came over. "He's in some kind of trance. Either that, or he's drunk. Help me get him away from the sand." TJ took one arm, and she took the other. They lifted him off the ground. He was surprisingly light.

"No! No!" Moon shouted as they walked his wriggling body out to the street. "The celebration. I have to be there!"

"What celebration?" TJ's arms wrapped around the smaller man's chest, restraining him from running back into the courtyard.

"We've waited so long. He's calling us."

"Who's 'us'?" Willet said. "Who's calling you?" She had a sinking feeling she knew the answer, but she wanted to hear him say it. He didn't. He just struggled. "We could lock him in the Jeep," she said. "Smoke would keep an eye on him."

Moon struggled with increasing strength. When they stood him on his feet, he broke out of their grip and ran back into the courtyard. They followed him. "All these people were hit by the red lights from the sand," Willet said. "Lars Lake and his crew were working here when the sand was shooting lights. Moon got hit too. They all have flames in their eyes, like they've been marked somehow."

Gem walked over to a man standing on the fringe of the group, studied his face and waved a hand in front of his eyes. The man did not react. She returned to Willet and TJ and confirmed Willet's suspicions. "O-Ka holds them in thrall. They have been summoned here."

Willet confronted Lars again and pounded on his chest. "Lars!" He didn't so much as look at her. "Lars, can you hear me?" She jumped up to eye level with him. He finally reacted. A flicker of recognition registered in his eyes. She grabbed his shirt and shook him. "It's me. Willet."

He looked down at her and stared. "Willet," he said, his voice dull.

"Yes." She held his cheeks between her hands and looked in his eyes. "You have to leave. Go out the way you came in." He stood immobile.

Willet heard TJ shout. She whirled around to face the sand. What she saw terrified her. A large hole had opened in the sand above the heads of the gathered crowd. It looked like a mouth, wide-open and without lips. The edges of the mouth were lined with triangular black teeth, like a Venus fly trap. Inside the mouth, sand rolled in waves where a tongue should be. Breath blasting out of it permeated the air with the stench of death, followed by a loud, long groan and a booming voice. *Aaaaahhhhhhh. O-Kaaaaaaa.* It was O-Ka, announcing himself. People in the courtyard cheered.

Long black whisker-like projections shot out from around the mouth and waved over the crowd, then sprang out and wrapped around the bodies of people standing close by. The people smiled as they were lifted into the air. They didn't struggle. The whiskers curled backward and quickly popped the people into the open mouth like potato chips. Their bodies disappeared down the long gullet without a sound.

Willet couldn't wait around to find out if O-Ka would eat everyone in the courtyard. She had to raise the biggest barrier she'd ever attempted. Glass was not the ideal solution, but it was quick, and she was sure she could pull it together. Her gravitational force sucked in particles of sand and streams of energy until a hot cloud formed. She took possession of it, pressing it between her arms and chest until it smoked. No longer able to stand the heat, she threw it into the air. As the boiling mixture spread over the crowd, she stretched and formed it, hoping the glass wouldn't harden until it had the shape she needed. It had to be curved. Otherwise, O-Ka's wiry whiskers might try to curl under edges of the glass and drag people out. The glass finally settled over the crowd, including Willet. The people underneath were not happy about it. They tried to push the glass up and away, but it had hardened into a heavy lid that could not be moved.

"Stay down!" Willet called out to everyone under glass. They pushed and shoved even harder.

TJ retreated to the low wall surrounding the courtyard and crouched down behind it, staying out of range of the grasping projections. He peeked over the wall and marveled as the Guardian spread the glass barrier. "That's my girl," he said under his breath.

At that moment, Dean ran into the courtyard and stopped, huffing for breath. TJ stood up. "Dean, get over here!" he yelled, waving frantically with his hand. Dean jumped over the low wall and ran to him. "Get down! Get down!" TJ yanked him down by the shirt when he got near enough. "Stay low and out of sight." Then his brain registered what his eyes saw. It was Dean, actually Dean, solid and physical. The strong jaw, curly brown hair and direct brown eyes were as familiar as a brother. TJ grabbed him by the upper arms and squeezed, felt those hard drummer muscles under his hands. "It's really you. I thought I'd never see you again. Not like this." He pulled Dean into a bear hug. "How did this happen? Never mind, we have a crisis in progress. The sand is swallowing people. You have to stay away from those long black things."

Dean stiffened. "Do you have fifty bucks?" he said, seeming to ignore what TJ just told him. "I need fifty bucks. The cab driver is holding Audrey hostage until I go back to pay him."

TJ searched Dean's face for signs of a joke. Dean seemed serious. He pulled out his wallet. "I have a hundred dollar bill. That's it."

Dean plucked the bill out of TJ's fingers. "That'll work." He stood and ran back to the street to rescue Audrey.

"You guys better get back here quick," TJ shouted after him. "We need help. And I want change for that hundred."

Chapter 46

The glass lid steamed underneath from all the panic breathing. People pushed and shoved. They banged on the glass with their fists. Claustrophobia drove some people to tears. Others gave up their struggle and dropped to the ground in exhaustion. They sat cross-legged, hanging their heads in despair.

Inevitably, the emotions of the crowd snaked out in hot wires and found their way to Willet, who was at the edge of the glass. The wires slid around her chest and legs, wrapped around her neck, and squeezed. She struggled to breathe. She would lose the fight if help didn't appear. It appeared in the form of a familiar furry gray creature with blue eyes. Smoke crept up from behind her, put one paw on her leg, and looked up at her with his eyes wide, as if alarmed at the situation. "Smoke," she gasped. "Help me." Smoke swelled into his bobcat form and his claws sprang out. He tore the wires from around her legs and then ripped the ones circling her chest. She struggled with wires around her neck, trying to get her fingers under them and pull them away. She was finally able to take a full breath. "Thank goodness you're here," she whispered, "Stay close in case I get caught up again." The bobcat hunkered down beside her. His blue eyes scanned every direction, alert for incoming wires. If anyone was upset by the sudden presence of a bobcat in their midst, Willet didn't care.

The sand mountain loomed above the foggy glass. Wiry whiskers from around the huge mouth probed at the glass, searching for a way around or through it. People suddenly got very quiet. She hoped they were aware of the danger they were in. It would make them easier to manage.

Dean was able to free Audrey from the clutches of the impatient cab driver with an extra-large tip. They ran back into the courtyard. The incongruous sight of the glass brought them up short. "What's this?" Dean asked. "Where's Willet?" Audrey demanded. Dean pulled Audrey by the hand to where he had left TJ. They crouched down beside TJ and Gem were both taking cover behind the wall.

"O-Ka summoned his victims, and the Guardian protects them under glass before they give themselves up," Gem summarized succinctly.

"O-Ka is an ancient cannibal," TJ added. "He's hiding in the sand, waiting for dinner. If the people under the glass come out, he'll eat them. It's a stand-off." He chewed his bottom lip, eyes shifting between the sand and the glass. "Something's gotta give."

They didn't have to wait long for that 'something' to give. A black projection, thicker than the others, sprouted from the sand and wrapped around the small bronze statue of the woman mounted on top of the fountain, snapped it off its pedestal and raised it above the glass. The statue was slammed down on the center of the glass with a resounding smash, and a web of cracks spread through the lid from the point of impact. The glass shattered, leaving everyone underneath it covered in shards of glass. New projections shot out and grabbed people, lifted them, and stuffed them into O-Ka's mouth, then curled out and grabbed for more. Thaddeus Moon was one of the first to go. Another long whisker sprang out, slipped around Willet's waist and lifted her into the air. Smoke jumped, trying to stay with her, but she rose so fast that the bobcat was left on the ground. He hissed and his fur stood on end.

Audrey screamed. "Will!" She ran toward the sand with TJ, Dean and Gem close behind her, and threw a hot ring into O-Ka's mouth. It disappeared down the open gullet. Dean raised his sword and slashed through the black whisker that held Willet. Willet began to drop. Another black whisker quickly snagged her and tossed her in between the jagged teeth. The wide-open mouth snapped shut after her, and the black whiskers retracted into the sand. The Guardian was gone.

TJ's shouts of anguish split the air. He hurled spears at the sand mountain as hard and fast as he could until he ran out of stones. Then he tried to dig into the sand with both hands to get inside that huge mouth. Dean stabbed his sword into the sand where the mouth had closed. Audrey threw ring after ring until her hands burned. The mouth didn't open. They turned to Gem.

Gem shook her head. "She must find her own way out now."

Chapter 47

Those left behind in the courtyard beseeched O-Ka to take them, but the mouth didn't open for them. Apparently, O-Ka had eaten his fill. The dispirited crowd slowly dispersed, leaving the Circle to deal with the aftermath. TJ was still trying to burrow into the sand to get to Willet. Making no progress, he gave up his assault and sank to his knees, shaking and cursing. Dean put a hand on his shoulder. "We'll get her back, buddy. We won't give up." Dean and Audrey helped him up and led him away to the ledge where Gem sat.

They didn't notice a man in a tailored tan suit standing in the courtyard entrance. He had salt-and-pepper hair and a close-cropped beard. His shoes were polished to a mahogany shine. The man stood silently, watching, then walked toward them. Gem tracked him with her eyes as he crossed the courtyard. "What is your business here?" she said.

"The Circle seems to be in a bit of a pickle," he said, appearing amused by the situation.

Gem frowned "What do you know about the Circle?"

The man smiled a broad smile full of teeth that contained no warmth. "Some of your members are causing quite a sensation on social media. There are videos of them making strange motions with their hands and large numbers of crows turning to dust. It's quite a spectacle. The word 'witchcraft' was used. What everyone really wants to know is, how were they killing the crows?"

"Damn, that's bad" Dean murmured to Audrey. "Sounds like the sword and rings didn't show up in the pictures. That's good." He looked sheepishly at Gem. "Sorry Gem."

The Guardian of California shook her head at Dean and Audrey. "You allowed yourselves to be filmed? That was careless."

"The crows were pecking people to death!" Audrey said. "We had to help."

"You might hear from the U.S. Government before long," the man said with a sly smile. "You could be an asset in national defense."

Gem turned a glare on him. "This is none of your concern."

"It seems you are minus a Guardian," he said. "I can help with that if you would allow me."

That got TJ's attention. "How? What can you do?"

The man got down to his real purpose. "If you would be interested in a business arrangement, I offer my services as a retrieval expert, someone familiar with the ways of, shall we say, the less savory aspects of the universe."

"What kind of arrangement?" TJ demanded.

"The terms are simple. I retrieve the young woman. You perform a task for me at a day and time of my choosing."

"The Circle of Augustus is not for hire," Gem said curtly.

"What's the task?" Audrey asked.

"That will be revealed at a later time."

Dean snorted. "We can't agree to do something when we don't know what it is. That would be stupid."

The man wasn't smiling now. "Do you want the lady restored or not? She won't last long where she is."

"Who are you?" TJ said.

"Lionel Stegner," he said with a slight nod of his head.

"Lionel Stegner." TJ nodded slowly. "Willet mentioned you. Not in a good way."

"I did meet her previously," he said with a sour smirk.

"Rather inexperienced for a Guardian, wouldn't you say? Pity it had to end this way."

"Just do it," TJ blurted out. "Get her out of there." No one else spoke.

Stegner shook his head. "I need the whole Circle to agree or there's no deal."

TJ looked at Dean and Audrey, who looked at each other, and then they all looked at Gem. Gem was looking at Stegner with ice in her eyes.

"We can't just leave her in there!" TJ said. "What other choice do we have?"

"This man is an agent of Jat," Gem said in a calm voice. "He cannot be trusted. We should consult with the Guardian Enclave, seek their help. Guardians do not bargain with the Deceiver."

"I won't let my sister die without a fight," Audrey said. Dean nodded in agreement.

"Clock is ticking," Stegner said. "Tick, tick, tick. My offer will expire in sixty seconds."

TJ's voice and hands trembled. "I don't know how to get to the Enclave. This might be our only chance." His face begged Gem for understanding.

"I will not stand in your way," Gem said finally. "Do what you must." She turned her back and walked away with Dora by her side.

TJ went chest to chest with Stegner and stared into his dark eyes. "If you don't get Willet out of that sand quick and in good shape, I will punch your teeth in and throw you down the Bunker Hill Steps head-first. Then I'll kill you."

"Do not threaten me, young man. You don't know who you're dealing with."

TJ laughed in his face. "I know exactly who I'm dealing with. Another one of Jat's flunkies. We've dealt with them before. They don't last long."

For a moment, it looked like Stegner might be angry enough to walk away, but he settled his shoulders and waved his hand toward the street. A man in camouflage gear walked into the courtyard carrying a Spike-MR rocket launcher on his shoulder. He aimed the gun at the sand mountain. "Say when, Mr. Stegner."

"What are you doing with that gun?" Dean said.

"We will fire a specially designed projectile," Stegner announced. "It will clear a path through the sand for anyone inside to escape."

TJ's left eye twitched. "That's an anti-tank weapon. You could kill everyone in the sand with that thing!" He looked like he could strangle Stegner right then and there. "And we haven't agreed to do anything for you yet."

Stegner went on. "The payload is made of crystal combined with other ingredients. It will be very effective. The Guardian denied me the crystal, so I had to take matters into my own hands and procure a crystal boulder by stealth. How ironic it is that I will be the one to rescue her." Stegner gave a casual shrug of his shoulders. "It is a bit of a gamble, though. Never sure how these things will go."

"What are the other ingredients? Dean asked.

"The blood of O-Ka combined with blood of his firstborn son, whom he ate."

A chill fell over the Circle. That sounded wrong on so many levels.

"O-Ka is ancient," TJ said. "Where would you get his blood, or his son's?"

A nasty leer spread across Stegner's face. "I have exceptional sources."

No one doubted who or what they were. This was a deal with the devil. The Circle searched each other's eyes for consensus. The unholy concoction in such a powerful projectile could have awful, unpredictable consequences. They all knew it.

"There has to be another way," TJ said finally. "It's too unpredictable. We'll consult the Enclave like Gem said."

"We need to do something before it's too late," Audrey implored. "But not this."

"Too dangerous," Dean agreed. "We're not doing it."

Stegner ignored them. He gestured to the man aiming the Spike launcher, who engaged the gun and fired it with a boom. A projectile shaped like a torpedo flew out of the stovepipe barrel and disappeared into the sand. The Circle shouted in protest as they watched the torpedo fly. They held their breath, waiting for an explosion. It seemed like time stood still.

Chapter 48

Willet tucked her head down and pulled her knees to her chest when O-Ka tossed her into his mouth. She felt the tips of pointed teeth slide over her back, and she landed on a gritty surface in the dark. O-Ka's thudding heartbeat jarred her bones and a wet, sucking sound from deeper in his throat made her skin crawl. As her eyes adjusted to the darkness, she could see that the teeth lining his lips were not his only teeth. Another arc of serrated black teeth loomed half way down the gullet, almost impossible to avoid. A thick liquid oozed up through the sand around her feet. *Does O-Ka digest his food, or does he just chew it?* She hoped the liquid wasn't digestive fluid. Her feet could dissolve away from underneath her, and her legs would follow. There was more than one way to die in this dark place.

Muffled screams and wails echoed off the high vault of the mouth. O-Ka had already started eating. A waterfall of chaotic thoughts spilled through her mind. *How do I help these people?* It was difficult to focus on a single idea, but one thought stood out. *It's just sand. Maybe we can push through to the outside.* It would have to happen fast. Shrieks rose to screams of pain, then faded away in moans of agony as O-Ka's teeth ripped people apart and he swallowed them. Some of O-Ka's devotees had met the death they sought so enthusiastically. Desperate now, she thought about her options. A large barrier protecting everyone would be useful, but she couldn't see where everyone was. She needed to survive long enough to help them. Her feverish mind latched on to a crazy image - a porcupine covered with sharp quills. It was a random thought, but a barrier formed around her as soon as she imagined it. Her fingers felt a smooth cold surface around her. She was surrounded by a circular enclosure made of metal. How this related to a porcupine, she couldn't guess, but when she pounded her fists against the metal, it rang like a bell. The people in O-Ka's gullet heard it. A chorus of voices screamed, "Help!"

The sand pile was enormous, but she knew the gullet led out of O-Ka's mouth at one end, the end where they entered. If she could roll her metal capsule in the right direction, it might act as a battering ram to break through the heavy sand to the outside. She tried to rock the capsule back and forth to get it rolling. The thing rose up and down as if it were on stilts. She finally got some forward movement but wasn't sure what direction she was going. She needed a push toward the mouth. "I'm here," she shouted. "Come to me. Help me push this metal thing toward the mouth, and we can all bust out." She kept shouting so someone, anyone, who could reach her. Anxious cries echoed in the gullet, and the sound of feet pounded and slid across the sand. Hands found the capsule and started to push. She hoped they were pushing toward the exit. The capsule started moving, making progress. *This might actually work.*

Before they got very far, pressure swelled underneath the capsule, lifted it and tossed it backward with that wet sucking sound, and the hands pushing her fell away. The capsule bounced from one side of the long throat to the other. Her head, back and every boney joint banged painfully against metal until the capsule came to a stop lodged somewhere deeper in the gullet.

People slipped down O-Ka's gullet. Their voices faded as they were sucked deeper. Other voices got louder, shouting and crying, more desperate than ever. She tried to rock the capsule to free it, but it was stuck. A crunching sound at the top made her look up. The tip of a black tooth had broken through the top of the capsule two feet above her head, and the metal had buckled. O-Ka's sharp teeth could tear the capsule apart and chew her like a soft candy center. It would be a painful death. Images of Thomas, Audrey, and Dean flowed past her mind's eye, their faces afraid and grief-stricken. If she was going to die, she wanted to make it count for something. She said, 'Swell' and pictured the capsule expanding around her. The metal capsule swelled according to her command.

"Push me down his throat," she shouted out to the others. "So he can't swallow."

Hands returned to the capsule. People grunted and swore as they pushed the capsule. She slid around inside it with every jarring motion. The capsule fell deeper into O-Ka's throat until it came to a stop, reaching some kind of choke point. She hoped the throat was effectively closed, but O-Ka had other ideas. A deep rumble rose from the depths of his throat. He was going to gag. "Watch out! I'm coming up," she shouted, hoping the people understood. A thunderous cough lifted the capsule and catapulted it out of the depths of his gullet with explosive force. If he spit her out, his mouth would have to open and everyone would be expelled along with her. That was the plan all along..

At that moment, something flew through the sand with a fast whoosh, so close that the capsule was sideswiped by a strong pressure shift. The capsule bounced out of control, hitting every side of O-Ka's mouth. Her skull and every bone in her body felt the impact. *No, No!* She had no way to steer the capsule back on course, but another hacking cough from O-Ka sent the capsule on a straight trajectory. She could only hope she was moving in the direction of escape.

She closed her eyes and sang HU, the only thing she could think of to do in that moment. The HU sound rang inside the metal capsule and vibrated right into her bones. Her breathing slowed. Her heartbeat slowed. Whatever came next, she would remain calm.

*****

In the courtyard, the Circle waited for any sign of Willet. The sand gave no clues. TJ turned on Stegner with clenched fists. "If she's hurt, I'll bust your windpipe!" He was about to throw a punch when O-Ka opened his huge mouth and belched a blast of sand and dust into the air. A lopsided metal orb studded with black spikes flew out of the open mouth, hit the ground hard and skidded to a wobbling halt. The orb split in two and hatched Willet like a baby chick. She sat cross-legged, holding her head and looking dazed. Bodies hurtled out of the mouth after her with arms and legs flailing. 'Oomph's and 'Oww's echoed in the courtyard, along with the uncomfortable sound of bones and skulls cracking as they hit concrete. People coughed up sand and wiped it out of their eyes. Others lay motionless. Body parts, bloody, broken and partially chewed, littered the ground. Those who could move crawled in circles on hands and knees, trying to find their way through the dust.

TJ reached her first. He ripped the pieces of the orb away and dropped to his knees beside her. "Will! Talk to me. Please."

"Ow," she said weakly. Her head dropped to her chest, and she rubbed her temples. "My head hurts. I might be concussed." She swallowed hard, sniffed at the front of her gray hoodie, and wrinkled her nose. "Ewww. I smell like the inside of O-Ka's throat." She sagged against him, trembling.

TJ wrapped his arms around her. "You do smell a little ripe, but I don't care. I thought I'd lost you," he murmured, planting kisses on her hair.

Audrey rushed over and dropped to the ground beside them. "Oh, Will. I was so worried," she sobbed. Tears ran down her cheeks. She wrapped her arms around both of them. "What happened in there? And what's that smell?"

"People were screaming and dying. It was awful." Willet's eyes rolled, unfocused. It looked like she might faint or throw up. "It smelled like hell."

"Let's get her away from the sand," Audrey said.

Willet was unable to get her legs underneath her. TJ and Audrey slid their shoulders under her arms and lifted her to her feet. They walked her slowly to the low concrete wall at the edge of the courtyard and helped her to sit down. Dean and Gem rushed over to them. They all wanted to know how she was, but she was too weak to say much.

Audrey took her sister's hands and rubbed them vigorously. "Her hands are freezing. And she's shaking. Definitely in shock."

TJ held her and rocked her until the shakes subsided. "He had so many teeth," Willet whispered. "He was chewing people... I couldn't reach them." Her body shuddered.

"Sorry to interrupt, folks," Dean said. "We've got a situation in front of us. We need to do something fast to help the people still alive or more will die. Will, are you well enough to deal?" She nodded weakly. "Give me a minute to get it together. We need to help them.."

Dean called 911. In the meantime, the Circle members got to work attending to the injured on the ground, staunched bleeding wounds, wrapping fractured bones with whatever fabric was at hand, and helping people breathe more easily if they could. Gem blew her icy breath on severe sprains and inflamed cuts. There was little they could do beyond that until the ambulances arrived.

Paramedics finally entered the courtyard and surveyed the scene. It was a shock even to those veterans of many accidents. "This place is cursed," one of them said shaking his head. "Last time I was here, it was heart attacks. Now it's whatever *this* is." The paramedics went to work with professional vigor, helping the injured and dealing with the dead. Another crew would come later to clean up the blood and unidentifiable human remains splattered across the courtyard. How could so many people be so injured a second time in the same place? No one would suspect that the pile of sand sitting silent and inert had anything to do with the tragedy if they hadn't seen it for themselves.

After the last of the dead and wounded were carried away by the ambulances, the Circle took a moment to regroup. Physically and emotionally spent, they had done what they could, but it seemed so little against all the carnage. Lives were lost. Some would be permanently disabled due to loss of limbs. Others would suffer from PTSD that may never leave them. Willet leaned against TJ. His solid presence sustained her.

Lionel Stegner chose that moment to march into the courtyard, flanked on each side by a uniformed soldier holding a semi-automatic weapon.

Willet saw him. Her body went rigid. "What's he doing here?"

"This isn't a good time," TJ growled at Stegner. "Go away."

"That is poor thanks for rescuing the woman. We'll take custody of her now. Until your task is completed." Stegner gave one of his leers and motioned to the two guards. They moved toward Willet. Dean and Dora blocked their approach. Audrey stood and tossed a hot ring over the head of one guard. That guard yelped in pain. His gun slipped from his hands as he slid to the ground, holding his neck.

"Don't make me do this the hard way," Stegner gritted between clenched teeth. "We have an agreement." The other guard raised his weapon.

Weak as she was, Willet sat up straighter and gave TJ an incredulous stare. "You made an agreement with this guy?"

"We didn't agree to anything," TJ said. "We told him NO. He's delusional."

"I made the rescue," Stegner growled. "It's a tacit agreement."

"A tacit agreement? You're kidding," TJ growled back. "I'll see you defend that in court."

"You think you rescued me?" Willet bristled at Stegner. She looked at TJ. "What is he talking about? I rescued myself! The people inside, we rescued ourselves!"

"This guy shot a torpedo made of the crystal into the sand. Supposedly to get you out."

"So that's what the sound was. He knocked my capsule off course and almost ruined our escape. He didn't save me!"

If Stegner heard, he went on as if he didn't. "I want assurance that your group will carry out its part of the agreement when the time comes."

Gem intervened before things got out of hand. She turned cold eyes on Stegner. "There was no agreement to turn the Guardian over to you. In fact, no agreement was made at all, to my knowledge."

"So, you're reneging?"

Gem gave him a stern look. "The Circle of Augustus does not break its word if a word is given. Custody of the Guardian is not negotiable, however."

Stegner and his other guard seemed ready to grab Willet by force. TJ pulled her closer, and Dean stood with tight fists, ready to defend her. If the guard chose to use a gun, there was little they could do to stop him. Then, a deafening roar echoed through the courtyard that shook buildings and rattled windows. Every head turned. A full-grown African lion was standing at the top of the Bunker Hill Steps. The pelt of the beast was golden brown, and the thick mane around its head shimmered with light. Its eyes were blue. The lion bounded toward them with fury in those blue eyes.

The guard with the burning neck fell backwards on his butt. The other guard pointed his weapon at the lion. "Fire!" yelled Stegner. Shots erupted from the gun. The lion leaped through the air over the bullets and landed heavily on the shooter, knocking him over and pinning him to the ground under his massive chest. The lion's jaws opened, long white teeth extended and pressed against the man's neck, held firmly at the point of puncture. The man whimpered and froze. The other man was foolish enough to reach for the gun he had dropped. The lion lifted a huge paw and batted it across that man's face, opening a deep gash across his forehead. The man dropped to his knees and held his head. When both men stayed still, the lion stood up and turned his attention to Stegner, his huge jaws open to show all his teeth. Saliva dripped from his canines. While the lion focused on Stegner, the two guards managed to wriggle backwards on their butts, scramble to their feet and run for the exit, leaving behind their guns and trails of spattered blood.

Stegner leaned over and tried to grab a gun. A long, curdling growl came from the lion that sounded like thunder, and a big paw slapped down on Stegner's hand. Stegner looked up into the eyes of an apex predator. There would be no further warning. A wrong move would bring death. Stegner slowly slid his fingers off the gun and backed up cradling his hand. Three deep scratches had opened on the top of it, studded with ruby-colored beads. His red-faced anger almost matched the color of his blood.

"Thank you, Smoke," Willet said quietly. Everyone backed up as the big cat turned and sniffed her, assuring himself of her well-being. Satisfied, he sat back on his haunches, close to her, never taking his eyes off Stegner. Another low growl vibrated deep in his throat

The lion's sudden appearance rendered the rest of the Circle speechless. Even TJ, who knew about Smoke, was astonished at the size of him. Blood drained from Audrey's face, leaving her chalk-pale. "That's a lion," she said, pointing a trembling hand at the huge animal sitting near them. "A lion right there. What is happening, Will?"

"I told you we had a cat." Willet smiled at Smoke. "Smoke protects me. He would have ripped this guy apart if I was in danger." She looked pointedly at Stegner. "Just sayin'…"

Dora was the only one not freaked out by the appearance of the lion. Gem's big black dog walked right over and sniffed at the lion's face and hindquarters. The lion bore the examination stoically. When Dora satisfied herself about the lion's identity as a fellow spirit animal, she sat down beside him, close enough to touch butt to butt.

Stegner kept his distance but was still seething. "This isn't over. You have a debt to pay. You'll be hearing from me," he said, backing away.

"I want to hear from you now," TJ yelled at him. "What do you want? Why are you dogging us?

"I've done my part," Stegner repeated. "You owe me."

"The lion let you live," Dean said reasonably. "Consider that repayment for whatever we owe. We're even."

"That wasn't the agreement," Stegner snarled.

TJ could hardly contain himself. "There was no agreement!"

"Clock is ticking," Dean mimicked Stegner. "Tick, tick, tick. Our goodwill gesture will be rescinded in sixty seconds. If you don't accept the payment, you'll have a lion sitting on your chest."

Stegner shook with anger but continued to spar. "If you don't fulfill your part of the bargain, you'll be sorry."

"We'll be sorry?" Dean shook his head. "What does that even mean? You're in no position to barter."

"It's all you need to know right now. Events are unfolding." Stegner shrugged.

Dean's sword flashed. The sharp gold tip touched Stegner's throat. "Make them unfold faster."

Stegner's eyes lit up at the sight of the glowing sword. Torn between fascination and desire, he pulled his focus back to the matter at hand. "It's not up to me. It's in the hands of my benefactor. It will be in your best interests to comply."

"You mean Jat?" TJ said. "Nothing he wants would be in our interests."

"Gentlemen, please," Gem said. "Mr. Stegner, regardless of any agreement, real or imagined, the Circle of Augustus does not engage in any action that would harm a living being in any way, physically, emotionally, mentally or spiritually. It is not up for discussion. You must understand that."

Stegner shook his head. "I'll let you know when I know." His unpleasant smile showed all his teeth. With a wary glance at the lion, he edged away to the courtyard exit.

Gem turned stern eyes on the Circle. "Do you see why we do not make bargains with the Deceiver or his lackeys? His bargains are full of lies, designed to trap the unwary. If the Circle is caught off guard, people could suffer." A hint of reproach flickered in her eyes. The message they conveyed was, 'I told you so,' but she didn't say it out loud, and no further lecture was given. Her weary Circle was relieved.

Chapter 49

Smoke padded off toward the Bunker Hill Steps, stopping long enough for a glance over his shoulder at her to make sure Willet was still safe, then leaped down the stairs and out of sight. Willet was sure they would find Smoke in the back seat of the Zinger when they returned to it. She noticed the bronze statue lying on the ground. *Source Figure*. O-Ka had broken it off its pedestal and used it as a hammer. She walked over and picked it up. The statue of a woman felt weighty in her hand. The lines of the woman's body flowed with graceful simplicity. It was beautiful, a work of art. She wasn't sure what to do with it, so she tucked it under her arm and returned to the wall where the Circle sat. The faces of her dear ones were beautiful to her. That they were all together was a miracle. Her sister was there, solidly and physically, and Dean was there, strong as ever. Terror, stress, joy and relief jumbled together inside her. It made her head pound. A migraine might start. She'd deal with it later. There were so many other issues to face.

It was getting toward sunset. Despite the rush hour bustle that filled the city, there was silence in the courtyard. After all the noise and chaos, it had a hollow sound. People dead and injured, mauled and blinded – it was devastation too great to absorb. The Circle stared at the blood spattered concrete where bodies had laid broken, too numb to speak. Willet slipped her arm around her sister's waist. Audrey hugged her close. Dean and TJ searched each other's face.

TJ seemed uncharacteristically at a loss. "Is O-Ka gone? Really gone?"

The mountain of black sand gave no clues. Eyes embedded in the sand held blank, lifeless stares. The network of currents between them was reduced to sporadic sparks, less active but not dead.

"We can't stay here," Dean said quietly

"I'd invite us to my place," TJ said with a sullen shrug, "but I'm in no mood to deal with Evelyn."

"We could go to my house," Dean said. "Manhattan Beach is closer than the desert."

"And then what?" Audrey asked. "Don't we have to do something about... all this?" She waved a hand at the sand.

"Yes, we do," said Willet. "I wish I knew what." She had no words beyond that. Even in its dormant state, she knew the sand still harbored a gaping hole in the Gate leading straight to the Underworld. They would have to close it before some other evil being slipped through.

Dean pulled Audrey to his side. "Right now, I want to do this." He pressed a gentle kiss on her cheek. She blushed and stood on her toes to press her lips firmly on his. They melted together into a kiss that went deeper and deeper.

Dean and Audrey clearly needed a moment of privacy. Willet and TJ walked to the other side of the courtyard and sat on the low wall. She turned to TJ and handed him the statue. "Take this please. It's kind of heavy."

He accepted the weight and laid it down on the wall beside him. "What are we doing with it?"

"We'll return it to its rightful owner. The Parks Department probably knows who that is."

They sat in silence and watched Dean and Audrey losing themselves in their own bubble of bliss.

"They'll need to breathe soon, won't they?" TJ said.

Willet sighed. "It's beautiful. Audrey waited for him, and now he's here. They deserve to enjoy this moment together."

TJ slid closer to her and laid his cheek against her hair. "You came out of O-Ka in a metal ball," he said softly. "You made that, right?"

"Yes."

"It was big. And covered in spikes. How'd you do it?"

"I pictured a porcupine with quills, the first thing that came to mind. Should have figured I couldn't create an actual living thing, but what I got was even better. The spikes made O-Ka gag and send us all flying through the sand out of his mouth." A look of anguish shadowed her face. "Wish I had saved more people."

TJ cleared his throat. "There's something I have to tell you about the crystal torpedo, Will. When Stegner made it, he mixed the crystal with the blood of O-Ka and of his son. No idea how he could have their blood after fifty thousand years, but he says he has sources. The crystal and the blood are in the sand now. I'm thinking that was his plan all along."

They looked at the sand with new distrust and loathing. The open Gate to the Underworld, the ancient blood, the crystal, the black sand from the Dragon Head Building – it was a recipe for something awful, courtesy of Jat.

Willet dropped her head into her hands and groaned. "I am so inadequate."

"What do you mean? You're doing great!"

"I'm just a woman with an extreme case of hyperacusis who can't handle noise. I have no business accepting this kind of responsibility. It's not fair to the city."

TJ put his arm around her shoulders. "You've learned to manage your hearing, amazingly so. Besides, you have the Circle with you. You have Gem. And you have that Guardian Enclave you told me about. We'll fight whatever comes out of the sand. You just need time to rest and recover after all you've been through. I can't even imagine what it was like inside O-Ka's mouth."

"It was a nightmare of stench, suffering and death. People screamed as they lost their lives. Just thinking of it makes my stomach turn."

"It's a miracle you made it out of there." He nudged her closer. "When I thought you weren't coming out of the sand, I couldn't breathe."

A newsreel of memories ran through her mind and brought tears to her eyes. She looked up at him. "I thought of you too. And Audrey and Dean. It kept me from giving up. I did what I could to help those people get out, but so many were hurt and killed. And the crows and the eyes – I foresaw it! How can I live with that?"

"You saved a lot of people too. They would have been chewed and swallowed without you. What I do know is, this city needs its Guardian. The Circle needs you. The sand is still there, and it might be even more of a threat than before. You lived to fight another day as Guardian. That's your path."

She wasn't sure the outcome merited her own good fortune. The Circle was back together. She felt the embrace of their love and friendship, without any wires to bind her. *Love has no wires.* She resolved to be the Guardian the city needed, no matter what it required of her.

"We can enjoy our own moment, can't we?" He pulled her into his arms and kissed her.

Her arms slipped around his neck. The warmth of their kiss melted any doubts between them. They were partners in love and life. Nothing would be allowed to change that. Not O-Ka. Not Evelyn. Definitely not Lionel Stegner.

Willet looked into his green eyes, those eyes that always reminded her of the ocean. A dreamy smile spread across her lips. "A moment will not suffice."

EPILOGUE

*** James Jain ***

Jain returned to Hope Place to look for the Circle. The courtyard was deserted, but the catastrophe that had taken place there was evident. The statue that used to stand on top of the fountain was gone, leaving a broken spike on the pedestal. The ground was stained with blood. He'd seen enough blood for one day.

He walked out of the courtyard with his hands stuffed in his pockets, destination uncertain. It was too early to go back to his sister's apartment. He could go to the park, sit on his favorite bench. Perhaps a puff or two on the pipe would put him at ease. No, that didn't seem right. He pictured Nick shaking his head. Nick didn't approve of Jain's smoking. Said it made him act like a 'dufus.' Jain was never sure exactly what Nick meant, but he knew it wasn't good. He wanted to be someone Nick would be proud to call a brother. He pictured his friend's face from better times, before all the weirdness messed up their lives. "Dude," Nick used to say. "You're my bro. No lie."

Jain needed to get his own life back. He needed a plan and thought again of paramedic training. How would he pay for it? He imagined several scenarios. With his skills, he could get a security guard job and work nights. Or go back to the private investigator gig. He was good at that. There were possibilities. He would make it work.

A breeze picked up and rushed across his skin, refreshing and cool. Trees rustled their leaves. He could swear he heard a familiar voice whispering, "I love you, man." His steps quickened. Wherever he was going, he wanted to get there quickly. His new life was starting now.

*****

Lionel Stegner sat in the back seat of a black Escalade and stared through the dark tinted windows as the vehicle slipped away from Hope Place, merging into the flow of city traffic. The scratches on his hand were still bleeding. He had it wrapped in a towel.

He held a phone in the long fingers of his uninjured hand and spoke quietly into it. "The payload was delivered."

A gravelly voice on the other end fired off several terse questions.

Stegner frowned. "Recovery was successful, but the agreement wasn't finalized. They balked."

The pitch of the distant voice rose.

"I'll make sure we get what we paid for, sir."

Another staccato series of questions came through the phone.

"As yet, no activity," Stegner replied. "I'm confident we'll see results soon."

The call ended, and Stegner leaned back in the leather seat. He was uncomfortable with the whole situation, and his hand ached. The Circle had proved to be difficult to manipulate. How dare they set a lion on him! He couldn't let that stand. His reputation would be tarnished. If they had cooperated, he could have worked with them. Now, things would have to get nasty.

Acknowledgements

Thank you to those who helped make this book happen. To Georgette LeBlanc for the early reading and feedback. To Cherie Kephart for the alpha edit, and to Mark Spencer for the beta edit. Cherie and Mark are wonderful writers, and Georgette is one of my dearest friends. It takes a village to write a book.